The Tangled Mane

Charlie Tyler

Published by SpellBound Books 2024

Praise for Charlie Tyler

'Superb! The Tangled Mane roars into life with dark secrets and tragic lives, careering towards a twisted climax. Cally is a fantastic new addition to the PI stable. I sense I'm in at the beginning of a cracking new detective series. Looking forward to more.'

T. Orr Munro, author of *Liars Island*

Praise for Charlie Tyler

'Superb! The Tangled Mane roars into life with dark secrets and tragic lives, careering towards a twisted climax. Cally is a fantastic new addition to the PI stable. I sense I'm in at the beginning of a cracking new detective series. Looking forward to more.'

T. Orr Munro, author of *Liars Island*

For Wilbo

Chapter 1
Mikey
2004

I WOKE with my sister's face a lion's whisker away from mine; her wavy, caramel hair tousled around her pillow. Lucy's soft lips were in their natural resting position; a gentle upturn to the edges; not a smile, but almost. She was on the edge of waking and her eyelids pulsated. I hoped her dreams offered her sanctuary. Maybe she was in Narnia. Back then, I don't think I had dreams. It was only after *it* happened, the nightmares began.

Early summer sunlight filtered through the dirty net curtains and gave the room a grey tinge. I could see the clock on the sitting room wall – the plastic handles stuck in the same position – batteries were a total waste of money. Time didn't matter to me; all I knew was, when the school holidays came around, there was a lot of daylight to fill.

It was the little things which made us happy and kept us going. We were free to do as we liked – Lucy, being the oldest at thirteen, was responsible for me; her nine-year-old brother. She also took on the role of Mum's errand girl.

Mum. It's hard to know how to describe her. We were something she knew she couldn't get rid of, but also something she didn't want. She wasn't cruel, but she wasn't kind. She simply didn't care and, by the end, I loathed her. She was a cleaner with regular nightshift work and she hated us being in the flat whilst she was 'sleeping' so school holidays for her were a huge nuisance – it meant she had to feed us extra rations too – not that she did. Though her various jobs paid okay, she spent almost her entire wage on drugs and often funded her addiction by other methods.

Our flat had one bedroom which Mum and usually another paying guest stayed in. There was a bathroom with ever increasing black spots rising north on the shower curtain; a sitting room with a squidgy poo-brown sofa and a kitchenette whose units were the colour of an overripe satsuma. Lucy and I slept on a mattress in the corner of the living room.

Lucy opened one eye and smiled. 'Morning, Mikey.'

'Morning.'

'You been awake long?'

'Not really.' I rolled onto my back and squinted up at the ceiling. There was a patch of damp on it which was shaped like a hippo emerging from a swamp.

Lucy sat up taking the duvet with her. I yelped. Despite the heat of the past few weeks, I shivered. Our flat never got warm as the only bit of sun it got, if there was any, was first thing – the rest of the day our side of *Hazleton Towers* lurked in the shade.

'What are we going to do today, Luce?'

She sighed and got up, tucking the edges of the duvet around me before leaning over to tweak my nose. As she manoeuvred around the mattress our book slid to the floor with a thump and she picked it up and balanced it on the windowsill. *The Lion, Witch and the Wardrobe* was the only book we owned, and we worshipped it. Fat Eddie had bought it for Lucy as a gift and since then she'd read it to me, over and over again.

Rubbing her hands across her thin arms, she went over to the little plastic table on the kitchen lino and perched on one of the two wonky chairs; it was garden furniture put out with the bins, but it did the job. Lucy was thin – we both were, but her hollow cheeks gave her an air of a mythical creature. She'd fallen from heaven, whereas with my black eyes and olive skin it was as though I'd emerged from the underworld, a dirty street urchin. Her big blue eyes blinked slowly as she lifted the scrap of paper with Mum's scribbled writing on it from under the jam jar.

'It's laundry day today, Mikey,' she said. 'Get yourself dressed and brush your teeth – then we can go.'

'Is there anything for breakfast?' I already knew the answer, but sometimes – sometimes Mum remembered to get some supplies in; a loaf of bread, milk, some cereal – she had to eat too. Lucy opened the tall cupboard and for a split second hung her head. Then she squared her shoulders and turned around. She smiled. 'Hmm! Well – I can offer you wool or jam, or both – take your pick.'

One of Mum's cleaning jobs was in a knitwear factory, another at *Bramble Preserves* and we never knew whether the stuff she brought home was given or stolen although I suspected the latter. She also worked in the offices of a building company and when she started there, we wondered if she would bring home bricks or rooftiles – instead she seemed to help herself to copious amounts of coffee and sugar sachets, and capsules of uht milk.

My tummy rumbled. I went into the bathroom, peed, splashed some water onto my face and rubbed some toothpaste across my teeth. I put on yesterday's shorts and tee-shirt which Lucy had hung on the hook behind the door. When I emerged, Lucy pushed a cup of coffee over to me. I opened two tiny pots of milk and tipped them in. She offered me a jar of jam and a spoon, but I shook my head and instead added a sachet of sugar to the coffee.

'I've got an idea,' said Lucy.

I sipped my coffee – the uht milk had given its surface a filmy layer. 'Uh-huh?'

'Doesn't football camp start today?'

I nodded, taking another slurp.

She kicked the big blue bag by her foot and it crackled. 'I think, if we shove all this in one wash and don't dry it 100% in the machines – we'll have some left over for...'

I slammed the cup onto the table, spilling a few drops. 'Hot dogs?'

Lucy grinned. 'Absolutely, Mikey. Hot dogs.'

We hurried down the stairs. We were on the ninth floor of *Hazelton Towers* and the lifts sometimes worked, but the smell of them made Lucy retch although it was only marginally worse than the smell of piss and decay which lingered in the stairwells. The lower down you got the more choking the bleach smell – apparently the ground floor was the only place which was ever 'cleaned' presumably by someone who threw a disinfectant bomb at it then did a runner.

We said hello to Mrs Slobberdown-yuck; a small bird-like woman with wrinkly skin and jet-black hair. She lived on the second floor with her parakeet called Gogo. If she saw us, she always reached into her handbag to furnish us with a peppermint. *Always*. Although they weren't the nice sort – they tasted more like the medicine Fat Eddie glugged from the bottle to stop him burping all the time. Fat Eddie was the only one of Mum's boyfriends who I missed even though he smelt of hot marmite and garlic. Whenever we saw him, he was either farting or belching, but he was always kind to us, unlike most of her bedfellows. He called Lucy, Loopy Loo and me, Kiddo which I liked. He also made Mum laugh. When he left Mum, as was inevitable, he handed Lucy an envelope with some money in it and a shiny leaflet with the number of someone from the council who 'was ready to listen'. The next morning, even though Lucy had hidden the envelope under our mattress before bedtime, both items had gone and Mum spent the whole week totally out of it.

There was a group of boys wearing baseball caps loitering on the square patch of balding grass outside the entrance to the apartment block. They stared at Lucy and made some horrible, leery-eyed gestures which I didn't understand. Lucy ignored them and I scowled and trotted at her heels, my bare knees bashing into the laundry bag. They whistled and cat-called after her, speaking in a language which I thought was English, but was also full of words I'd never heard before.

The moment we crossed the High Street, we went into *Linda's Launderette* – the scent of washing power was so overwhelming I started to sneeze. There were only a few other customers inside, sitting on a line of metal chairs and staring at their flip screen mobile phones. We marched to the end of the aisle and picked an empty machine on the bottom row. Lucy took out our detergent which she'd decanted into a plastic bag and tipped it into the drawer. The plump, grey-haired lady behind the counter was folding a pile of washing and putting it back into a crackly bag with a zip. She grinned at us and waddled over brandishing a huge bottle of fabric conditioner.

'No,' said Lucy, shaking her head. 'We can't afford it.'

'Tsssk,' said the woman and sploshed a bit into the drawer then ruffled my hair.

I sniffed. 'It smells like that flower we had on the windowsill once – what was it, Luce?'

'Hyacinth,' she said. 'You're right. It does.'

'Says its grape and cherry blossom,' said the woman, squinting at the bottle as though she'd never seen it before. She had a name badge pinned to the collar of her white overall which said she was called Penny and I thought the name suited her. 'Leave me the money for the drier and I'll set it going for you.'

'You sure?' asked Lucy handing over two pound coins. Penny gave her one of them back and grinned; her crooked teeth glinting under the glare of the strip lighting. 'Let's see what we can do with that – I happen to know there's one of them which isn't so hungry as all the rest.' It was another little kindness which, over the years, I'd forgotten about because when things went bad those were the memories which came bubbling to the surface, the good ones lost in the deep.

We rushed past the discount stores and cheap booze outlets before we got to the end of the road and took a sharp right turn. I could see Walkers' Common in the distance and heard the faint sounds of people shouting; balls thudding, and whistles blowing. The closer we got, the stronger the smell of fried onions.

Walkers' Common was made up of cultivated parkland with a lake at its centre. The black iron gates were thrown open and we walked straight in, immediately dazzled by the mass of peach and yellow frothy flowers which filled the rectangular flowerbed. Paved paths, lined by sycamore and lime trees, led off in various directions. To the left was a children's playground and beyond that lay the football pitches and tennis courts. If we went right, we would have ended up in the undulating meadow peppered with straggling gorse bushes and squat pines, the dog walking brigades' favourite route. Straight ahead led onto the popular path which encircled the lake and where Walkers' Café was situated. This café was always busy no matter the weather and even sold doggy cupcakes which cost more than an entire loaf of bread. I admired the hot chocolate from a distance; it was served in a glass with oodles of cream and topped off with a flake bigger than my hand – the stuff of boyhood dreams, if I'd had any.

We certainly couldn't afford a goat's cheese and prosciutto panini from Walkers' Café, but during footie training *Harvey's Hotdogs* van would park on the tarmac between the pitches and the playground. His food was as cheap as chips; the inside of the sausages was the colour of candyfloss and the hotdog buns tasted like wool, but Harvey – even though he probably wasn't called Harvey, let us help ourselves to as much sauce as we liked and was very generous with the fried onions. It was the only time, when not at school, I got one of my *five a day*.

'Hello you two. Long time no see. What'll it be today?' he said, flashing his gold tooth at Lucy. His dark hair curled up on his shoulders and was shiny with grease.

'Two hotdogs please,' replied Lucy.

'Nothing on mine today, Harvey,' I piped up. 'I'll have it plain.'

'Right you are, Sir,' he said.

Lucy gave me a sideways glance and a frown. Then she grinned. 'You sharing it with someone?'

I pressed my lips together and nodded.

She looked down at the change in her palm. 'Well, you don't have to.' She smiled at Harvey. 'Make it two with all the trimmings and can I have an extra sausage on the side, please.'

'Anything you want, love,' he said.

'Thanks,' I whispered. 'Aslan will be so pleased.'

We walked back onto the damp grass, shaded by the boughs of several ancient chestnut trees and I watched a squirrel scuttle around a fat trunk and disappear into the budding conkers. The soles of my feet squelched against my flipflops as we headed down to the lake. I caught a noxious whiff of drains and the bright green algae blobbed around as a dabtail ducked under the surface. The edges of the lake were covered in white dots which from a distance looked like blossom petals but was actually bird shit.

I had wrapped the spare sausage in a flimsy paper napkin whilst trying to divide the salty, greasy meat so each mouthful of woolly bread was topped with it, but my stomach overrode my patience.

'Don't gobble it or you'll need Fat Eddie's pink medicine,' said Lucy, picking at hers with her fingers.

I stuck my neck out and made a noise which I hoped sounded like a turkey, but in my head, I couldn't even think of the cry they made, so I just ended up saying 'gobble gobble' and shaking my head, my cheeks puffed out like a hamster. Lucy laughed. I loved making her laugh.

We screwed up our napkins and threw them into one of the many litter bins which lined the park walkways.

Half-way round the lake was another split in the path shaped like a -V. The right slant took you to the other side of town. It was known as The Village and was full of boutique clothing stores, delis and coffee shops which made Walkers' Café seem cheap. There, women in soft velvet tracksuits, hair in swishy ponytails, emerged from behind the jangling doors, sipping juices every colour of the rainbow but which, when I went past, all seemed to give out the same aroma as the cucumber stuff I chucked off my plate at school. The left fork was where we were headed.

'Mikey?'

I tipped my head on one side and grinned. Her blue eyes twinkled in the sun.

The game was about to begin.

She grabbed hold of my hand. 'Okay. So, you win the lottery. You get one house to live in *forever*. Which would you choose?'

The path narrowed and we crossed over a cattle-grid, though no cattle were to be seen, nor do I reckon had ever been there since ye olden days, and headed down a dusty path, lined with waifish elms and a thick wedge of blackthorn and brambles. It wasn't the best time of year to play this game because the trees were out in their leafy magnificence, but it didn't matter – I knew what they were shielding; this was where Millionaires' Row began.

Behind the brambles ran a tall fence which was topped with barbed wire. At intervals there were gates which were shut, their keyholes rusty. In my entire nine years I'd never ever seen anyone emerge from behind them. Why would they need to use the park full of common people when they had their own beautiful gardens? Some of the houses had another layer of brick behind the fence. But if you didn't mind getting a bit scratched or streaked with moss then a few of the wooden panels offered a hole; a knot through which to view what was behind.

Of course, we knew exactly which one the other would pick. Lucy; the cream house with magenta shutters and emerald rooftiles. That particular spyhole offered the perfect view of a kidney shaped swimming pool; bigger than the local lido and filled with water which looked turquoise. I smelt smoke and, as I pressed my cheekbone against the rough wood, I could see a man flapping his hands over a barbecue while a woman in a red bikini stood next to him, laughing and sipping from a wineglass the size of a goldfish bowl.

Lucy nudged me. 'Your turn, Mikey.'

We fought our way along the wrong side of the hedge, Lucy holding back a vicious looking thorny strand until I'd snuck past. Three gates down stood a grey-bricked house with two turrets shaped like ice-cream cones at either side of the slate roof. At the centre of the top window sat a telescope so big it must have been able to see exactly what the astronauts were up to in space. But, it wasn't the castle or the telescope I wanted, it was the creature that lived within. It was Aslan. I pressed my face to the gap in the wood panel, and just behind it stood his big, iron-bar cage.

I gasped.

'What is it?' asked Lucy.

'He's...he's gone.'

Chapter 2
Cally
Present Day

Cally checked off the crates. *How the fuck had that happened?* One of the boxes of vintage champagne had disappeared. Right from under her nose. She was standing in the security office leaning over Steve's dandruff-speckled shoulder and trying not to breathe because his skin gave out an odour similar to boiled cabbage and onions. Meanwhile Paula, whose own perfume was something straight out of the eighties when shoulder pads were still in fashion, was spooling back through the footage, her frizzy canary-coloured hair growing in volume due to the exertion caused by having to stand up for more than a minute at a time.

'See. There's the van,' said Paula tapping a violet acrylic nail at the screen. It set Cally's teeth on edge – just how Paula managed to function with nails that long was a mystery to Cally who was a keen gardener and had difficulty keeping hers scrubbed clean. Cally's gaze fixed on the screen, watching as the van pulled up outside the back entrance to the club and a short, stocky man with a shaved head, wearing a tee-shirt which barely stretched over his biceps, came out with his clipboard then unloaded the boxes. It was Bulag; a thoroughly unpleasant thug who also happened to be a member of a local criminal gang who called themselves The Cobras.

'There's Bulag,' said Paula. 'He's one of the usual delivery men. See – twelve cartons come off the lorry.' Paula fast-forwarded the footage then tapped her talon at the images of the twelve boxes, it was as though she was spelling it out in morse code.

Steve coughed and leant forward releasing another soupy waft. 'Then, see, Nori arrives, checks them, signs the receipt and he gets the porters to take them to the cellars. Somehow, from getting off the van and going to the storeroom, one of the boxes goes missing.'

Cally ran her fingers through her short red pixie cut – it was, according to her fiancé Dan, like living with an extra from *The Lord of the Rings*. That, also according to Dan, had been a compliment. Cally had disliked the cut and colour right from the start, but she'd needed a change in appearance for her latest undercover role and she thought this style would make her look edgy and hip, not as though she should be dancing by moonlight around a fairy-ring. Cally worked for a PI agency run by her boss, Miriam Kershaw, a well-respected and well-connected ex-copper who maintained strong ties with the local police force. A few months ago, Miriam had received a phone call from the General Manager of The Phoenix, Gloria Cavel, who reported that one or more of her staff were stealing from her, but despite her best efforts, had yet to catch them. So, Miriam decided to send Cally in as a Trainee Assistant Banqueting Manager. When Cally discovered that a couple of the porters had ties to The Cobras, Miriam passed the information on to her police contacts who asked if she wouldn't mind sharing any further details which, of course, Miriam was extremely happy to do in order to keep open the reciprocal channels of communication.

In her entire 32 years Cally had never been so exhausted – the club was for high profile clientele and they expected perfection. The weddings were the worst – the most recent one she'd overseen had the mother of the bride demanding the flower arrangements on the table be replaced one hour before the guests arrived because 'the red wasn't red enough'.

So far Cally had ascertained that the produce went AWOL en route from the back storeroom to the cellars but where it was vanishing to was a complete mystery. This was happening in plain sight, and it was beyond frustrating. She knew she was missing something, but she simply couldn't figure out what it was.

She strongly suspected Nori, the Food and Beverage Manager, was involved. Nori was a middle-aged man from Malta with a droopy black moustache and receding hairline who spoke in an accent which grew more difficult to understand the more irritated or stressed he was. It made taking commands from him at a function almost impossible. He also threw Madonna-esque Vogue poses which, if the waiters witnessed, had them falling about with laughter. He was, however, good at his job and his diva persona was a match for even the most difficult of clients.

Cally's walkie-talkie beeped. Nori's voice shouting something about her needing to be in the ballroom right now, making sure the name places matched the table plan.

She turned to the security guards. 'Keep the tape – don't wipe over it.' She caught a look – the briefest of smirks between them, but before Cally could process it Paula busied herself pulling the tape out of the machine and handing it to Stinky Steve. Then she flipped the switch on the kettle and sank into her leather chair which creaked in protest.

Cally hurried across the hall then through the double doors to the ballroom. It was a modern, purpose-built, vast space whose dark wood panelling and chequered tiled floor with intricate balustrade and orbital chandeliers made it look older than its twenty years. It had a vaulted ceiling, and a sweeping staircase led up to a gallery which was sometimes cordoned off for VIPs only. This route up to the gods also led to the most exclusive bedrooms in the club, including the bridal suite from whence the bride could choose to make a grand entrance or hasty exit.

Cally had been looking forward to this wedding. Although the bride-to-be was a little bit petulant and ditzy, her mother had been nothing but delightful to work with. Cally wasn't fazed by superstars or money and although the Camblys were wildly rich, they had been very down-to-earth with their vision, reigning in their wannabe Instagram superstar, *LuellaBoo,* when her grand designs had got out of control. Yes, they had wanted the best, but they'd also insisted on local produce for the menu with the food, booze and flowers all sourced from neighbouring businesses. Choosing the cake had been Cally's favourite part of the job and she was invited along to test the most beautiful Fiona Cairns creations. Luella wouldn't try it because she wasn't eating any carbs before the big day, so Val Cambly, the mother-of-the-bride, and Cally had picked out a luscious red velvet creation with creamy frosting and covered in pink marzipan hearts. Cally's mouth watered at the thought.

It was a crate of the Welland Valley vintage sparkling wine which had disappeared. It cost a fortune and had a very noticeable dry gooseberry flavour which, if they switched with a more basic fizz, would be obvious to most palettes. Maybe she could hold back the alternative for the toasts when half of the guests would already be sloshed.

She went into the ballroom and breathed in the scent of the lilies on the table then caught sight of a lanky waiter holding a plastic bucket in one hand and a pair of scissors in the other.

'What are you doing?' she asked.

'I've got to cut the pollen off to stop it marking any of the guests' clothes. Nori also hates it if it stains the tablecloths.' He held up a hand, streaked with orange lines. Cally shuddered at the sacrilege then took her clip board and started to check off her table plan against the place names behind each setting.

'Cally, darling. So glad you're here.' She turned to see Val Cambly sweep into the room. She was tall and lean, her long pale green dress clinging to her sinewy figure. Her hair was in rollers and her face was devoid of any make-up but covered in a thin layer of pearlescent cream which made her skin glisten. 'I need you to come with me.'

'Of course,' Cally set down her clipboard. 'How can I help?'

Val put a lean arm around her and squeezed. 'Well, I have a little bit of bad news to break to Luella and I think it would be best coming from you.'

'You mean, you want her to shoot the messenger.'

Val laughed. 'Yes. One of the members of the string quartet has gastric flu and so can't come. The other three are fine, but unless they can get a friend to cover, they'll have to change the playlist so it's more suitable for a trio.'

'I'm sure they'll be fabulous whatever the outcome.' Cally tucked her clipboard under her arm and gave a little frown. 'You know. I don't think I'd pass on that news just yet. It may resolve itself and I bet you anything that when Luella starts down the aisle she won't notice.'

Val sighed and the roller which had chewed up her fringe, wobbled. 'Probably. What do you think about the weather forecast? Awning or no need?'

Cally squinted out of the window. The stone steps from the terrace down to the lawn were now dotted with metal planters, tied around the middle with magenta ribbon and containing individual pink and white roses. She could see staff traipsing up and down the stairs, setting up the chairs for the ceremony. The weather had recently been very unpredictable with sudden downpours, but today the sky was clear, and it felt light and warm. 'I think we'll be okay, but we can get the awning up faster than Wimbledon centre court, if needs be.'

'You're an angel,' said Val. 'Come on. Let's go and see how far Luella has got with her hair and make-up. I need to take a few photos so I can make her an album for when she gets back off her honeymoon.' Now wasn't the time to mention the fact that a crate of their sparkling wine had gone missing.

They climbed up the staircase which was twined with foliage and Cally rearranged a tendril of ivy sticking out at the wrong angle. At the half-way split, Cally and Val took a left turn and then went under an arch towards the bridal suite. A young woman with very tanned long legs, wearing silky shorts and matching button up tee was banging on Luella's door.

'Mum. She's not answering,' said the woman, her curly blond hair trailing down her spine and stopping just short of her pert backside. She had bright blue eyes, curved dolly eyelashes and big, pouty lips. This had to be Val and Bill's younger daughter: Sasha. She looked a bit more like Val – her features not as angular as those of her sister. 'I've been trying for, like, ever.'

'Perhaps she's in the bath,' said Val, pulling a key card out of her purse. She brushed her daughter aside.

They entered the room which Cally had described to Dan as being the most beautiful hotel suite she'd ever set foot in. The wallpaper behind the sumptuous emerald velvet bedhead was of a woodland scene and the tips of the pine trees folded over onto the ceiling then vanished into a hand-painted starry night. When Cally first did a tour of the hotel, Gloria had let her sit on the bed and she leant back against the bronze and gold-fringed cushions and stared out of the sash window which gave the most wonderful view of a meadow, stretching down to the River Welland, complete with frolicking lambs. Cally was determined that one day she was going to decorate her and Dan's bedroom in a similar style although she'd be getting her wallpaper from Dunelm not Liberty's of London.

Cally registered that the turquoise voile curtains had been tied back and there was an empty teacup on the bedside table, but the room was silent which was unlike Luella who was always listening to music, searching for soundtracks to accompany her life on screen.

'Darling?' said Val, then repeated the question.

The bathroom door was closed, and she knocked, then put her ear against it. Nothing but eerie silence. Cally felt a shiver run down her spine. The next moments she would recall later as though in slow motion. Val tried the handle – it opened. She hesitated before entering the room. Seconds later she was screaming. Cally ran towards the door. There in the bath, under the water was Luella; naked except for a towel wrapped around her hair. Cally barged forwards and helped Val drag her out of the tub; the water was cool and devoid of bubbles. She also noted that there was a wet bikini in the sink and one empty champagne flute resting on the side of the bath. She began compressions, but the girl was a corpse. Her bloodshot eyes wide open and glassy, skin clammy, her lips blue.

'Call for an ambulance,' Cally shouted, but it was too late. LuellaBoo had been dead for some time.

Chapter 3
Mikey
2004

I CLAWED at the air behind the fence with my grubby fingers, willing him to materialise. Aslan never left his cage.

'Do you think something's happened to him?' I asked, my voice a whisper.

'I don't know.' Lucy nudged my shoulder. 'Here. Let me have a look.'

'He's not there,' I said, a small sob catching in the back of my throat as I relinquished my viewing platform and stared up into the boughs of a wispy ash tree.

Lucy stooped into position, sucking in her breath. 'There's a man in the corner of his pen, right next to the entrance and...he's got a broom. He's cleaning it – that's what he's doing.'

The scratchy fence panelling prickled through my flimsy tee-shirt. 'But where *is* he? He's never allowed out. Maybe, they're cleaning it because he's...he's dead.'

Aslan was the very predictable name I'd given the magnificent creature who lived in the cage at the bottom of the garden belonging to the castle house. Lucy always played along and, although deep down I knew he wasn't really a lion, he fitted into my fantasy world and made the impossible seem tangible. He was massive, the size of a small pony, and I think his fur was meant to be fluffy, but up close it was matted and dotted with bald spots and his golden mane always had bits of straw tangled up in it. Aslan spent most of his day pacing the perimeters of his cage, often shaking his head from side to side as though trying to rid himself of a terrible idea.

The first time I ever peeped through the fence panel into his garden, Aslan was waiting for me; staring through the bars as if I was expected. I gasped as he swam into focus taking in his dark, red-rimmed eyes and his slobbery jowls which drooped, giving him a mournful expression. Then he lifted his nose and gave a series of short, sharp sniffs. In return, I told him he was a good boy and poked a handful of stale crusts I had brought for the cygnets through the gap. He lowered his head to sniff them, then snaffled them up.

After our first encounter I got Lucy to take me to visit Aslan whenever we could and each time we went I took an old knife with a serrated blade with me and sawed away at the edges of the hole. By the end I could fit my whole hand in. I never had much to offer him, but he didn't seem to mind. Although he always had food and water, he recognised me as being cast from the same neglectful-shaped mould and we both took comfort from that. When he pressed his body up against the bars, I knew it was so I could reach in to tickle him, and he shut his eyes and growled with delight.

I couldn't comprehend a life without Aslan. Tears prickled behind my eyes as the brush scratched across the cement floor. Then came a sloshing sound and my nostrils tingled with the smell of strong disinfectant.

Lucy elbowed me back into position. 'He's putting down straw for his bed.'

I watched as the man in dark blue overalls scattered armfuls of it across the floor. Next he filled up the tin bucket from a standpipe outside the cage door and set it down, followed by a metal tub overflowing with biscuits and bloodied meat. The man went outside the cage, took a set of keys from his belt and locked it before pressing something on a small right-hand post. There was clinking and whirring and from out of the ground emerged a metal meshed box with Aslan squashed up inside, his expression more hangdog than ever at this humiliating sequence. When the coop was level with the floor, one side sprung open and Aslan stepped out and moved towards his new bedding. The man pressed the button again and the cage disappeared into the ground. 'Right you are then,' he said before walking off with the broom under his arm. Aslan, all of a sudden, lifted his head and stared at the gap in the fence panel then came thundering over to me. My face was wet with tears.

'Good boy!' I reached for the sausage in my pocket and unwrapped it. A few bits of the navy tissue stuck stubbornly to the layer of grease, but I didn't think Aslan would mind and poked it through the bars with the paper still attached. He chowed it down whole, letting me scratch his nose whilst he swallowed and licked his lips.

Lucy placed a hand on my shoulder. 'Come on.'

I nodded. 'I'll be back soon, buddy,' I said, kissing my fingers and pressing down on his nose. He sighed and trotted over to his new patch of straw, kicking it around a bit until he'd got the layout just right then he slumped down on his side and I could see his ribs rise up and down.

We were quiet on our way back to the launderette. It was a happy silence where each of us were busy thinking, and by the time we left the park I noticed Lucy's hands were full of twigs; green, spindly ones, not the snapping sort.

'Why've you got them, Luce?'

'Ah! You'll see,' she said, tapping the side of her nose.

We got our laundry from Penny. She'd folded each item and

put them back inside our bag – they were dry as toast and smelt delicious. I couldn't wait to get our fresh sheets back on the bed. There was only so much dawdling and hanging around the place we could do so, after a while, we tiptoed back into the flat and waited for Mum to get up. We sat on our fragrant duvet and I watched as Lucy's dainty fingers set to work on her twigs, bending and tying them with strands of peach wool from one of the spools in the cupboard. As I stared; the grooves in my forehead grew deeper and, knowing my curiosity was at bursting point, she began to giggle.

She held up a trivet of twigs garnished with wool.

'I'm making a dream catcher,' she said.

'It looks like a spider's web. What's it for?'

'It's not finished yet, but when it's done, I'm going to hang it on the edge of our curtain rail, and it will be above our heads while we sleep. It will give us good dreams.'

'How does it do that?' I asked.

'Ssh! You need to be quiet while I'm doing it. I'm wishing for stuff as I go along – that's what the little knots of wool represent – the dreams.'

'Can you wish for Aslan to come and live with us?'

'I'm wishing for lots of things, but I can't tell you what, because if I say them out loud they won't come true.'

After another few minutes of us sitting in silence, her expression changed and her eyes kept darting to the bedroom door.

'She should be getting up now,' said Lucy.

'Do you want me to go and have a look?' Mum was less violent towards me because I was younger.

She nodded and I went over to the bedroom door and flattened my ear against it. It was quiet. There were no sounds coming from within; none of the creaking, grunts and moaning Mum usually made when she was getting up. Slowly, slowly I pressed on the handle and pushed it open.

It was dark inside. The curtains were closed, but the bed was empty, the duvet crumpled to one side.

'She's not here.'

Her room smelt sweet and sour at the same time. I turned on the light and its dull glow bounced off a foil take-away carton making a little spark of silver. Her clothes were strewn across the floor like stepping-stones and I was of a mind to see how far into the room I could get without touching the carpet. 'Perhaps she's gone already.' My voice went up at the end – half question, half hoping.

Lucy hovered in the door frame. She shook her head. 'We've been back for ages. She wouldn't have gone that early.'

She spun around, seized by a thought, and hurried over to the row of keys which hung by the front door of our apartment. Each key had a name and code on its fob and underneath every hook was a sticker with the day of the week on. Lucy ran her fingertip across them. 'They're all here.'

An unwelcome worry was creeping into my head, but I could see it had already sprung fully formed into Lucy's. 'Is her bag in there?' she asked, her voice trembling.

I turned back to the dressing table, wondering if I could eat the piece of breaded chicken which was stuck onto the foil carton by something which had dried like tar.

'Yes.'

'Bring it to me.' Her words were now abrupt and urgent.

I grabbed the faux leopard-skin bag and, as I did, Mum's hairbrush and a sticky tube of ruby lip gloss tumbled out. Lucy snatched the bag out of my hands and rummaged through it. She pulled out Mum's purse and undid the popper, fingers rifling through. She shook her head. 'But her bank card is here.' Her eyes narrowed. 'That's weird.'

'What's weird?'

'Mum wouldn't have gone out and not taken her bag.' She

carried on searching. 'Here are her keys and her phone's here too.' The cheap pay-as-you go. Lucy unlocked it and began pressing a series of buttons, chewing her lower lip as she scrolled through. 'There's no messages of any interest and she's still got credit.' Lucy put the bag down and walked into the bedroom, recoiling at the sweaty body aromas which clung to the sheets. She opened the wardrobe and pulled out the drawers. 'Nothing's gone.'

'Apart from Mum,' I added.

Lucy walked over to the kitchen area, and I followed. By this time my stomach was churning with hunger and I reached for a couple of jam jars from the tall cupboard. I took the dirty coffee spoon, which was still on the table from breakfast, gave it a rinse under the tap, then dug in. I had become quite the confiture afficionado; no longer just settling for the mere likes of raspberry or strawberry. No, my favourite combination would start with a few heaped spoonfuls of plum and greengage chutney and finish up with spicy ginger and rhubarb for dessert. On that day, however, the fear of wondering if we had been abandoned made the usually satisfying flavours curdle on my tongue.

Lucy drummed her fingers on the table. 'She'll lose her job.'

'Do you think she's left us?'

'Nah!' She shook her head, but there was a little vein pulsing at the side of her temple; she was worried too. 'You know Mum. Most likely she's fallen down in a ditch or something.'

My spoon hovered in the air.

'Not hurt – just out of it,' she added as a hurried afterthought.

'What will we do?'

Lucy went back into the bedroom and came out waving a £10 note – it could have been gold bullion or a treasure box from the bottom of the ocean such was my delight. 'Mikey. I have a plan. What day is it today?'

'It's Wednesday, I know cos I heard the bin lorry clanking about this morning. Woke me up.'

She went back to the peg board and ran her finger along the days. 'That means, today is Cambly Homes. Good. I've helped Mum with that one a few times. I know where the office is, what to do and where she keeps all the cleaning stuff. We'll go now and then on our way back we'll treat ourselves to a pizza or a how about a kebab from Alfie's.' She waved the money again. 'It's the least she can do to thank us for us saving her skin.'

I jumped to my feet and saluted – a whole pizza doing a cart-wheel in my head. Lucy took her small handbag and put Mum's money inside. 'You got your key Mikey, just in case?' I patted my pocket and nodded. We set off back down the eighteen flights of stairs and retraced our route from the morning until we got right into the middle of the park. Lucy was speed walking, her mouth set in a determined line, and I had to beg her to stop a couple of times, my body folded in half as a stitch spliced down my sides.

This time, we took the right-side of the V and headed towards The Village. The park was still full of people buzzing about even though it was eight o'clock in the evening and although the café was shut, people were sitting at the tables, drinking from cans, smoking – some eating take-aways whilst the bins overflowed with empty packets, bottles, and squashed tins.

As we moved away from the lake, I turned to stare at the water which had turned golden in the sunset; the patches of emerald algae were almost navy in the ebbing light. The entrance to The Village from the park was festooned with white fairy lights and, as we passed under their glow, it was like stepping into another world. This was a place where the pavements weren't uneven or full of cracks sprouting weeds. Most of the units on the side facing the park were restaurants; their food smells mingling as their large windows, flung wide, spilled forth tables dotted with tealights onto the street. We passed a clothes shop where the backdrop was entirely white, including the faceless mannequin – all the model was wearing was a scarlet hat and towering crimson stilettos. I don't know why but it made me laugh and Lucy laughed too and went cross-eyed. We ducked down a narrow passage and under a wrought iron arch which had 'Cambly Homes' weaved into its curlicues. Lucy pressed the doorbell and the large man with a shiny peaked cap looked up from the screen on his desk. He smiled and gave us a wave and the door buzzed open.

'Where's Mum then?' he asked, grinning. His front two teeth stuck out at a funny angle and were a sandy colour, but I knew I shouldn't be unkind about that as some of mine had turned battleship grey. I scratched my head.

'On her way,' said Lucy. 'We're just going on ahead to make a start.'

He raised a sandy eyebrow and poked out his tongue, licking it across his fat lips but Lucy didn't notice, she was already pressing the button for the lift. When I turned to look behind me, he was still staring at her. I scowled at him, and he stuck up his middle finger then hooted with laughter.

Lucy tapped the code for the entrance into the keypad and we went in. The recessed lights along the main corridor were on, but the glass fronted rooms leading off the runway were in darkness. I started as I caught a glimpse of people huddled together, deep in conversation, but a second look revealed it was only a large plant with leaves shaped like a giant's outstretched hand. Lucy went straight to the cupboard and unlocked it; then pulled out the stuff we needed. She handed me a duster and polish.

'Every single surface, Mikey. Use lots of it.'

I nodded.

She stooped down, fiddling with a plug and then the room filled with loud rock music. Slash's soaring guitar solo to *Sweet Child o' Mine* wrenched through my body and had me turning the can of polish into a miniature air guitar. Lucy laughed and flicked her rubber gloves against my forehead. Then she took a deep breath and pointed to the sign with TOILETS on it. 'Wish me luck. I'm going in.'

After I'd polished every single desk, Lucy gave me a different bottle and cloth and I had to go around and wipe each phone handset. By the time I'd finished that and made a few pretend calls to Will Young and Robbie Williams, Lucy had done the bathrooms and was now in the kitchen, washing up the dirty crockery. The final job was my favourite – hoovering. I loved how the little red-faced machine trundled along behind me as I sucked up everything in sight with its nozzle.

Mid-way through my route the power stopped. I started at the jolt of silence, then fell to my knees to see what Henry had swallowed to block his throat.

'Who are you?' came a loud male voice.

I was so surprised by the intrusion I farted. I turned to face a towering man in a navy suit, plug socket dangling from his hand.

'I...' I clamped my mouth shut, my gaze turning towards the kitchen door. Lucy had taken the radio inside when I started the hoovering and she was singing, her body swaying in time to the music. She must have realised it had gone quiet and she shouted out.

'Mikey – what are you doing? You can't possibly have finished yet.'

She sighed and came to the door, her hands in bright yellow gloves too big for her, her hair falling out of the messy bun on her head. Her body tensed when she saw the man and she lifted her nose in the air, as though trying to appear taller.

'My word! The work force gets younger by the minute.' The big man was smiling now. He had incredibly white teeth which seemed almost blue under the halogen spots. I couldn't tell how old he was, but his hair seemed a little too dark for his leathery, tangerine skin and his eyes were so black it was impossible to see the pupils. He made my scalp prickle, and I gave my head a ferocious scratch.

'I'm Lucy.' My sister's voice was clipped, the words slow. 'My mum cleans here, but she's not feeling well so we're filling in. I know exactly what to do; I've helped her before.'

The man changed his stance and stood with his legs slightly apart thrusting his hands into his pockets. 'You have, have you?' His voice was treacly, and a smirk nestled at the corner of his wide, rubbery mouth.

'Well, pleased to meet you, Lucy. I'm Bill. Bill Cambly. I own the place. I just stopped by to pick up a set of keys but now I'm here...' He ran a finger across the desk then examined the tip. 'Very good. Very good.'

'I did that,' I said, my voice nothing more than a squeak which he ignored. Bill took a step closer to Lucy. 'You look like a very clever young lady. I reckon you could turn your hand to anything if you wanted.'

Lucy shrugged but she was smiling. She'd taken her gloves off and was tidying her hair.

'I think, if you're after some extra holiday work, I've got just the thing. How old are you?'

She cleared her throat. 'Sixteen.'

'Good. I'm holding a small, exclusive lunch party here tomorrow and I promised my wife I'd get someone extra in to hand out the drinks and canapés.'

Lucy nodded. 'Can my brother help too?'

Bill wrinkled his wide brow then turned and stared at me as though he'd only just clocked me. 'He's too young.'

'Then I can't do it,' said Lucy. 'We come as a team. Thank you though. Now, if you don't mind, I'd best get on.' She turned.

Bill's jaw clenched and his dark eyes narrowed. He gave a big sigh. 'Okay. Okay. The kid can hand out napkins or something, but he doesn't get the same rates as you.'

Lucy turned and smiled, her cheeks dimpling. 'Deal. When do you want us?'

'Turn up at eleven. You need to be in a short black skirt and a white blouse. The kid can just look presentable.'

'Thank you,' said Lucy. She gave a little wave, another beaming smile and then went back to the sink. Bill stood for a while staring after her.

'Could you put the plug back in?' I asked.

He turned, once again looking through me as though I was invisible. Then he grabbed something from behind the reception desk and left. I had to flip the switch back on myself.

Chapter 4
Cally

DI DAN MACKEY and his team were first to arrive on the scene. Dan immediately sent Val, Sasha and Bill to their hotel suite accompanied by a police liaison officer for support, and surreptitiously to observe their every movement. Gloria Cavel, the General Manager, grave-faced, had listened to Dan's instructions.

'But it's just an accident, isn't it?' she said, her pale face mottled like a half ripe strawberry – it made her green eyes shine, as though made from glass.

Cally, standing silent in the wings, had opened her mouth at this comment, but Dan cut her off with a warning glare. 'Probably, but we'll need to treat it as suspicious until we know exactly what happened.' As they left the office, he beckoned for Cally to accompany him. Cally turned in the doorframe and watched as Gloria reached for a nearby gin bottle, poured herself a large measure then knocked the whole lot back. Cally avoided the temptation to glance at her watch; there never was a good time for neat gin.

Dan led Cally out of the room and they went up the back staircase to Luella's bedroom. He handed her a pair of latex gloves and a couple of elasticated shoe protectors which she placed onto her black converse before entering the bridal suite. Cally noticed that the bouquet of roses she'd sent up to Luella's room the evening before were turning brown at the edges, as though mortified by the events surrounding them. Two people in crime scene suits were shuffling about in the room; one bagging up evidence and the other taking photos; flash bulbs periodically filling the room with a burst of dazzling white light. Thankfully, Luella's body had already been removed.

'Well – this is a nice surprise,' said Dan, looking around before ducking down to plant a kiss on her lips. Cally pulled away. 'Dan – no,' she hissed. 'Not appropriate.' She glanced to see if the forensic officers had noticed, but they were preoccupied with their work.

Dan looked wounded. 'We are in the bridal suite, and you are my fiancée,' he said, a tone of petulance in his voice.

She sighed and gave his gloved hand a surreptitious squeeze. 'Yes. But we're both at work and it's hardly a romantic setting – there's been a dead body in the room.'

He ignored her and stared up at the chandelier hanging from the central ceiling rose. 'Did we cross this venue off our list?'

Cally rolled her eyes. 'As if this was ever on the list to start with unless you've got a secret Swiss bank account you've been keeping quiet about.'

Dan sighed. 'I'm just worried *The Coach and Horses* isn't swanky enough for Lady Calista Cranleigh-Simmonds.'

'Firstly, don't call me that. I've told you a hundred times, Mum and Dad turned their back on that lifestyle before I was even a teenager. Second, our venue is perfect and, third, please don't ever use the word swanky again. EVER.'

She loved him, she had tried not to; he was neanderthal, crass – often archaic in his views; divorced with daughters that were closer to her in age than she was to his, but she couldn't live without him. And, as for Dan, he'd thrown himself wholeheartedly into the relationship and even Rolly, her Jack Russell, had been won over, that is, he no longer growled if they sat cuddled up on the sofa together as long as there was space for him in between. Plus, Dan was more than happy to go for long walks in the countryside with Rolly, especially if it ended up with a pint or two at the village pub.

Cally had been caught off guard when they had been strolling around Rutland Water and Dan went down on one knee, pulling a diamond solitaire out of his jacket pocket, at the same time keeping Rolly at bay with a biscuit. She'd said yes to his proposal without thinking.

After that, events had steamrollered along. Dan de-camped into Cally's sprawling house in Stoneygate which her mum, Helen, had persuaded her to move into before she'd set off travelling the world with her new partner, Ken. Dan and Cally had even talked about the prospect of having kids. Cally didn't necessarily want them, and it wasn't something she'd thought much about, but she needed to know if Dan was against it. He'd just grinned and said he didn't mind either way but felt that practice was always a good thing. Yes – Dan was a buffoon, but he was her buffoon and she loved him, and she also loved his boundless enthusiasm, most of which was currently being channelled into their wedding preparations.

Dan made a harumphing noise and pulled out his notebook. 'So, tell me exactly what you saw.' They shuffled into the bathroom which had been processed and was now empty. Cally shuddered, closed her eyes, and recalled the events. 'The sister, Sasha, was in the corridor, hammering on the door. She couldn't get in but the mother, Val Cambly, had a key card, so she entered and when we saw there was no one in the main part of the room, she knocked on the bathroom door which was closed.'

'Time?' asked Dan, scribbling down her words.

Cally perched on the edge of the sunken bath and stretched her feet out in front of her. 'It was about 9.30am when Val and I went up to her room. Previously, I'd been in the ballroom checking the seating plan arrangements for the wedding breakfast. Val came down from her room which is on the opposite side of the staircase to the bridal suite and invited me up to Luella's room to see how she was getting on.' She wrinkled her brow.

Dan's eyes narrowed. 'What?'

'It's probably not connected, but this morning a crate of sparkling wine went missing.'

Dan tapped the tip of his pen against the notebook. 'Hmmm. And what do you always tell me about coincidences?'

Cally shrugged. 'That they shouldn't be overlooked.'

He raised a dark eyebrow. 'How are you getting on with your investigation?'

She sighed. 'I've got absolutely fuck all to go on. It's like watching a Derren Brown magic trick. The stuff comes off the van and then somehow one or two boxes disappear into thin air – right before my eyes.'

'Bloody Cobras. They're a sneaky bunch. Any chance this Luella could be involved with them?'

'I doubt she'd stoop that low. The father, Bill Cambly, owns a yacht-building empire worth billions and Luella spends...spent her entire life shopping or pampering herself – and filming it.' Cally clapped her hands together. 'That's a point – her phone pretty much tracks her every waking movement, so I'd get trawling through that footage straight away; you'll get a great timeline.'

'Excellent. Will do.' Another scribble: square brow furrowed; his tongue poking out with concentration. 'So, what happened after you'd seen that the bathroom door was shut?'

'Val knocked on it. There was no answer. She listened then tried the handle and it opened so she went in and saw Luella slumped in the bath under the water. Val screamed. I rushed in, and we pulled her out, but I think she'd been dead for some time.

The water was barely warm.' Cally turned and pointed at the gold-plated tap end. 'See that bottle of expensive bubble bath?'

Dan peered at the dark vial with a purple rose emblazoned at its centre.

'I could smell it in the air, but there were no bubbles in the water.'

Dan nodded his head. 'Good. What else?'

Cally stood up and walked over to the sink. She tapped the rim. 'In this basin – there was a bikini. Which I thought was odd.'

'Why?'

'Why would she have a wet bikini?'

Dan shrugged. 'Maybe she'd taken an early morning swim. I can check that with the security footage at the spa.'

Cally drew her index finger across her forehead and sighed. 'Honestly Dan – don't your daughters teach you anything? Her hair was in a shower cap and then wrapped in a towel. She did *not* want it getting wet.'

Dan's face remained blank and he stared at Cally's fringe, as though hoping it would give him inspiration.

Cally smoothed down her own embarrassing haircut. 'Dan, if you've had expensive hair extensions and are about to have it styled, the last thing you want is to get chlorine in it. But, just suppose she'd been swimming and was rinsing out her bikini to take on honeymoon, she'd have it soaking in a sink filled with cold water. So, you need to check if the bikini is soaked in bath water.'

Dan's eyes grew wider. 'Why?'

'You don't have a bath in a bikini.'

He frowned, opened his mouth to say something then shut it again.

'I mean – it's weird. Unless she had someone with her in the bathroom.' Cally pressed her knuckles against her temple. 'Now I come to think of it, there was a champagne flute on the side, but only one.'

'That we know of.' Dan made a note. 'Right. Anything else?'

'Yes. She was half made-up. Her face was covered in foundation, but nothing else.

Dan scratched his unruly salt and pepper hair. He held up his palms. 'Please don't be cross, Cally, but I just don't understand what you're going on about.'

'It's strange. If you're having a bath to relax before you get ready, then you wouldn't start putting on your make-up until afterwards. You'd have the bath to open the pores then do make-up and hair.'

'Did she have...' Dan waved his hand around his head, '...you know, *people*, coming in to do that?'

'No. That was Luella's thing – she did a lot of Instagram posts about hair and beauty styling. She and her sister, Sasha, were doing everything themselves and Sasha was going to film it to broadcast later.'

Dan ran his finger down his notebook. 'So, just to recap, you didn't see anyone else in the corridor?'

'No.'

Dan scratched his stubbled chin. 'I think everything points to it being an accident, but I'm not ruling out foul play. Especially not with what you've just told me.' He stared at her. 'Now, am I right in thinking you have a relationship with the parents?'

Cally's shoulders sagged as she remembered Val's sobbing when the paramedics called time on the chest compressions, and it had finally sunk in that her daughter was dead. 'Yes – just the mum really. I like her.'

'That could be very useful. I want you to go and see her now and stay there for a bit. Make a note of anything odd or suspicious and report back to me.'

Cally frowned. 'As you know, Dan, I don't work for the police, and I'm not sure Miriam will like me doing you yet another favour. I'm already spying on The Cobras as an extra job to add to my already hefty workload.'

Dan clasped his hands together. 'Please. For me. I'll be going to interview them all separately later, but you're so good at getting people to open up. You might go down a rabbit hole and find out something useful without it even occurring to me to take that particular tunnel.'

She nodded then hung her head, already feeling the grief weighing her down. It was the last place she wanted to be.

Dan took her hands in his and kissed her forehead. 'Be careful.'

She gave him a hug then pulled away. 'I will.'

Cally left Luella's room and went down the steps towards the ballroom, crossed the small half-way landing and stood there, watching the staff below, talking in hushed voices. They had begun to dismantle everything, stacking towers of chairs against the panelled walls. The double doors to the ballroom opened and in came Nori gesticulating wildly with Bulag behind him pushing a parcel trolley, no doubt to retrieve some of the wine. Cally was about to move on, but something about Bulag made her stop in her tracks. His wrist was in a cast. He looked up at her and she pointed to the injury. 'Ouch – that looks painful.'

He shrugged. 'Only one week to go before the plaster comes off.'

'How did you do it?' she continued.

He winked at her. 'A little disagreement.' He shoulder-bumped Nori. 'You should see the other guy.'

They sniggered.

'Idiot,' muttered Cally under her breath before running up the stairs on the opposite side, emerging onto the other corridor. The ceiling on this side was flat with large lantern lights spaced at regular intervals which let in the natural daylight and showed up every scuff and stain on the plush royal-blue carpet. Cally was pondering what would happen to all the beautiful lilies when the hairs on the back of her neck prickled and she swung around. She was being filmed.

'Oh – oh no!' she said, her hands flying to cover her face. She peeped between a gap in her fingers and recognised the mass of blonde hair. It was Sasha. 'What are you doing?' she asked.

Sasha pulled the camera away from her bronzed face, her expression incredulous. 'I'm filming for Luella. It's what she would have wanted.'

'*Really?*'

'Oh yes. I've taken over her account – the follower numbers are already skyrocketing.' Sasha pressed her lilac-clawed hand to her heart. 'She'd have been sooooo delighted.'

Cally gave a cough as she tried to gather her thoughts. 'Er. Right. Anyway, Sasha, I can't be on film. It's...it's against my contract. All to do with the non-disclosure clauses we have to sign when we're employed at The Nix.'

Sasha pouted. 'But you'll spoil the real time sequence.'

Cally folded her arms. 'Sorry. But I absolutely can't be in it.'

Sasha ran a long acrylic fingernail through a curl of her hair as though she were combing it. She tutted then placed a hand on her hip. 'Well, I'll just have to patch up the film with some other footage, I suppose.'

'Good.' Cally pointed to the door. 'Can I go in and see your parents?'

'If you want. I mean, I really wouldn't unless you want to join the pity party.'

Cally didn't want, but nevertheless she took a deep breath, opened the door and went in.

Chapter 5
Mikey
2004

'Hey, Sleepy head. Time to get ready.'

Lucy was standing over my side of the bed. I propped myself onto my elbows and she held out a white cardboard box, placing it under my nose; it was full of dusty chunks of pale pink and yellow.

I pushed my spine up against the wall and, as I took a deep breath, I inhaled a powdery sweetness which made me splutter. 'What is it?'

'Try some.' She shook the box and the cubes shuffled around, making a scratching sound against the waxy paper.

I selected a pink cube, sniffed it like Aslan always did before he ate anything, and took a nibble. A delicious sweetness filled my mouth. It wasn't a harsh flavour, like jam, but was gentle and left a curious, perfumed aftertaste on my tongue. I took another bite – a big one this time, and then I swallowed. 'It tastes like jelly babies but nicer.'

'It's Turkish Delight. Rose and Lemon. You've got a rose one.'

'Turkish Delight! No way!'

'Yes. Just like Jadis gives Edmund.'

I was speechless. I'd seen her slip the hexagonal box into the bags with our kebabs last night, but I didn't know what it was then forgot all about it. Lucy touched the dreamcatcher and smiled. 'It's working.' She paused, lowering her gaze. 'By the way, Mum's back.'

My grin vanished.

'It's fine. I told her we did the job for her, and she was really pleased.' Lucy's eyes remained focused on the floor. I knew she was lying. She rolled her shoulders back. 'Anyway, we've got a job today, haven't we? And if we do good then Mr Cambly will give us some more work. Plus, we'll get paid in cash after we've finished, and it will be enough to get us each another treat.'

I rolled out of bed, landing with a thud on the floor which made Lucy giggle. I crawled over to the plastic box in which all my clothes were stored and searched for what to wear.

'Can you do my hair and make-up, Mikey? You're so good at it.'

I grinned. I *was* good at it. Thanks to Topsy, our neighbour's cat, we had an endless supply of glossy magazines – payment for Lucy taking care of her when Mrs Hudgens went to stay with her daughter and grandkids. It didn't matter that the magazines were out of date; I wasn't interested in the articles about health or relationships, it was the beauty sections which fascinated me. I could draw – my art teacher had wanted to take Mum to one side on parents' evening to talk about my future, but she never showed up – I doubt Mum even knew the name of our school let alone what a single one of the teachers were called or taught. But, much as I liked drawing on paper, there was something special about drawing on skin; the closeness; the intimacy.

Lucy knew how much I studied the magazine and so one time, when Mum went out, she raided her make-up bag which hung from a hook behind the bathroom door. My first commission: a smoky blue eye with black, winged liner and a frosted lip. I was slow and although Lucy didn't look quite the same as the model on the cover, the expression of joy as she examined her face in the bathroom mirror was priceless – I wanted to bottle it.

The magazines may have been out of date, but the classics never changed and soon I knew how to perform all the basics and had expanded my talents to incorporate hair braiding too.

For the Cambly job I'd decided a vibrant matt lip with nude eye palette would be a good way to create the illusion Lucy was older than she was. For the hair I was going to fluff up her curls and tie back the top section, letting the rest fall onto her shoulders but then as I combed, I noticed them; little white dots hitching a lift on the tines. I knew I needed to act fast and before she could protest, I plaited it in a tight French Braid. Just thinking about the lice made me start to itch all over and I had to concentrate on keeping my hands balled up in tight fists.

Lucy looked lovely. I'd mention the lice to her when we got back this evening – my heart plummeting at the thought of having to spend some of our earnings on nit shampoo.

I picked out my best shorts and a white tee-shirt which was a little bit stained but smelt of the purple grapey flower from the laundrette's fabric conditioner whose name wouldn't stay inside my head.

When we got to the entrance of Cambly Homes we were met by a slender woman in a tight-fitting, knee-length dress which was white and covered in black spots. She was pleased to see Lucy and pointed for her to go and stand with the other young people dressed in black and white, then she turned to me, a frown across her brow.

'And you are...' her voice trailed off. She tipped her head to one side and her curtain of glossy, almost purple, hair swung with her. I'd seen that colour advertised a lot recently.

'I like your Ober-jean hair,' I said. She blinked; her silver eyes disappearing into a crease of lines as a huge grin spread across her face, showing her big white teeth and small gums. Her sparkling earrings wobbled.

'Val, daaaaarling,' said Bill, sidling up to her and planting a loud kiss on her cheek. He was wearing a blue blazer and the silk handkerchief frothing at the breast pocket matched Val's dress. His chinos had a crisp pleat and his Gucci loafers (no socks) looked box fresh. He'd undone too many of the buttons on his cream shirt and little curls of his dark chest hair poked over the edges like hundreds of spiders' legs. The gold chain around his neck was thick and shiny and I recognised his aftershave as one we'd had a sample of in the magazine; it smelt of mint tea and furniture polish and had an exotic name neither Lucy nor I knew how to pronounce.

'This is Lucy's brother. I said he could hand out the napkins.' He winked at me. 'A very important job, hey kid?'

'Mr Cambly. You're such a softy,' purred Val, picking at his gold chain with her shiny fingernail. She punched Bill gently in the chest – she was wrong – he was rock solid. 'You're going to make a great dad. Can't you just see us with two gorgeous daughters?'

'As long as they look like you, Mrs Cambly. What did I do to deserve you?'

Val kissed him on the lips; it made a squelching noise, and then looked at me and held out her hand which I took, and she squeezed it. 'Come with me to the kitchen, young man, and I'll get you those napkins. Bill's right, it's a very important job.' Her palm was soft, but the diamonds on her rings dug into my skin. She talked all the time in a gravelly voice and I only had a few seconds between each question to give my replies: Mikey Jones; Nine; Flat 439 Hazleton Towers. Once we were in the kitchen, she leant over me, reaching up into a cupboard and stopped suddenly. She gasped.

'Oh! *Oh!*'

I tilted my head up to look into her wide eyes. 'Can't you find them?' I asked.

She bit her lip – a thin line of peach sticking to the edge of her top front teeth. She smoothed down her skirt and hurried over to the door and shut it, shooing away a simpering woman, who wanted to make Mr Cambly a cup of tea.

She stooped so she was eye-level with me. 'Mikey. I'm really sorry but I'm going to need you to go straight home.'

I frowned. 'Why?'

'Your hair, Mikey. It's crawling with lice. I'm so sorry honey.'

A burning sensation crept across my cheeks and my scalp tingled.

'But listen – it's no biggie. Why don't...'

The room went blurry as I bolted for the door.

'Wait! Mikey. Please wait.'

I didn't wait, I ran. Lucy was still in the huddle of penguins on the terrace, and she didn't see me which was just as well. I ran all the way home and let myself in with my keys. I went straight to the kitchen drawer and took out the scissors then proceeded to cut off all my hair. Afterwards, when I saw myself in the mirror, I cried and had to search in my clothes box for my winter woolly hat which made my head itch almost as much as the lice had. I looked like I had a disease.

I climbed into bed and waited for Lucy to come back, but she didn't return, not even when Mum was getting up for work. When Mum left her room, I pretended I was asleep and I heard her come across and for a while she stood over me, sniffing, but she didn't say anything. The front door slammed shut and I stayed still. I wasn't sure if she had a man staying over, so taking a deep breath, I tiptoed over and peeked in. It was empty. Knowing I was alone took away some of the heart flutters – I really didn't want to tell Lucy I had lice and that she had them too. *Where was she?*

I must have fallen asleep and then I heard the rattle of the key in the lock. It was Lucy.

She went to the bathroom, staying in there for a few minutes, and then she walked around her side of the bed, picked the dream-catcher off its hook and smashed it into pieces. I supressed a gasp. I was to blame – I'd embarrassed her. Had she been sacked? But if she had that didn't explain why she was so late. My stomach gave a loud rumble.

'I'm sorry Mikey,' she said. 'I'll get us something good to eat tomorrow. I promise.'

I didn't say anything.

She reached out to stroke my hair. 'What the...?'

Chapter 6
Cally

CALLY LOUNGED on the sofa in her sitting room, her calves on Dan's lap. Between large gulps of rosé wine, Dan half-heartedly massaged her feet and picked through the box of chocolates to find her anything with a caramel centre. Rolly had manoeuvred himself so he was stretched out along the back cushion, squashed up next to her thigh, his head resting on her left knee. He was exhausted from doggy day care but couldn't quite give in to sleep and sporadically opened one eye to check Cally was still there.

'How were they – the Camblys?' asked Dan, placing a chocolate marble on her kneecap. Rolly's whiskers twitched at the scent, but she whipped it into her mouth before he realised what was causing it. The hem of the curtains in front of the French windows ruffled in the summer's breeze and beyond them Cally could see her tub of bright orange marigolds knocking their bonnets together. She'd been meaning to get into the garden to do some dead heading but after they'd cleared away the supper things, the draw of the sofa had been too tempting.

'That wasn't caramel,' she said, her mouth full of praline.

'Oh, sorry,' said Dan pushing his tangerine-rimmed reading glasses off the top of his head and onto his nose; he thought they made him look 'hip' when, in fact, they screamed middle-aged crisis. Unfortunately, his daughters had told him exactly that and it had made him determined to persist in wearing them just to be contrary. He peered at the menu selection. 'So?'

She swallowed the chocolate. 'Oh – you know. Awful. I still can't believe it.'

He took a sip of wine then went back to a forensic examination of a chocolate in a rose-gold foil wrapper. 'You saw the fiancé too?'

'Yes. Jonty van der Kelt. He and the best man were staying in a guest house on the outskirts of Leicester and only came to The Nix after we'd found Luella's body. Poor chap was distraught.'

Dan nodded. 'His alibi is solid. Bless him. He's a bit...'

'What?'

He unwrapped the foil, leant over and popped the chocolate into her mouth. He tapped the side of his head. 'He's not exactly the smartest tool in the box, is he?'

'This is caramel,' she said, giving him a thumbs up. She patted her tummy. 'No more, or I'll explode.'

'Me too,' said Dan sucking in his stomach. 'I want to look good for the wedding photos.' He reached down to his side of the sofa and pulled out a magazine, handing it to Cally. 'This is for you,' he said, helping himself to another chocolate.

Cally stared at the cover. It was a bridal magazine and the model on the front beamed at her from behind a vertiginous veil. For a split second she saw Luella's face staring out at her – haunting dark eyes imploring her – *to do what?* Cally blinked and the image was gone.

'You'd look fabulous in the whole meringue thing,' said Dan. 'Oh, by the way, I was thinking of asking Miriam to say a few words at the wedding.'

Cally, mid-sip, spluttered. 'Why?'

'Because she was the one who introduced us.'

Cally thumped her fist against her chest. '*Dan*, I was tracking down a husband who was having an affair.'

'Yes, but who also happened to be a serial flasher.' He grinned. 'If it weren't for your razor-sharp eyes, we'd never have identified his you-know-what in the line-up.'

He leant over and kissed her cheek. Rolly gave a warning growl and climbed higher onto Cally's lap, dislodging the magazine onto the floor. Dan laughed and tickled the back of his head, between his silky ears. 'It's alright old fella, you can have a fancy outfit to wear on the day too.'

Cally took a sharp breath in then forced a laugh. 'So... are you allowed to tell me anything more about what the pathologist said? Off-the-record, of course.'

Dan reached towards the coffee table and handed Cally her glass of wine. 'Did you know Luella took Bonsai?'

Cally wrinkled her brow.

'Otherwise known as, phenazepam?'

Cally took a sip of rosé and rinsed the chocolate from her teeth, wincing; the wine now tasted like vinegar. 'No. I wasn't aware that Luella took anything like that – it wasn't part of her girl-next-door image. Have you spoken to her parents about it?'

'Not yet, but Dr Death says the early indication is she had a heart attack, most likely brought on by the combination of phenazepam and alcohol. The actual cause of death, though, was drowning.'

Cally shook her head. 'That doesn't feel right. I'd be interested to hear what Val and Bill have to say about it.'

'Maybe she had the drugs to help her sleep and took it as a one-time thing to settle her nerves, not realising she shouldn't mix it with booze.'

'Would you experiment with something like that on the biggest day of your life? I'd check her medical records, but they can't be prescription drugs – they're illegal over here.' She yawned

– the combination of lots of food and alcohol was making her feel sleepy. 'You know I think I'll give Rolly a run around in the garden then head off to bed. It's been a long day.' She stood up and stretched, her joints clicking. Rolly immediately leapt off the sofa and went over to the French doors pressing his nose against the glass and leaving a greasy smudge.

'Do you want me to join you?' asked Dan, who had already picked up the remote control and was flicking through the sports' channels – she found it intriguing and endearing that Dan would happily watch tiddlywinks if it were televised.

'No, you're alright. I think I need a bit of time to clear my head – it's buzzing.'

She pulled on her gardening crocs and picked up a semi-bald tennis ball then headed out into the dusk. The sky was violet, morphing into a sheet of indigo but the moment she stepped onto the patio the security lights flicked on, bathing her in white light and casting spiky shadows onto the lawn. She bounced the ball on the patio a few times, revving Rolly into a woofing frenzy, then lobbed it as far down the lawn as she could, towards Nonna's apartment at the bottom of the garden; Cally's former residence and where her mum and Ken now stayed when they came to visit. Rolly charged after the ball, his tail wagging like a windscreen wiper in a rainstorm. There was a small shed at the side of the house, and she unlatched the door and breathed in the scent of creosote and fermented grass clippings. She grabbed a trug from the corner and pulled Nonna's floral-handled secateurs off a shelf which was sticky with cobwebs. Cally's heart jolted thinking about what Nonna would say if she could see the state of her precious garden. She peered into the gloom and saw Rolly snuffling at something hidden under a blanket of pine needles.

She crouched before the nearest terracotta pot and pulled at the spindly weeds which were threading through the marigolds. The moment her fingertips touched the soil she felt her body relax; her breathing and heartbeat slowing as the jumble of thoughts in her head began to separate from each other, dissolving the angry fizzing in her head. As she snipped at the golden petals, she tried to remember what had caused the knot in her chest in the first place. Despite the horrible tragedy involving the Camblys, there was something niggling at the back of her mind. *Yes!* That was it: how was the thief, or thieves, stealing from the hotel?

She clipped the dead flowers, dropping them into the trug and turning over the soil with the points of the secateurs. Rolly made an appearance, dropping his ball onto the backs of her calves. She threw the slimy thing in the air a few times then hurled it into the shadows and, once again, off he scarpered. She switched to a different pot; and knelt beside one she'd filled with scarlet geraniums, inhaling their earthy smell. Sasha popped into her thoughts and though she tried to sweep her to the sides, the image of the young woman glued behind the camera remained. Cally had been baffled by Sasha's desire to document everything – even her parents' raw grief wasn't off limits. She recalled how irritated she'd been when Cally spoilt her timeline. Her fingertips froze, half-submerged in compost. What was it she'd said? *I'll just have to patch up the film with some other footage.*

She remembered the sly look Stinky Steve and Paula had given each other. She leapt to her feet. *Of course!* They were in on it.

Dan appeared at the door; a grin plastered across his face. He beckoned her with a frantic flap of his hand. 'Cally. You've got to come and see this. Come on.' Intrigued, Cally kicked off her shoes, washed her hands and went back to the sofa. Dan had paused the TV and waited until she was sitting down again.

'Wait until you see this. It's your old pal Misha Carlton.'

Cally gave an involuntary grimace. Cally, before she became a PI, had been at stage school with Misha and did not like her one bit. It was part jealousy and part that she simply didn't like her, but the undeniable fact remained: Misha had beaten her to a role in *Downton Abbey* and then gone on to become a superstar. No matter how much Cally swore it wasn't just a case of green-eyed envy, the worse it looked for her especially as she'd quit acting altogether after that crushing disappointment. Unfortunately for Cally, the local media was saturated with Misha's image at the moment as the film she was currently starring in was being shot in Market Bowden.

Dan pressed play. There was Misha Carlton sitting behind a long table with a glass of water and microphone in front of her; flashbulbs going off every few seconds. She'd grown her hair and corkscrew, caramel ringlets bounced onto the tops of her elegant shoulders. She was wearing a tight-fitting navy polo neck and a thick coating of black eyeliner made her green eyes stand out. Her skin was a flawless peachy colour with a dusting of blusher to highlight her angular cheekbones.

A journalist shouted from the middle of the crowd of people: 'So, your latest film *Mother's Ruin* is set in rural Ireland and is all about what it's like to be a mother bringing up small children during a conflict. Is motherhood something on your agenda, now you and Henry Carmichael are happily married?'

Misha gave a tight smile which didn't show her pearly white teeth. 'No,' she snapped then followed it with a forced giggle. 'I mean, we're both far too busy to unload the dishwasher let alone think about becoming parents.'

A male voice at the back of the room piped up: 'But if you were to have a baby, have you got any names?'

Misha's eyes narrowed and the muscles in her jaw clenched. She spoke through gritted teeth. 'Like I said – starting a family isn't something either of us want at the moment.'

'But...' continued the man. The TV camera panned around to catch a glimpse of the persistent questioner, other journalists also turning, craning their necks to stare at a hooded figure at the back of the room. 'If it's a girl, how about Jad–'

There was a crash as Misha leapt to her feet – her expression one of both fury and horror. She slammed her palms against the table, pushing herself to her feet and muttered something about needing some air before storming out, knocking over the glass of water in the process.

'Jeez!' whistled Dan. 'She really doesn't want kids. Anyway, the news channels are full of her little tantrum – she's not done herself any favours especially as she's playing the role of an inspirational mother.'

Cally grinned.

'I thought you'd like it,' said Dan, moving over to lock the doors behind Rolly who had emerged from the garden carrying a stick twice the length of his body.

'Oh – I'm not smiling about her,' said Cally moving to Rolly's biscuit jar and shaking it to try and distract him from taking the large branch upstairs to bed. 'It's rather sad, don't you think? Why do people assume having kids is on everyone's agenda? Or perhaps she can't have kids and the journalist pressing her for information hit a raw nerve.'

Dan scratched his head. 'So, what are you smiling about?'

She held up her palm and Rolly sat back on his hind legs, dropping the stick and opening his mouth in anticipation of the Bonio about to fly through the air towards him. In one swift, fluid movement, Cally threw the biscuit then stooped to swipe the stick which she put on the kitchen island. She moved over to Dan who was at the sink pouring them both a glass of water. She wrapped her arms around his middle and squeezed.

'I'm smiling because I've figured out exactly how the goods are going missing from The Nix, and I can't wait for tomorrow morning to come around so I can get the whole damn lot of them arrested.'

Chapter 7
Mikey
2004

THE NEXT MORNING Lucy was very quiet. She'd gone out first thing to buy nit shampoo from the chemist in town. The bag she came back with was a different one to the chemist around the corner – she'd probably gone to the big pharmacy in the centre, in case she bumped into anyone she knew. Not that it's polite to ask anyone what they are buying in a chemist, but some things are more embarrassing to be seen with than others. Our pillowcases were back in the laundry bag along with all the towels. She'd also had to buy a disposable razor to shave off the uneven patches of fuzz clinging to my scalp. She couldn't have been too angry with me because she'd been to the pound shop and bought me a black baseball cap which had 'Cool' embroidered in silver above the rim. She also came back with a McDonalds breakfast – a proper sausage and egg McMuffin – not the cheap version we sometimes got from Sid's café. At the time, I remember thinking, despite her grumpy mood, she must have earnt herself a tidy sum of money.

I ate slowly, chewing each mouthful to make it last as long as possible.

She took little sips of coffee which she drank black, like a grown-up.

When I'd finished, I folded up the wrapper and took a sip of orange juice. 'You promise you didn't get sacked because of the lice?'

She shook her head; her jaw clenched. 'I told you. They paid me but said there was no more work.'

I knew I probably shouldn't have pursued my line of enquiry, but something didn't make sense. I fiddled with the brim of my cap, bending it into a more rounded shape. 'But...but Mr Cambly said there would be lots more work and you stayed so late. They must have thought you were a very good worker to keep you there for so long.'

She shrugged and stared at the back of the sofa where a bank of fluff from the carpet had collected in a ragged line. I wanted to ask why she'd smashed the dream catcher, but she had an aura about her; a thick layer of misery which enveloped her skin and made me tongue-tied.

The silence was interrupted by a loud rapping at the door. Both of us started then stared at each other unblinking. The rhythmic knock sounded again, and Lucy's eyes darted towards Mum's bedroom door, both of us weighing up which was worse: Mum being woken up prematurely, like a grizzly brown bear evicted from its hibernation cave, or what was waiting for us on the other side. Lucy nodded for me to take a peep and I went over, stood on tiptoes and squinted through the spyhole.

I turned to Lucy and frowned. 'It's Val Cambly.'

Lucy's already pale face drained of any remnants of colour.

Lucy hissed, 'no!' at exactly the same time I opened the door.

Val stepped in, all smiles; diamante encrusted sunglasses pushed back on the top of her head making her glossy purple-black hair curl up behind her ears. She was wearing a thin denim jacket over a white tee-shirt, and long white linen trousers finished off with wedges, bright pink toenails peeping out from the ends. The long trail of beads bunched around her neck were the same colour as her toenails, but her fingernails were French manicured, each crescent tip a perfect arc of white. 'Hello.' She bustled in, lavender and vanilla following in her wake, and she put two large shopping bags on top of the work surface arranging her Gucci handbag next to them.

'Is your Mum in?' she asked, her eyes widening as she took in her surroundings although she was careful to keep her smile fixed.

Lucy pointed to Mum's door and pressed her finger to her lips. 'She works nights.'

Val made an -o with her mouth and nodded. She didn't, however, lower her voice. 'Right. Well – I hope you don't mind but I've brought you a few things.'

I put my hands on my hips. 'How d'you know where we live?'

She smiled and tapped the side of her head. I pointed to my chair and Val brushed off a clump of congealed egg and sat down.

'Do you want a drink?' I asked. 'Coffee?'

'You drink coffee, Mikey?' I nodded and stood next to her. I hoped she wouldn't recognise the empty sachets strewn across the table as being stolen from the kitchen in her husband's office.

'Thanks, but I'm okay,' she said, her gaze falling on the sticky table, flitting from the MacDonald's wrappers to the dirty mugs. Another wave of heat spread across my face as I imagined seeing our flat through the eyes of a stranger. Val was too perfect to be sitting in it, certainly not when dressed in white.

'First,' she held up her index finger. 'Oh! Be a love and pass me those bags, Mikey.' I handed them to her, and she delved into the first one – it was that expensive plastic, the one which doesn't break or rustle. She put a box of lice shampoo onto the table. 'You might need another dose,' she said to Lucy. Then she looked at me and lifted off my cap, her silver bangles jingling. 'Ah! Mikey – I see I was too late.' She gave a sad smile. 'Never mind. The cap looks very *cool*.'

'I also have this for you,' she went back in and then pulled out a toothbrush and some toothpaste – 'you know, Mikey, it's berry flavour.' She pointed at a picture of a googly-eyed strawberry. 'Just a bit of brushing every morning and before you go to bed and those teeth will be as shiny as a new penny.' I took the toothpaste and pulled off the lid. I gave it a hard squeeze, but nothing came out. Val took it off me, unscrewed the lid and peeled off a silver film which she flicked into the MacDonalds rubbish. 'There!'

I stared at the pink blob oozing out of the neck.

'Why don't you go and try it out?'

I shrugged as though I wasn't bothered one way or the other, but I took my time choosing which colour toothbrush to have (turquoise) and the toothpaste tasted like bubble-gum. I couldn't help feeling a bit prickled and out of sorts, though, because it meant Val had noticed my grey teeth.

When I went back into the room, Val was standing in front of the tall cupboard, unpacking the rest of the stuff and putting it onto the empty shelves. I spied a big loaf of bread, some tins of beans and soup, and a string bag stuffed with satsumas which smelt like Christmas candy.

Val was talking over her shoulder to Lucy while she arranged everything. 'It was Bill's idea and I think it's wonderful. A couple of times a week. Filing and that sort of thing.'

Lucy stared at the backs of her hands.

'You're sixteen Lucy – you need to start thinking about what you want to do when you leave school. This would be great for your CV plus you can earn some money. He's seen something in you which he – *we* want to nurture.'

Lucy stayed quiet. It was embarrassing. Val was being so kind and yet here Lucy was sulking about something.

I tried to chivvy along the conversation. 'What about me? Is there anything I can do?'

Val shut the cupboard door and leant her back against it, folding her arms across her chest. 'Yes. We've thought about that too. There's a little snug room at the back of the office which no one uses because – well, I don't know why and it doesn't matter, but I thought I could put in a couple of beanbags and cushions and maybe you'd like to stay there and watch TV while Lucy's working.'

I jumped into the air. 'Yes! Yes! Oh! Wow! I can watch MTV like the others. You know it's just non-stop music? Non-stop music.'

'Is that so?' Val grinned.

I nodded. 'When I'm grown up, I'm going to be lead guitar in a band. I'll sing too and –'

'No,' said Lucy in a loud voice. She'd scrunched up her features so they looked pinched and ugly.

Val frowned. 'Why ever not?'

'Luce,' I whined. 'Please, pleeeease, Luce. It's such a good idea.'

The door to the bedroom opened, there was a waft of weed, and out stumbled a man in baggy y-fronts with black printed handprints on each of the saggy bum cheeks. He was thin and any skin which wasn't covered in tattoos was pale, almost blue. He stared at us and said: 'What you fucking looking at?' Then it seemed to register that there was another adult in the room. He turned back to the bedroom. 'Shez. Sheryl – there's some weird lady in the flat.'

Val's eyes narrowed, her mouth a flat line.

'Who the fuck are you? You a fucking social worker?' he asked. At that, I heard a thud and a few seconds later Mum lunged out of the room, the hem of her tee-shirt caught up in her pants. Her skin was mottled, like a slice of tinned corned beef, and a thick green-blue vein snaked down her right leg. Her lank, brown hair clung to her scalp and she smoothed it behind her ears; her nicotine stained fingers trembling.

Val took a deep breath in through her nose and put her hands in her jacket pockets.

'What's going on?' Mum's bloodshot eyes were wide with confusion and worry. She sniffed. 'Lucy? Who's this? A teacher?'

Val stepped forward. 'I'm Val Cambly.' She held out her hand, but Mum just stared at it as though the gesture was beneath her.

Val raised an eyebrow and shrugged. 'Lucy did some waitressing for us the other day and we were very impressed by her work ethic. I'm here to offer her a summer job.'

Mum's expression morphed from fear to relief and then she set it at scorn. 'She doesn't need a job. I work.' The man coughed, scratched his arse then went into the bathroom slamming the door behind him.

Val ran her tongue across her top teeth but said nothing. She busied herself folding up the plastic bags and she dropped them into her handbag which she slung over her shoulder, holding onto the gold chain as though it were a safety belt. 'Yes, Mrs Jones. She does.' She turned to Lucy and clamped a hand on her shoulder. 'Come to the office tomorrow afternoon. Wear something smart but don't worry, I can sort you out if needs be. Mikey you be there too.' She turned to Mum and tilted her nose into the air. 'If you guys don't show, I'll be back, and I won't be on my own. I have a good friend who works for the local council; children's department as it happens...' She raised an eyebrow, her gaze sweeping across the room and lingering on a crumpled piece of foil and syringe which lay on the threshold of Mum's bedroom. The thought hung in the air along with the stale smell of marijuana as she stalked out of our flat.

Lucy swallowed. Mum scowled. The tattooed man lit up a joint.

I couldn't understand why I was the only one who was deliriously happy with the outcome.

Chapter 8
Cally

CALLY WALKED along the corridor towards Miriam Kershaw's office, the static from the nylon carpet sparking beneath the soles of her shoes. Miriam was what her mum, Helen, would call a 'blue-stocking' and who Dan described as 'a sheep in wolf's clothing'. Cally knew Dan's assessment was wrong; he was far too archaic in his belief that women always had a warm and fluffy side. Miriam had retired from a lifetime of service in the police force five years' ago and there was no soft-centre nestling within Miriam Kershaw – what you saw was what you got. For Cally, Miriam epitomised the sort of self-awareness and control she could only aspire to. Her watchful silences had the ability to make Cally feel like confessing to all sorts of misdemeanours she had and hadn't done.

Miriam was in her late fifties with a willowy figure. No matter what day of the working week, she looked exactly the same; dressed in a charcoal grey suit with her dyed curly morello-cherry hair worn loose around her shoulders and a smidgen of blue-black mascara cocooning her green eyes. Cally would have loved to know what she wore on her days off – Dan who had worked with her on the murder squad said he reckoned she didn't ever change, not even for bed, but Cally leaned towards a rugby shirt, bootcut jeans and black, non-branded trainers.

Thankfully for Cally, Miriam liked her and after Cally's acting career had come crashing down and she realised that she couldn't survive as a jobbing gardener she had applied for a post at Miriam's fledgling PI agency. Since Cally's arrival, Miriam had taken it upon herself to assist with enhancing her skills, promising her a promotion and generous pay rise at the end of the year if she kept up her good performance record.

Cally stood outside Miriam's door and smoothed down her hair. She assumed she had been summoned to her office to receive a quick burst of praise which would be followed up by a new case. Cally had already resigned herself to saying goodbye to her brief stint of brushing shoulders with the rich and famous at The Nix before heading off to whatever joys awaited her; the case before this had been a series of garden shed burglaries and before that, a graffiti artist who couldn't spell or draw but really had it in for someone called Barry.

Cally lifted her hand to knock on the door then paused. She could hear raised voices coming from within. When there was a lull in the conversation she rapped loudly.

'Enter,' came Miriam's low voice.

Cally opened the door and saw Miriam sitting at her desk with Dan leaning against the windowsill next to a vicious-looking cacti. She did a double take: first, what was he was doing there? He'd had a phone call in the early hours, showered and then left without making her a cup of tea or letting Rolly out and she hadn't heard from him since – not even a love heart and a yawning emoji. Second, what had they been arguing about? Perhaps Miriam also thought that Dan and Cally's first encounter wasn't worthy of its own special wedding speech.

'Come in. Sit,' said Miriam, pointing to one of the two faux leather chairs opposite her desk. Cally perched on the one on

Miriam's left, which permitted her to see Dan out of the corner of her eye; she could feel his gaze upon her. She tilted her chin upwards and opened her blue eyes wide in the hope her boss thought she looked bright and alert rather than tired and a tad hungover. After she had told Dan about her breakthrough, they had decided to crack open a mini bottle of champagne to celebrate.

'First,' said Miriam interlocking her slender fingers, neatly trimmed nails unvarnished, 'well done for catching the hotel thieves. Gloria Cavel is delighted. Talk me through it.' Her desk was devoid of anything except an A4, hard-backed, lined notebook with a gold-lidded ink pen cradled between the pages.

Cally nodded and smoothed her hands across her suit trousers. 'It was something Sasha Cambly, Luella's sister, said – you see she's always filming everyone and everything. When I spoilt her action sequence, she said she'd cut me out and paste in a section to make it look as though it was part of the real-time filming.'

Miriam pressed her thin lips together. 'Hmm.'

Cally swallowed. 'When I was in the security office at The Nix, I caught a glance between the security guards which I couldn't place. Looking back, I now know they were laughing at me. But you see, later in the day, I saw Bulag, one of the Cobra men, taking back some of the wine from the abandoned wedding breakfast. I spotted his wrist was in plaster and he quite happily told me he'd had it in a cast for a while.'

Miriam raised an immaculately plucked eyebrow.

'It was only when I was in the garden last night, I realised the footage of him on the tape I'd seen that very morning showed him getting out of the van with no plaster on his wrist.'

Miriam pressed her fingertips together and nodded. 'Pre-recorded footage. Clever.'

'Yes,' said Dan. 'My colleague said the security guards were in on it and are now being very helpful, claiming they were forced to take part in the operation. Bulag, however, is staying quiet, but with the other two squealing he's not going to get away with it. Plus, now we have the CCTV evidence as proof which some lucky detective will have to go through frame by frame.'

'Excellent,' said Miriam, clapping her hands together, her gaze turning back to Dan.

'Over to you, then, DI Mackey.'

Cally looked at him and he gave a sheepish smile.

'I'm sorry to say this, Cally, but I'm afraid I've received some very bad news.'

'Oh?' Cally's mouth went dry. Rolly then her mum sprang into her head, but she didn't have time to berate herself for it being in that order.

The afternoon sun emerged from behind a fat cloud, its rays lighting up half of Dan's face, and Cally noticed the bags under his eyes – he looked exhausted. 'Bill Cambly killed himself last night. He's dead.'

'What?' Cally lurched forwards, her elbows banging against the desk, sending a jolt of excruciating pain up each arm. 'But... but how?'

'He shot himself in his London flat, using his own revolver for which he had a legitimate licence.'

'Because of Luella?' Cally felt the bile rising up her throat. *Poor Val. Poor Sasha.*

Dan bit his lower lip then let out a puff of air. 'Here's the thing. He left a note saying Luella's death was all his fault.'

Cally became aware of a flimsy plastic cup of water being placed in her hand.

'In through the nose and out through the mouth,' said Miriam, perching next to her on the desk. Cally took a sip then set the cup down and gave a few slow, deep breaths. She could see Dan clenching and unclenching his fists, no doubt, trying to squash the urge to come over and envelop her in a hug which would have been very unprofessional for both of them.

'Are...are you telling me,' said Cally, 'that Bill Cambly killed his own daughter?'

Dan shook his head. 'I don't think he killed her himself – but the phrasing of the note indicates he was somehow involved.'

'But how?' asked Cally.

Dan shrugged. 'We've no idea at the moment.'

Miriam reached behind for her notebook and flicked back a page, her eyes scanning the surface for something. 'But the police are sure Luella's death was murder because of several other reasons.' She clicked her fingers. 'Dan. Explain.'

'Yes. Like you suggested, Cally, we went back through Luella's film footage and on the morning of the wedding she films herself having a cup of tea in bed and she's chatting about how excited she is.'

Cally raised a hand. 'What does she look like? I mean – clothes and make-up.'

Dan took a few seconds to check his notes. 'Her hair is down and she's wearing no make-up. Then her phone rings and she answers, then immediately cuts the film. That's the last footage of her and it was taken at 7.30 am. We traced the number and it was–'

'– a burner phone,' said Cally with a sigh.

Dan gave a small smile and raised his palms in the air. 'But, of course.' He paused. 'The costume in the sink was indeed soaked in bathwater not chlorine but, and this is the most interesting thing, the phenazepam in her system was administered via her... what's it called?' He patted his cheeks.

'Foundation.' Cally frowned. 'Wow! That's really odd.'

'I've told Dan that we'd be happy to continue to do some more surreptitious digging into the Cambly family for him,' said Miriam, checking her watch, 'if you're happy to do so, Cally.'

'Of course. I'd be happy to.'

Miriam held up an index finger, 'but that's not all. Another case has come to The Phoenix which needs our attention.'

'Oh?' Cally could see Dan shaking his head at her; his mouth set in a flat line.

Cally turned her gaze back to focus on Miriam.

'Yes. A celebrity has received some intimidating items through the post and her husband came to talk to me about arranging some low-level protection. He's already a member of the club so he and I have decided they are going to stay in a suite there until we know what we're dealing with.'

Cally nodded. She could hear Dan clicking his tongue against his teeth. 'So...'

'So, I'd like you to stay under cover at the hotel. From there you can do some more digging about the Camblys' personal lives to help our *very* good friends, the police.' Miriam glanced at her Rolex. 'If Val, with whom I believe you have a good relationship, decides to confide in you, she will expect to be able to contact you there. Gloria Cavel has found a quiet room in the beauty salon from whence you can operate.'

'But I'm meant to be the Trainee Assistant Banqueting Manager.'

Miriam flicked her hand in the air. 'Not a problem. Gloria's going to tell the staff, if they bother to ask, you're doing some marketing work for the re-vamped spa. Whilst there you can keep a close eye on our celebrity as they're staying in an apartment which you'll be able to see from your office window.'

A sudden wave of shock washed over Cally, making her hands tremble. 'I still can't believe Bill shot himself. That's just terrible. Poor Val and Sasha. Just horrible – in the space of only a few days too.'

Miriam steepled her long fingers together. 'Indeed. Any questions so far?'

Cally looked at Dan who was scowling. 'Is there any reason why DI Mackey looks so unhappy about the situation?'

Miriam snorted. 'So, you noticed the face like a slapped arse? Even though this has absolutely nothing to do with him, Dan thinks this is too much work for you and he wants the protection job to be done by someone else.'

Dan opened his mouth, but Miriam held up her hand. She narrowed her green eyes and stared at Cally. 'Is it too much for you?'

Cally shook her head. 'No. Not at all.'

While Miriam picked up her desk phone and dialled, Dan tried to get Cally's attention, swiping his hand across his neck and mouthing 'no' but Cally glared at him then looked away. The job sounded perfect – unlike Dan, she could multi-task, besides, she owed it to Val to help get to the bottom of this terrible mess.

'Send him in right away.' Miriam slammed down the receiver.

After a few minutes, the door opened and in came a short, muscly man with a mop of blonde curly hair. He had piercing blue eyes, and his smile dimpled his cheeks to reveal a set of perfect, white teeth. He was vaguely familiar. The man was clearly nervous, rubbing his hands together and blinking his long eyelashes fast.

Miriam gave the man a huge, simpering smile and pointed for him to sit in the chair next to Cally.

'Henry Carmichael,' Miriam purred, 'meet PI Cally Simmonds – one of our finest. I have appointed her to work undercover at the hotel, keeping a close eye on you and your wife.'

Henry looked at Cally and swallowed. 'Gosh. Thank you so much.' His voice had a slight West Country burr to it. He glanced at Dan.

'This is DI Dan Mackey who is here on another matter, but I don't think it will do any harm if he listens in on this too.'

The men nodded at each other.

'Now Henry,' continued Miriam, 'although we've already spoken in great detail, I think it would be best if you explain to Cally yourself why you are concerned.'

Cally took her notebook out of her handbag and flicked to a clean page. Henry scratched his head then placed his palms flat on his thighs. 'Um...Yes. Sure.' He swallowed again and Miriam passed him a glass of water in a horrible plastic cup – a far cry from the iced, mint-infused water at The Nix. He took a sip then smacked his lips together. 'So, these past few months my wife has been acting very strange.'

Cally raised an eyebrow.

Henry tipped his head to one side. 'Yes. I know what you're thinking. She's having an affair and wants a divorce.'

Cally gave an apologetic smile.

Henry shrugged. 'That's what I thought to start with. In our world...'

'Which is?' asked Cally.

'Oh! Sorry. I'm an actor – so's my wife.'

'Right.'

'Well – the nature of the job is such that we often spend vast amounts of time apart holed up with other lonely actors in similar situations.'

'Sounds like you need counselling and not a PI,' said Dan, his tone clipped.

Henry gave a small, dry laugh. 'I hear what you're saying, but if you let me explain, there's more to it than that. You see, I bought a flat in The Village part of Market Bowden. A mate of mine needed a quick sale and so I got it for a great deal. Honestly, you should see it – it's got plans for development which I'm working on with an architect as we speak.'

Dan rolled his eyes, but Miriam was sitting behind the desk, resting her chin on her hands and gazing at Henry with a look of utter adoration. Cally had never seen such an expression cloud her face before and it was throwing her concentration. Miriam licked her lips and simpered: 'Sounds wonderful. Such a desirable area too.'

'Yes. I love it, but rather foolishly I bought the flat as a surprise for my wife and she wasn't pleased although I was certain she'd come round once we'd settled in.'

'And?' asked Cally.

'And she hated it and almost the moment we moved in she started getting weird fan stuff through the post.'

'What sort of stuff?' Cally's pen was poised.

He shrugged. 'I know this is going to sound really strange – it was pom poms – dozens of them. There was one time when I came into the kitchen and Misha was holding a pink bobble hat to her chest and crying her eyes out.'

'Why? Was it badly made?' asked Dan. Both Cally and Miriam glared at him, and he shrugged and mouthed '*what?*'

'Was there ever a message attached?' asked Cally.

'No. Never – and the postmark was local.'

'How strange,' said Cally, frantically scribbling. 'But nothing has escalated beyond these pom poms.'

'No, and whoever it was, has stopped sending them now, but it's taken a bizarre toll on her. She recently stormed out of an interview about her latest film and wouldn't tell me why.'

Something at the back of Cally's mind fluttered its dusty wings.

'But the final straw was when she was watching the news last night and she collapsed.'

Cally's eyes widened. 'OMG? Is she okay?'

'Yes. Thank you. It was a panic attack, brought on by stress, but I need her to feel safe, so I've booked her into The Nix and Miriam said that you'll be able to keep an eye on her.' Miriam fluttered her eyelashes.

Cally supressed a giggle. She coughed. 'Yes. So, Mr Carmichael–'

'Henry.'

'Er...yes, Henry, I'll do everything I can to make her feel safe and protected, hopefully without intruding but it sounds to me that what your wife really needs is a bloody good rest.'

Henry sat back and sighed. 'Absolutely. She's leaving the flat first thing tomorrow and I've got her booked in for a personal beauty session with a superstar make-up legend. Have you heard of him? JayDoll? He's a social media influencer – not that I've ever come across him before. Apparently, according to Gloria, he only comes to The Nix once a quarter and getting an appointment with him is like winning the lottery, so I thought it was too good an opportunity to miss, but apart from that I'm going to make her stay in our room and rest.'

'That sounds like a perfect plan.' Cally grinned. 'Oh! By the way, I forgot to ask; your wife – what's her name?'

'Misha. Misha Carlton.'

Chapter 9
Mikey
2005

ALMOST A YEAR PASSED. I think I was the happiest I'd ever been which was in complete contrast to Lucy. If I'd been but a few years older I might have probed the changes in her behaviour, but at the time I thought her sullen attitude was a sign that she was on the cusp of adulthood – a destination I wasn't yet ready to join.

Lucy was never unkind to me. She continued to look after me in a way that Mum never had, but it was as though something had shifted; there sprung an invisible barrier between us. Before, we'd been partners, now I was a child and she the adult. She didn't speak to me like she used to, and she didn't share her dreams. Even Narnia had lost its shine and though I was careful to put the book in a prominent position on our bed every night, she never touched it, and I was left to read it to myself.

Lucy had her own smart phone which Bill Cambly had bought her for work. I, however, wasn't allowed to touch it which seemed very unfair as she was always playing *Snake* or *Doodle Jump* on it, and I'd have loved a go. One time when she was in the shower, I'd picked it up for a look and noticed there was a screen lock – well, it wasn't very difficult to figure it out; it was my birthday. The screen was full of messages from someone called Bly

Mac. Message after message popped up all with attachments. I opened one and a photo started to download, the wheel spinning, percentages increasing, fuzzy pixels morphing. From over my shoulder there was a scream and the phone was knocked out of my hands, falling onto the table with a thump. Lucy, wrapped only in a towel, wet hair dripping all over the floor, snatched it up and held it to her chest. 'What the fuck are you doing? How dare you?'

I stared at her; my cheeks flooded with colour and my mouth hung open at the harsh tone of her voice. 'I just...'

'Did you see anything?'

I wrinkled my brow.

'Did. You. See. Anything?' Her voice steely; clipped.

I shook my head. Tears prickling my eyes. 'I just wanted to play Doodle Jump,' I said, a sob stuck in the back of my throat.

'It's for work. I've told you before – it's not for you to play with.' She sighed and reached out a hand to ruffle my hair. 'Mikey. If it gets broken, then I'll be in big trouble.'

I stood up, kicking the chair from under me and sending it scooting across the lino, anger rising through my body. 'How do you think I'm gonna break it? I'm not a baby, I can handle a phone.' I desperately wanted to storm off, but it was late and there was nowhere for me to go. Instead, I went over, picked up our book and flung myself onto the mattress. Lucy came over and squatted beside me.

'You want me to read it to you?'

Even though I couldn't think of anything I wanted more, I shook my head and stared at the picture of Mr Tumnus, standing under the lamp post; a guilty look plastered across his stupid goaty face.

During the school term, Lucy only worked on Saturdays but, in the holidays, she spent most of her time at the office. I never saw what she did, hidden away in the corner of Bill's private room, slatted blinds closed. Instead, I hung out in the cosy cupboard which Val had turned into a little boy's dream den. There was a mini fridge stocked with cans of sugar free soda, a biscuit barrel full of digestives and a fruit bowl bursting with apples, satsumas and bananas – all for me. There were books, magazines and lots of plain paper and drawing pencils plus I had my own colour TV. It was the only time I watched TV on account of us not having one in the flat, and I binged on pop music videos, cartoons and American sitcoms. She'd even bought me a guitar – an acoustic one she said she'd found in a charity shop, and a book on how to play the chords. Between reading, watching TV, drawing and learning the guitar, I'd never been so busy nor so content.

At that time in our lives Mum disappeared from the flat for longer spells, the keys on the noticeboard, decreasing one by one along with our supplies of jam and wool, but now Lucy had some money coming in, we didn't have to worry as much about where we were going to get food from. I also got a newspaper round and diversified into leaflet delivery which put an end to me going into the office on a Saturday. Bringing home money and contributing to the grocery bill made me feel a foot taller although I still couldn't see out of our living room window without standing on a chair.

Unfortunately, I never saw much of Val because she had a different job, something to do with cosmetic marketing, but it meant she was always leaving Lucy little bags of make-up samples which I experimented with, a lot of the time on myself. I loved how it made the pit of my stomach fizz and whirr when I caught sight of my reflection in the mirror, and I started to grow my hair long. When Val did pop into the office, she was pleased to see I was looking after my teeth and some of the second set had come through not too shabby looking. Though they weren't pearly white, if I didn't smile too much, no one noticed them. I was happy and I guess this showed because, after a while, I found a few friends to hang out with after school – other guitar nerds who dreamed about getting a band together despite our very noticeable lack of talent.

I wrote my first song: *The Lion's Roar*.

Due to Lucy's work, I mostly visited Aslan on my own, each time taking a handful of biscuits I'd bought him from the pick and mix at the local pet shop. He loved them, especially the ones shaped like a tiny sausage roll.

For my tenth birthday, as a surprise, Lucy took me to Twycross Zoo. We caught the number 15 bus from the town centre, and she let me sit on the top deck, right at the front so I could look down and see the top of the driver's balding head. She'd even packed us a picnic and it was full of my favourite things; little sausages, pickled onion flavoured Monster Munch, corned beef sandwiches made with white bread, and a large bag of iced gems. She said we'd get a birthday ice cream when we were there. That late autumn day, it felt like I was hanging out with the old Lucy. As we stood outside waiting for the gates to open, the sound of monkeys calling to each other broke out; it was a deafening mix of wailing, screeching and booming, and she put her hands over her ears. I squatted and swung my arms down so my knuckles trailed the floor, and I threw my head back and mimicked the sound – she laughed and patted my head telling me I was a good baboon, and that my banana breakfast was on its way. Our first stop was the kiosk where we bought hot chocolates with all the trimmings and Lucy handed me the map of the grounds so I could plot our way around.

I saved the best spectacle until last.

When we reached the lion enclosure, Lucy reached out her hand and grabbed hold of mine. The lion was pacing up and down, shaking his head from side to side and swishing his pom pom tail.

'Just like Aslan,' she murmured, and I noticed there were tears in her eyes. She pressed her lips together and gulped. 'Sometimes I wish things could go back to how they were,' she said, gazing at a small child who was holding his toy lion up to the cage and squealing with delight.

'How?' I asked.

'So that it was just the two of us and we could lie on the bed and read about Narnia.'

I folded my arms. 'Huh! I don't. Do you miss being hungry? Do you miss the lice and my rotten teeth?'

Lucy pulled away from me and wiped her eyes with the back of her hand. 'No. That's not what I mean.' Her dreamy expression vanished, and her voice was sharp. 'You don't understand. How could you – you're just a kid.' My stomach tightened. That was the last thing I had wanted to do; spoil our precious time together.

I threw my arm around her and kissed her soft cheek. 'I do know what you mean. We don't spend much time together anymore and I miss that too. Thank you for today. It's been the best day. EVER.'

Suddenly she grabbed my arm, taking a sharp intake of breath. Her brow wrinkled with confusion and surprise.

'You okay?' I asked, startled by her reaction.

She swallowed and gave a little moan. Then she shook her head. 'Yes. I'm fine. Something I ate. Probably best get home.'

We'd eaten the same things and I closed my eyes and pressed my belly to assess if I too felt odd. I didn't and she let me have another ice cream for the road. We got on the next bus home, but this time she didn't want to go back to the top deck, which was fine by me. We sat in the frail people bit and she closed her eyes and leant her head on my shoulder for the entire journey. I had to tap her awake when we got to our stop. She said the pains in her stomach were probably just women's things and I felt my cheeks flush because we'd done a bit about it in biology and it sounded revolting.

She said she couldn't climb the stairs to our floor, so we caught the pissy lift which was working despite the sign saying *Out of order* and the moment she was inside the flat she shot into the bathroom and threw up in the loo. I ran the cold tap for ages and poured her an icy glass of water which she glugged down in one go. She wiped the back of her hand across her mouth and said she felt a bit better, but she smelt funny. I led her over to the mattress and made her lie down on the bed, then I took her trainers off; her feet were very cold, so I put a thick pair of fluffy socks on them and lay down beside her. She drifted off and so did I.

In the middle of the night, I was woken by the most terrible noises coming from the bathroom. They sounded like a cow had been caught in some horrible trap. Someone was thumping on the ceiling, shouting 'SHUT THE FUCK UP.' Lucy wasn't lying next to me anymore. I leapt out of bed and rushed into the bathroom.

Lucy was sitting on the floor, legs outstretched, her back against the bath. Her face was jaundiced and a line of sweat above her upper lip glistened in the dim light. 'Get Mum,' she groaned. She was clutching her stomach; there was liquid on the floor and her underwear was wet and bloody. The room smelt sour and eggy.

I didn't knock on Mum's door. I barged straight in, but it was empty. The air damp and cold. I should have known she wasn't there – the noises Lucy was making were far too loud even for her to ignore. My mind was racing but I knew what I needed to do. I scrabbled about the place and found Lucy's phone on the table. I went back into the bathroom and held it up to her. My stomach felt loose and my knees were trembling. 'Shall I call for an ambulance?'

By this time, Lucy was on all fours, arching her back and mooing. 'It's too late,' she gasped.

That was it: my sister, my beloved sister was about to die, and I would have no one left in the world to care for me.

I passed out.

When I came round, I was lying on the bathroom floor with a blanket over me, and a cushion tucked under my head. The room smelt of disinfectant – the stuff Lucy put on my cuts. I sat up with a gasp, expecting to see Lucy's dead body lying on the floor but she wasn't there; instead, I spotted two bulging black sacks tucked underneath the sink. I got to my feet, my stomach roiling and stumbled out of the room. It was no longer dark, and the room was filled with grey light. I could see Lucy, sitting up in bed, her back against the wall, holding something in her arms. Her expression was odd; peaceful and at the same time, bewildered.

I came over, rubbing my eyes, unable to comprehend what was in the bundled towel she was clutching.

She looked at me, her blue eyes wide, and patted my side of the bed.

'Mikey. Meet Jadis.'

Chapter 10
Cally

HENRY HAD BEEN AWAY for a night filming a toothpaste advertisement in Harrogate but was catching the milk train back. He'd phoned Cally in the evening to say he'd organised for a car to bring Misha over to The Nix in the morning and that she was going to check-in with Cally outside the treatment room. So, at a quarter to nine, Cally positioned herself outside JayDoll's pop-up treatment salon, drinking a hazelnut latte and reading an article in 'Women's Health' about the most effective way to intermittently fast. She was jolted out of her headspace by someone stomping down the stairs, a large, wheeled suitcase bumping on every step behind them.

It was a slim man wearing a flared denim jump suit with supersized collars, and boxy white trainers and when he opened the door, she was hit by a waft of bergamot and lime. As he breezed into the room, turning on the lights, he called over his shoulder. 'I take it you're my VIP nine o'clock?' his voice was feminine, lingering on the vowels, and it set Cally's teeth on edge.

Cally stood up, looking for somewhere to deposit her half-drunk coffee. The minimalist waiting area, all taupe and white cube sofas, didn't have anything as unsightly as a litter bin. 'What? Yes. No. I mean, sort of.' She perched the take-away cup by the edge of her chair and followed him in. The treatment room was a mirrored shell lit up by halogen spots and Cally winced at the numerous unflattering versions of herself projected around the walls. At the centre of the room was a massage table and she counted three spindly chairs on casters abandoned around the room. Apart from that, it was empty barring his enormous Louis Vuitton suitcase.

'Come on in then. Don't be shy.' The man, presumably JayDoll, pointed to one of the chairs and Cally sat down folding her hands across her lap.

'This whole thing – it's not for me,' she said.

JayDoll tutted then sat down on another chair and rolled over to her, the soles of his trainers squeaking against the wooden floor. He stared into her face as though she wasn't there, and Cally felt colour flood her cheeks. He was curiously attractive with burnt-biscuit hair, tied up in a bun and his face was angular; his olive skin was silky smooth and coated in a flawless covering of foundation which exactly matched the underside of his chin. His eyelashes were fake and dotted with tiny jewels and underneath the lower lash was a dusting of silver glitter. His lips were full and lined with a nude pencil, shaded in with a glossy pink coating.

JayDoll lifted a manicured finger, and hooked it under her chin, tilting her face upwards. 'Girlfriend. You have good bone structure. I can work with this. But...' he opened his eyes wide and tweaked her scarlet fringe. 'This hair. Ouch! What happened?'

Cally felt the burn on her face grow deeper. 'I...I told you – this appointment isn't for me. I'm just here to make sure your client arrives here safely.'

JayDoll snapped open the locks on the suitcase and rummaged around, pulling out various bottles of foundation which had *Dollymix* in gold italic writing on the side. He opened a tube and dabbed a pea-sized amount on the back of his hand. 'Well – whoever she or he is, they aren't here so why don't you let me do my thing.'

Cally pushed her chair back and got to her feet, placing her hands on her hips. 'Thank you. No. I don't want your *thing*. I'm happy with how I look. Now if you don't mind, I'll wait outside. You know your client is Misha Carlton, right?'

JayDoll raised one colour blocked eyebrow and shrugged. 'No, I didn't, but it makes no difference to me who they are. Every client is special to me.' He held out a hand and placed it on Cally's arm. 'Sorry, if I offended you.' His voice had lost its campness and had morphed into a regular male voice with a slight Leicester accent. 'I got out of bed the wrong side this morning.'

Cally nodded and couldn't help but give a small smile – he looked so earnest. 'My hair is truly awful. I've been told I look like a Lord of the Rings extra. It doesn't help that I'm five foot nothing either.'

JayDoll threw back his head and laughed; a loud, booming sound which echoed around the bare walls. 'Oh my God, you totally do. A beautiful one. An elf not an orc.' He beamed at her, and his dark eyes sparkled.

Cally held up her hands and covered her eyes. 'Wow – you could blind someone with those gnashers.'

'Thank you. I'm extremely glad you like my Turkish teeth.'

'I didn't say I liked them. I was dazzled by them; they're white bordering on the blue.'

'Touché! But blue is better than beige. When I became more visible in the public eye, I had to get them done. I was brought up on a diet of jam and more jam, so my adult teeth came through a nasty shade of grey.' There was a pause. He pressed his lips together. 'Let's start again. What's your name?'

'Cally.'

'Nice to meet you, Cally. Please call me Jay. So, Cally, what are you, some sort of VIP liaison officer for The Nix?'

Cally nodded. 'Kind of. I'm working in the spa to try and improve the marketing side of things.' She waved her hand as though he would know exactly what she meant by her sweeping generalisation. 'And you? Gloria says you only come here for a few days a year but get paid a fortune.'

He grinned. 'Yes. It's part of the deal to stock my brand and my brand *only*. So, I rock up and hold a few masterclasses or give a few one-to-ones for the very special.' He winked. 'At least let me sort you out with a wonderful foundation – as an apology for being so rude. I really do know what I'm doing.'

Cally looked at her watch. 'Five minutes then I really must go and find out where Misha has got to. She should be here by now.'

He tutted and flapped his hand. 'Don't you know, daaaarling, celebrities are always late. She's probably sitting somewhere with a skinny mochaccino; baseball cap and shades on, reading the gossip columns with not a care in the world.'

Cally sat back down. A plastic bag had fallen out of Jay's suitcase and her foot caught in the handle, spilling the contents onto the floor: dirty black trousers, black hoody and trainers caked with white-flecked mud. 'Sorry,' she said as she kicked it across the floorboards.

Jay's face clouded and he bundled the items back into the bag. 'Early dog walk,' he said then stood up. 'Excuse me, just one second. I'm going to put these things in my locker – I don't want to stink the whole room out.' He was gone for a couple of minutes then returned – his face friendly and smiling again.

'You have a dog?' asked Cally.

'Yes. A little angel called Dolly. I love her so much.' He pointed to his lock screen which had a photo of a teddy-bear faced creature with a pink bow threaded through its top knot. 'She's a Dandy Dinmont.'

'Oh! She's adorable. I have a Jack Russell called Rolly,' said Cally taking out her phone and showing him her screen. 'I don't know what I'd do without him. He has to go to doggy day care during the week, but it's worth every penny.'

'I have a round-the-clock dog sitter when I'm away,' said Jay.

Cally laughed. '*Of course* you do. And does Dolly have her own chef too?'

Jay laughed and pointed his fingers against his chest. 'Do I sound like a diva?'

Cally shrugged. 'Maybe.'

He fluttered his eyelashes, and the jewels caught the light and cast rainbow sparkles on the floor. 'I suppose I do have a superfan: *BabyDoll123*, who knows my every movement and comments positively on everything I post. You should get one. It's good for the soul.'

Cally clapped her hands together. 'Yes. Having a superfan definitely makes you a diva.'

He dabbed a bit of foundation on her face and blended it in with his index and middle fingers. 'Cally. I'm not just saying this for the sake of it; you have lovely skin.'

'Thank you.' His face was an inch away from hers and she could smell the coffee on his breath.

He dabbed some more of the cream onto his fingertips. 'You know, I only got into this business to make my sister happy.'

'She must be very happy now.'

He said nothing, but pushed his chair away, narrowing his gaze, his eyes flickering over her face. 'You look perfect.'

Cally's phone rang. She glanced down at the screen and saw it was Henry Carmichael's number.

'Sorry. I need to take this.' She pushed herself away and Jay moved over to the sink in the corner and busied himself rinsing out his make-up brushes.'

'Is she with you?' asked Henry.

'No. She hasn't shown up yet.'

'What? Where are you?'

'I'm waiting for her in the spa.'

There was a moment's pause, and she could hear laboured breathing. 'She should have been there ages ago. I've just arrived at The Nix. Stay where you are. I'm on my way over.'

Cally turned to Jay who was wiping his hands with a white fluffy towel. 'Sorry, I have to go, but thank you for your time.'

'Wait.' He handed her the tube of foundation and a card with his details on. He lowered his gaze and a red glow appeared at the top of his cheeks. 'I mean, if you ever fancy a dog walk when I'm in town...'

Cally gave a cough of surprise. 'Thanks. That would be...fun.' She put the card in her pocket and hurried up the stairs into the lobby where she was met by a pink-faced Henry whose upper lip was glazed with sweat.

'Where is she?' he asked, clenching both fists.

The sunlight streaming in through the glass walls in the lobby was dazzling and Cally had to shield her eyes against its glare. The make-up on her face seemed to harden under the heat and her skin felt pinched and taut. 'I told you; she hasn't arrived.'

Henry tapped the toe of one of his loafers against the parquet floor. 'But the car picked her up at 7.30am. It's only a fifteen minute drive.'

Cally stepped into a shadow cast by a large vase of wilting irises. 'Have you called her?'

'Her phone's switched off.'

'Right. But I take it you've spoken to the driver?' asked Cally.

Henry ran his hand through his dishevelled curls and shook his head.

'Give me the number,' said Cally. Henry took a moment to scroll through his contacts then held up his phone with the number displayed. Cally dialled, putting her phone on speaker.

''Ello,' came a male voice.

'Hi. Are you the driver who picked up Misha Carlton from her flat in The Village this morning?'

'Yep. That's me.'

'And can you confirm that you dropped her off at The Nix as pre-arranged.'

'No.'

Henry's jaw fell open.

'No. Why not?' asked Cally.

''Cos she asked to be dropped off at the entrance of Walkers' Common which I thought was ridiculous because she was only in the car for a minute, if that. She said it was a lovely day and she wanted to take her yappy little pooch for a walk. So, I did just that. Dropped 'em Village entrance side and I took her suitcase to The Nix and left it with them lovely ladies behind the reception desk.'

'She seemed alright? Nothing weird happened on the journey? Any phone conversations you happened to overhear?'

'Nope. Although, it was straight after she took a short phone call she asked to go to Walkers' Common.'

Cally's ears tingled. That sounded like she was heading into the park to meet with someone. 'Right. And how did she seem after the phone call?'

'Same. She was quite rude and miserable to start with, so nothing changed there.'

'Thank you for your help.' Cally ended the call. 'Okay, so it sounds to me like she might have been meeting up with someone. Does she have any friends around here?'

Henry shrugged. 'She's been filming nearby so it could be anyone, I guess.'

They walked along the gravelled path back towards the main part of The Nix, up the steps which still contained the flowers for Luella's wedding though the ribbons around the planters had gone. They crossed the terrace and into the Members' Lounge which was laid up for breakfast and where a few people were sitting at the tables, reading newspapers, and picking at sugared pastries; the mingling aromas of burnt cinnamon and smoked haddock made Cally's stomach turn. Heading out of the bar area they found themselves back in the tiled corridor which was lined with the idyllic Toile de Jouy wallpaper. Cally's gaze fell upon a smirking shepherdess whilst Henry focused on Cally, waiting for her to decide what to do next. Cally drummed her fingers on the pedestal table. 'Let's see if she's checked in and gone straight up to her room. You know, on balance, I think she just got side-tracked and did a detour. She's probably at a café in Walkers' Common and has lost all sense of time. Maybe she did it on purpose – perhaps she had no intention of keeping the appointment with JayDoll. That sort of thing isn't everybody's cup of tea.'

Henry nodded. 'That's a possibility, but in light of all the things we discussed yesterday, I'm uneasy about the whole situation. She promised me she'd come straight here.'

Cally checked her phone. 'She's forty minutes late. It's not a huge amount of time, but considering her phone's off, we do need to find her asap.'

The petit woman on reception with large brown eyes and a dark, glossy bob, so shiny, her hair looked like it was made out of porcelain, informed them Misha hadn't checked in but that her luggage had already been sent to her room.

'What now?' asked Henry, his eyes darting all over the place.

'Let's go to The Village and see if we can spot her,' said Cally. 'We can assume that when she leaves, she'll take the route which leads straight towards The Nix so, with a bit of luck, we'll probably meet her on our way there.'

As they went down the main entrance steps Henry's phone beeped. He stopped to look at the screen then went pale and sank to the ground.

'What's the matter?' she asked.

Without saying anything he held up his phone and Cally took it from his grasp. There was a picture of a woman, tied up, hands bound, her eyes shining with tears and staring at the camera. It was Misha. The message attached:

If you find her, you can set them both free. If you don't, Misha will die, cold and alone.

Chapter 11
Mikey
2005

THE ARRIVAL of Jadis marked the beginning of the end for our lives. I don't know how Lucy imagined this would work out. That, at the age of fourteen and ten, we could provide a secure home for Jadis and bring her up in our shitty flat with our drug addled mum and her collection of boyfriends, pimps and customers. But I had never wanted anything more in my entire life – I wanted Jadis to be our responsibility and for Lucy and me to bring her up with me in the starring role of father figure.

I sat next to Lucy, reaching out my finger to touch the baby's tiny, clenched fist. The thumbnail so small and perfect. 'Why didn't you tell me you were *pregnant*?' The word sounded alien.

Lucy's lower lip quivered. 'I...I didn't know?'

'What?' I snorted, shaking my head. 'How is that even possible?'

'I thought...' she held one hand to her forehead. 'I've never had a period – I didn't think it *was* possible.' She gave a bitter laugh. 'Turns out I was wrong.'

Thoughts tumbled around my head and I couldn't get them into order. I had so many questions.

'*How?*' We'd done a bit about the reproductive system in biology, and I knew that there had to have been this mysterious thing called sex involved. She opened her mouth to say something then clamped it shut again. Looking back, I guess it was quite an ambiguous question to answer at that particular moment in time.

I shook my head. '*Who?*'

'I couldn't help it,' she said. 'I didn't want to. I didn't, but *he* made me.' Tears started running down her cheeks.

The way Lucy stressed the 'he' was as though I knew exactly who she was talking about, but I didn't have a clue. I kept thinking of all the boys in her class, but my mind hit a blank – she only mentioned them in passing, there was no one who stood out. I stared at Jadis' tiny, scrunched up face; and her lower lip quivered; it was funny. I leant over and kissed her soft forehead and she smelt of biscuits: malted milks.

'*When?*'

'All these questions, Mikey,' said Lucy staring ahead at the broken clock. 'I'm so tired.'

'But what are we going to do? We can't keep her here. I mean, shouldn't a doctor have a look at her? At you.'

Lucy closed her eyes. 'I just want to go to sleep.' Her spine was slipping down the wall and she stretched out her arms and gave me Jadis. I set my niece, flat on her back, between my legs on the duvet. She was snuffling. 'Hello, you,' I whispered, kissing the tip of my finger and pressing it onto her mouth. 'It's all okay. Uncle Mikey's here.' I liked how grown up it made me sound.

Lucy handed me her phone and I took it, a blank expression on my face.

'You need to text Bill,' she said.

I smiled. 'Of course. Bill Cambly.' I nodded several times. 'Yes, yes. Why didn't I think of that before? Val – she'll know exactly what to do.'

'No,' said Lucy, smoothing the bedcovers with her palms. 'He'll have to take care of her. I can't. Not on my own.' Her voice had become slow and scratchy like she had something stuck in her throat which she needed to cough up.

My heart wobbled and I wanted to protest; to say that I would look after Jadis, but I knew in my heart it was impossible.

I swallowed. 'Yes. Bill and Val will be the perfect people to take care of her, until we can sort ourselves out,' I said.

Lucy stared at me; her eyes narrowing. 'Mikey. He's the father.'

'What?' I exploded with laughter. 'Bill? You're joking.'

Lucy's sad face and silence provided me with the answer.

'But...but he's – he's a man.' This was all wrong. 'Do you love him? What about Val?'

'Enough of the questions,' she snapped. She closed her eyes, and the room was quiet for a few moments and all I could hear was the drumming of my heart. 'Send him a message.' She clawed at the phone. I picked it up and tapped in the code for the lock screen which was still my birthday.

'He's the only one who messages me on it.'

I nodded. 'He's Bly Mac?'

She grunted. 'Jumbled up Cambly.'

'I don't know how to send a message,' I said, my tone petulant. I was still pissed off she never let me touch it, although now it made more sense why she didn't. She sighed, opened one eye, and curled the tips of her fingers, gesturing for me to hand her the phone. Her breathing was very slow. I handed the phone back to her and she squinted at the screen and pressed something. 'Now type,' she said, pressing her head back against the pillow. Her hair was a frizzy mess – her skin clammy.

She hadn't deleted all the messages. There was a string of one liners from him: **I need you. Where are you? I have to taste you.** *Taste?*

I rolled my eyes at Jadis. A flood of disappointment and

disgust washed over me. What did she see in him? How could she do that to Val?

'Type: *I'll meet you tonight at 7pm in the usual place.*' Her breathing was shallow; her voice rasping as I pressed the keys. 'Hit the arrow button at the end of the line.'

There was a whooshing noise and a small envelope sign saying *delivered* appeared underneath the message. Little dots rippled across the screen.

I held it up to her, not understanding: **Gr8**

'Good. Mikey, listen carefully. Tonight, you've got to take Jadis to the show flat on the ground floor of the new Cambly Homes block.'

'The ones being built down the street from the posh entrance to the park?'

'Yes. I've got a key to get into the building and the flat – it's in my purse. Get there early. Leave Jadis in the flat and come straight back here. He mustn't see you. Do you understand?' A blob of saliva trickled down one corner of her mouth and the skin on her arms had goosebumps.

'Yes.'

She gave out a monumental gasp then rolled over onto her side, curled up in a ball and within seconds was fast asleep.

'Just you and me kiddo,' I said to Jadis. I manoeuvred myself off the mattress and shuffled her a bit further away from Lucy. I had a dragging feeling in my stomach; a sense of the inevitability of the situation coupled with a sudden rush of anger directed towards Mum. If she'd been a better parent we wouldn't have been in this situation or at the very least, she would have been able to take care of Jadis.

I've never experienced love like it. I now know it's an unconditional bond which is foisted upon us by nature, but at the time it felt like something heavy was squashing my heart. The need to do what was right for someone else, not purely what I wanted, wasn't something I was used to doing. I decided, as my only avuncular act, I would give Jadis to her father with her looking as presentable as possible, rather than it seeming as though we were putting her out with the recycling. I emptied out a vegetable box which we'd got from the market and, selecting the softest pink towel from the clean laundry pile, I made a nest for her. I placed Jadis inside and she wriggled a bit, but then settled again. I noticed Lucy had wrapped her up in my old tee-shirt which had a faded picture of Jimmy Hendrix on it. I grabbed a piece of paper from the table and wrote a note in my best handwriting which said: 'You are my daddy. Please look after me. My name is Jadis Jones. When I'm older please take me for a walk around the park to see Aslan – it is Mummy's best thing to do.' I ran and fetched a pink, green and white pom pom which I'd made one rainy day using the last of the factory wool and I placed both items in the cardboard cradle.

It got to 6pm. I wondered if I should wake Lucy so she could say goodbye to Jadis, but she looked so peaceful, I decided against the idea – it would probably only make Lucy sad and Jadis wouldn't gain anything from it.

No one stopped me in the street. I was just a kid carrying a cardboard box. I had worried that Jadis would start crying and that someone would stop me and ask me why I'd stolen a baby, but she didn't once wake up although I could hear her making cute little sucking noises and when I peeked in, she'd put her thumb in her mouth.

I arrived early at the building site – there was no one about. The sky was indigo and speckled with stars and lit by a fat, orange moon; Lucy said it was called a blood moon and that it would be even bigger in a couple of days. There was a chill in the air and I wished I hadn't set off in just a tee-shirt. That's the thing about warm September days – they have a sting in their tail. The block of flats rose behind the wire enclosure, like a giant's jenga game. Some of the lower tiers were almost complete, but higher up the tower were gaping holes, thick coils of wire poking out, and I could see glimpses of the brick building on the street behind. The moon lit up the patch of rubble in front of the flats and a digger sat, its bucket lying prone against the rocks as though saying his prayers before nodding off for the night. I crept through the gap in the mesh fence which surrounded the entire site and unlocked the metal front door with the chubb key. It swung open into a dimly lit hallway and my nostrils flooded with wafts of fresh paint and varnish. The floor was strewn with pointy plastic lids, nails and scraps of wire and absolutely everything was covered with a layer of white dust. Some of the doors leading off from the lobby were open, revealing spaces, split by wooden beams and kitchen islands swaddled in thick plastic. The show flat was the first one on the left of the main entrance. I used the second smaller key to open the glossy sugared-almond pink door and stepped onto a wooden parquet floor. I turned the light switch on and peeked into the first room and although, at first glance, the magenta velvet dining chairs and floor-length curtains embroidered with dusty pink hydrangeas took my breath away, a closer look at the sumptuous banquet laid out on the glass table revealed that the food on the plates was plastic and also a bit dusty. It was nothing but a giant doll's house. It was disappointing; like biting into a toffee apple and finding an onion beneath the honeyed shell.

I wasn't sure where to put Jadis. There was a nursery all kitted out with jungle animals and there was even a crib and changing table, but I thought she should be visible the moment Bill walked in, or he might do an about turn. A tiny bit of me wanted to see his face when he stooped down to check what was in the box blocking his path. The look of puzzlement and then utter surprise as he registered it was a baby. I couldn't picture his expression when he read my note and realised that the baby was his – was there a look for that?

How would he tell Val? Hey, daaaaarling, look what I've

brought home from work today. What would she say? He didn't deserve her, but I knew Val would be a good mum. The best. I also knew how much she wanted kids because she'd said so when we first met. Two little girls. Well here you are Val, I thought: *Here's your first girl and she's a beauty. And you haven't had to go through any of the shit Lucy did to get her.* It was cold in the show home, but when I leant over to kiss Jadis, her sweet breath was warm. She was still sucking her thumb. I knew she needed food, but Bill would have to sort that out – I didn't have a clue what or how to feed her.

'Don't worry my little girl. Daddy will be here soon. I'll see you again, I promise.'

Bill would be there. It was going to be alright. He was rich. She wouldn't want for anything.

I ran all the way home, my feet dragging across the pavements as though they were made of lead. When I let myself into the flat, Lucy was still curled in a ball, but I could hear her crying.

I sat down and took her hand.

'It'll be okay,' I said. There was a lump at the back of my throat but I gulped it down. I needed to be strong for Lucy. 'Bill's got her now, so she's safe, but that doesn't mean he'll always have her. Let's get you better first and then we can figure out what to do.'

She sobbed; her breath coming in short gasps. 'I told him no, but he wouldn't stop.'

Those words made the hairs on the back of my neck stand up. Thinking about him and what he did would have to wait. 'Luce. Do you think you ought to get checked out at the hospital?'

She groaned then turned over; I saw she was lying on top of a blood-stained towel. 'Mikey, can you get me some sanitary towels.'

I hesitated. 'Sure. What sort do I get?' but my question was met with gentle snoring. I made myself a quick sandwich then headed back out into the night, this time wearing a coat. I dumped the black sacks into the dustbin and headed along the high street to the late-night chemist and got a pack of heavy-duty sanitary pads and a packet of those special vitamin tablets which fizz when you put them in water but don't taste as nice as you think they are going to be. I lingered as I walked past the baby section, amazed by the range of nappies and tins of formula milk – it was an expensive business bringing up a baby and the whole milk choosing thing was a lot more complicated than I thought it would be. That wasn't our problem now.

When I got back home, I set to work making the flat as clean as I could. I'd done a detour around Walkers' Common to clear my head and to get some fresh air and it had made me feel loads better although my coat and face had got a bit savaged by the brambles. I opened the windows to get rid of the stale human odours and I bleached the floors. I was the epitome of the perfect modern-day man. By the end of the next day, I'd done the laundry and gone to the supermarket and Lucy was showered and sitting at the table, wearing clean clothes, eating buttered toast and drinking milky tea. I remember braiding her hair which, prior to washing was beginning to resemble our hessian doormat, and I was happy and filled with a sense that all was right with the world. Lucy began fretting that Mum still wasn't back, but I told her not to worry; we were doing just fine without her. Better, in fact.

I went to top up the teas and I noticed Lucy's phone on the work surface. I'd put it there to charge. A couple of messages had popped up on the screen and, not wanting to bother her, I glimpsed at them.

In that instant my world crumbled to pieces.

Chapter 12
Cally

Cally had never seen the wrought iron gates of Walkers' Park shut during the day, and for the first time she noticed the iron curlicues at the centre of each panel; one depicting a dragon, the other a sword-wielding knight in armour. Tiered cerise blossom from a horse-chestnut tree pressed through the lower bars of the gate and made the police officer on sentry duty look as though he was wearing a feather boa. Cally told him she had an appointment with DI Mackey and the officer garbled something into his radio. After a few seconds he nodded, and the gate creaked open.

It was such a beautiful summer's morning and, in the distance, the surface of the lake shone as though it had been sprinkled with gold dust. Henry broke into a run towards the squad of police officers all huddled together wearing high-vis jackets; some were clutching take-away cups of coffee, others taking chunks out of bacon baps oozing with brown sauce; fuelling up whilst waiting for their instructions which would probably involve being on their feet for the rest of their shift.

'Henry, where are you going?' called out Cally, breaking into a trot behind him. Then she heard woofing and the fluorescent-coated police officers fanned out to reveal Henry's dog at the centre of the posse, tugging at its pink gingham lead; the matching bandana was dirty and tangled and the lower half of the dog was caked in dried mud. Henry dropped to his knees and the dog leapt onto him, licking his face, and wagging its tail. For a few seconds Henry seemed to forget the image of his wife tied up inside a cell as he showered the dog with kisses, repeating the name Mabel over and over again. He fumbled in his pocket and a couple of poo bags tumbled out along with a broken dog biscuit which he gave to Mabel with a flourish. She sniffed then licked it before pushing the fragment away with her nose, no doubt, her tummy already full of bacon or sausage donations.

'Where did you find her?' asked Henry, still crouching and rubbing the dog's topknot.

'Just roaming about near the café,' said the large male officer with piggy eyes and a sandy moustache who had been in charge of holding onto the lead. 'Reckon she's been all over the place though, judging by the state of her.'

Cally tugged at Henry's shoulder. 'Come on.' She'd spotted Dan near the café next to the fountain which had a stone lily pad at its centre, complete with a yawning frog who spurted water out of its mouth although at this angle the jet appeared to spout forth from Dan's crown. He was stooped over, muttering something into a walkie talkie, large bap held aloft in his other hand. He didn't see them approach and when Cally slipped her hand into his he startled and pulled away, leaving Cally's palm coated with a sticky smear of tomato ketchup. When he saw it was Cally he gave a sheepish smile. 'It's granary bread,' he said, polishing off the rest of the bap in two large bites then wiping the evidence off his lips with a paper napkin which he drop-kicked into the litter bin.

Cally rolled her eyes.

'I'm stressed,' he said pulling a sad face and patting his tummy. 'You know it makes me hungry.'

Dan shook Henry's hand. 'Hi Henry. We met before in Miriam Kershaw's office. I'm DI Dan Mackey.'

Henry nodded.

'We're going to find her. It's only been a couple of hours since the taxi driver dropped her off at the park. I know it's hard but try not to worry.'

'Anything useful from the CCTV that you can share with me?' asked Cally.

Dan stooped to retrieve the cup of coffee he'd balanced on the mossy bevelled edge of the fountain. 'Misha enters the gates, Village side, at 7.40 am and appears to head towards the lake with the dog, then she disappears and doesn't re-emerge.'

'Fuck!' gasped Henry. 'Do you think she could have somehow tripped and fallen into the lake?'

'No. No.' Cally pressed Henry's arm. 'The lake is only knee height. It's man-made.'

Henry let out a puff of breath.

Dan took a gulp of coffee, and a line of frothed milk coated his upper lip. He pointed to the gates with the dragon and knight. 'We'd have expected her to leave via that entrance if she was heading for The Nix but if she wasn't going there then there are several other exit routes she could have picked so we're checking all the traffic cameras in the area.'

A couple of flies buzzed around Cally's head and she swatted them away. 'The meadow section is a wide stretch and, by the looks of the dog, she's been frolicking in the mud.' She stared into Dan's eyes. 'I assume you've taken samples from her claws. It might indicate where she's been.'

Dan nodded. 'Yes, and parts of the meadow never seem to dry out, even in a heatwave, so those results are going to be very helpful. Unfortunately for us, the meadow has lots of renegade exit routes made by dogwalkers so they can get out from there without having to go back through the park. Anyway, that's where we're prioritising our search.'

'Right,' said Henry. 'Well, that's where I'll go then. They'll let me help?'

'Er... best not,' said Dan. 'They'll have a proper search line going. Leave it to the plods – that's what they're good at.' He looked at Cally for support.

Cally gave Henry's shoulder a sympathetic squeeze then turned back to Dan. 'I think the meadow isn't the right place to search for her. The cell looks metal lined to me. Someone's basement? Are you checking the nearby houses?'

'Yep. We're sending a team out to go door to door, but Cally – this is a police matter now, you can't be seen to be interfering.'

She frowned and wagged a finger at him. 'Er, I think you'll find I'm acting on behalf of my client and, unless he tells me otherwise, I'll do whatever it takes to find his wife.' Dan grimaced. She paused for a few seconds then forced a smile onto her face. 'I take it you still want my help with that other matter? The Cambly murder.'

Dan sighed then shrugged. 'Okay, okay, you win, but just keep it low key and don't get in the way.'

Cally took Dan's coffee out of his hands and had a sip – it was disgusting. He was lactose intolerant and the almond milk mixed with hazelnut syrup was overpowering and far too sugary even for her; she winced. She'd have serious words with him this evening – no wonder he couldn't shift any weight if he was eating whatever he liked the moment she wasn't with him. 'Weird that there's no money involved. Do you think there's something personal going on here?' She turned to Henry who was now cradling Mabel in his arms, despite the fact she was quite a hefty pooch. She'd seen a dog like that recently, but she couldn't remember where. Henry gave a sorry shrug, his blue eyes shining with tears. Cally needed to get him away from here. She moved closer to Dan and whispered in his ear. 'I'm going to take Henry back to his flat and have a snoop.'

Dan nodded. 'Good idea. I'll be bringing him in for questioning in an hour or so, but in the meantime, I'll send someone over to get Misha's laptop. Can you have a good look to see if she keeps a journal or a notebook. We need to find out who the other person is who needs setting free and why. Whoever it is, they aren't visible in the ransom photo.'

'Sure. Perhaps the kidnapper has got a very personal grudge against Misha – a jilted lover maybe.' She tapped her forehead. 'Also, the fact Misha's been so jittery suggests she's been trying to handle him or her on her own, possibly for some time now so I reckon there will be clues to their identity amongst her personal belongings. On the plus side...'

'There's a plus side?' asked Dan, raising an eyebrow.

'Yes. The note also suggests there is something which Misha or Henry can do to resolve this situation – that it's not too late.'

Dan drained the last of his revolting coffee and smacked his lips together. 'I agree.' He tapped the side of his nose. 'Let me know what you find out.'

Henry, Cally and Mabel walked out of the park towards Henry and Misha's apartment. Her stomach was rumbling, and she realised that it was now mid-afternoon and, so far, she hadn't had anything to eat; the skinny latte at the spa didn't count.

The flat was the sort of thing you might see on the cover of an interior design magazine. The entrance resembled that of an airport lounge VIP area and required a special fob for one to gain access to the pale, pine-floored lobby. The moment the doors slid open, motion-sensor lights lit up the area with a peachy glow. Straight ahead loomed a wall of black, metal letter boxes, all neatly labelled and with a row of succulent plants standing sentry along the top. To the left hand-side of the wall stretched a corridor ending with glass double doors which opened out into a garden; Cally spied a patch of grass and some wooden chair legs.

Henry's flat was the first door on the right. He unlocked it and, as Cally entered the flat, her lungs filled with the scent of lavender, and she couldn't help but give a contented sigh. The entrance hall had a set of wall-mounted hooks which were overloaded with coats and beneath sat an overflowing shoe rack – Cally had never seen so many trainers in one place: most of them spotless. There was a small cloakroom to the right and to the left was a passageway with two doors leading off it. The area straight ahead fanned out into an open plan living space. It was light and airy with buttermilk cream walls and Cally was immediately drawn towards the floor to ceiling window and she pushed the dusty-pink curtains aside to stare at the garden. The lawn was a juicy emerald colour, flanked on all sides by a mossy brick wall, the lower half of which was hidden by a line of white rose bushes, possibly White Swan. The furthest wall was smothered by golden-leafed ivy which Cally noticed was strangling a passion-flower and her fingers itched to get out there and prune it free from its constraints. A narrow patio surrounded the lawn with polished teak benches stationed at various intervals so one could admire the garden from all angles.

'Wow!' said Cally, turning to Henry who gestured for her to sit on the distressed leather sofa which Mabel had already leapt onto and was busy nesting herself into a caramel throw whose tatty edges indicated that it belonged to her.

Henry checked his watch. '1 o'clock. I need a glass of wine.' He gave Cally a sheepish smile. 'Have one with me. Please.'

'As long as it's not Chardonnay,' said Cally. 'I absolutely hate Chardonnay.' Henry gave a grimace of agreement and moved towards the kitchen area. She would only have a sip of hers, but she hoped with some wine down him, Henry might relax a bit and become talkative. Through the double doors Cally could see glimpses of duck-egg blue shaker units and some sort of marble clad island above which hung a batterie de cuisine laden with copper pans glinting under the halogen spotlights. She heard the fridge door open then the musical chime of wine glasses knocking together. Henry came in clutching a perspiring bottle of something plus two enormous balloon glasses which he set down on the walnut-topped coffee table, brushing aside a couple of film magazines to make space. He sank down and unscrewed the lid and, as he poured the straw-coloured liquid into each glass, it was accompanied by a satisfying glugging sound.

'You knew Misha at drama school?' he asked, pushing the wine towards her.

Cally took the glass in both hands and pressed her spine into the squishy leather cushion behind her. She wondered if she should reveal her complicated feelings towards Misha but decided against it. She wasn't there to make friends. She needed to stay aloof. 'A bit. We weren't in the same social circle.'

Mabel shuffled along the sofa and placed her head on Henry's lap. 'Not friends, then.'

Cally took a sip of wine and let it wash around her mouth; it tasted like a slice of gooseberry tart mixed with wine gums. 'Mmmm! This is delicious. No. Not friends. But I always admired her acting talent.' Her cheeks flushed with the effort it took to produce the lie – she really was a terrible actor, no wonder she wasn't given the role in *Downton Abbey*.

'Yes.' He smiled. 'She's fabulously talented. Puts me to shame.'

Cally turned to stare into his eyes which were the colour of bluebells. 'You and Misha. You're happy, right?'

Henry eyes narrowed.

Cally took a deep breath. 'Look. There's no point sugar-coating this. I'm not being nosy. The brief has changed – I'm making it my business to find your wife.'

'Won't that be a job for the police now?'

'Yes, of course, but while they're out there searching for her and following up any physical leads, I get to find out what makes Misha Carlton tick. That's where the real clues are – the kidnap message is personal and cryptic, so I think the answer lies with your wife and it also means I need to know *everything* about her, you and your relationship. Sometimes it's the things you might think are irrelevant which hit a chord, so don't be coy – I need to hear it all.'

Henry let his gaze fall upon Mabel and he made his fingers into a spider shape and massaged her head; the poor dog was exhausted and the mud on her paws had dried leaving a coating of white dust.

Cally cleared her throat and carried on. 'I'm convinced either Misha or you have a connection with the kidnapper which we can get to if we dig deep enough.'

Henry drained his glass and smacked his lips together. 'I...I suppose we haven't been getting on very well recently. She's been in a pretty solid bad mood.'

'Since?

'I suppose since we moved here.'

'When was that?'

'March.' Henry refilled his glass, leaning over to top up Cally's but she placed her hand over the rim.

'I'd love to, but I can't. I've got to drive later.' She set her almost full glass down and pushed it away from temptation, pulling her notebook out of her bag. 'And, am I right in thinking that when you moved here in March this year that's when the pom poms started arriving?'

Henry swirled the wine around, staring at the centre of the vortex. 'Yes. So, I guess I'm the one to blame for all this, as the move was down to me.'

Cally made a note of the date. 'Okay. What else can you tell me...the press conference walk-out seemed to be centred on whether or not you were going to have kids. Is that something you discussed – having kids?'

He gave a shrug. 'Yep. I wanted them. She didn't.'

Cally tilted her head to one side. 'And you thought she might change her mind.'

He mirrored her gesture. 'I suppose later down the line, yes. In the meantime...' he held up Mabel's floppy paw and waved it. 'We got ourselves a Mabel.'

Cally reached out her hand and shook Mabel's paw and Henry smiled making his dimples appear. 'The name the journalist mentioned in the TV interview – Jade, perhaps, or Jaden. It's unusual. Does it mean anything to you?'

Henry folded his arms and shook his head. 'Absolutely nothing. I don't know anyone called Jade or Jaden and, as far as I'm aware, neither does Misha.'

A few moments of silence passed while Cally thought of more questions to make Henry open up a bit more. So far, there was no conversation, just her interrogating him – she supposed he was in shock, unable to get the vision of Misha out of his mind. 'Tell me what Misha was watching the night she collapsed.'

'She was watching the news.'

'Yes, but what time and what channel?'

Henry threw back his head and stared up at the glitterball light which hung from the centre of the ceiling. 'BBC 1. 9.30 pm.'

'That's local news then.' Cally pulled her phone out of her bag and hit on her BBC iPlayer icon, scrolling through to the news channel. Henry got up and padded into the kitchen and Mabel shuffled along the cushion and flumped her head on Cally's lap. Cally went back a day and pressed play, fast-forwarding the news items. She could hear Henry opening and closing cupboard doors. She went back to the screen; there was something about a water sewage leak, a minor royal had visited Leicester Cathedral to see

King Richard's tomb, and then the news that Luella Cambly had been found dead in her bridal suite at The Phoenix. Her spine tingled and she hit pause.

Henry walked into the room carrying a large bowl, heaped with Twiglets.

'Did either of you know Luella Cambly?' asked Cally, staring at his face, watching for tell-tale signs that he was lying.

Henry's expression didn't falter. He shook his head. 'You mean, that poor daughter of the billionaire who died on the morning of her wedding day?'

Cally nodded.

'No. I mean, I've vaguely heard of her on Instagram, but that's all. I don't follow her. I'm certain Misha didn't know her – she hates social media.'

Cally could feel it at the back of her mind – a shadow lurking that she needed to draw out. She wrote Luella's name down and underlined it, twice. This was getting her nowhere. She cleared her throat. Time for a different tack. 'Talk to me about Misha's early life.'

'She didn't really talk much about her childhood because, from what I can gather, it was a bit traumatic.'

'Oh?' Cally edged forward in her seat.

'Yes. She was born in the UK but was adopted when she was fourteen and her new parents took her over to live in the USA.'

Cally remembered that when they'd first met at drama school, Misha had a slight American twang to her voice which, at the time, she thought was an affectation – a pathetic one.

'Right. Well, we'd better talk to her parents and let them know what's going on.'

Henry put a couple of Twiglets into his mouth and crunched. 'No can do. I'm afraid they're both dead. Died a while ago in the Californian wildfires.'

Cally sighed. 'How awful. Poor Misha.'

Henry held up a Twiglet and pointed it at her. 'But she has an aunt who lives in Boston.' He checked his watch. 'I can call her if you like. I ought to tell her that Misha is missing before she hears it on the news.'

'Yes. Please do and then I'll ask her some questions. Just background stuff that may be useful.'

Henry got up and wandered over to a sideboard which was the same colour as the units in the kitchen. On it were several hardback lifestyle books facing outwards, a googly-eyed lion statue and a row of expensive-looking candles, still in their cellophane wrapping. Two laptops sat on the bottom shelf and Henry unplugged his and brought it over to the sofa.

'How come you left your laptops behind?' asked Cally.

'We agreed this was going to be a complete break for us – use the stay at The Nix as a time to recharge, ditch the temptations of the internet. Once we were there, we were only going to check our phones in the morning.'

'Admirable,' said Cally who would happily ditch the social media but not her virtual farm which needed tending to every day... or Candy Crush which was essential when killing time on a stake-out.

Henry placed the laptop on the table between them and dialled. Suddenly the black screen lit up and revealed a woman with bronze skin and platinum hair set in a gravity defying quiff.

'Hi Aunty Cleo,' said Henry, waving.

'Hello, Henry dear, what a lovely surprise,' said Cleo, her voice husky. She was cradling a mug of coffee and each finger bore a ring studded with a gemstone the size of a marble. Her expression was one of constant surprise but the crepe skin around her neck proved she wasn't quite as young as her face would have you think. Her lemon-yellow linen shirt billowed as a breeze came in through the patio windows and the sea sparkled in the distance causing Cally to choke back a whine of jealousy.

'Aunty. I'm afraid I have terrible news,' said Henry, placing his head in his hands.

Cleo set down the coffee with a bump and some of it spilled over the rim. 'Oh! Jeez. What? Misha's okay?'

There was a split-second pause. 'No. She's been kidnapped.'

Cleo stood up showing her slim waist in a pair of white fitted jeans and then she sat down with a bump, realising she had nowhere to go. She fanned her bejewelled fingers about her head. 'What's happened?'

'We don't know, I'm afraid. She's being held hostage, but we have no idea why yet. So let me introduce you to Cally here. She's a private investigator and she wants to ask you some questions.'

Cleo jabbed a manicured nail into her chest. 'Me? Why me?'

Cally tilted the screen towards her and waved. 'Because I need to know if there's anything about Misha's past which might shed light on her current situation.'

Cleo nodded. 'Okay.' She picked up her coffee and took a gulp. 'Fire away.'

'If you could start by telling me when you first met Misha.'

'My sister, Barb and her husband Graham Hamble...' she paused and made the sign of the cross then cleared her throat. 'They adopted Misha when she was fourteen and they moved her to California to give her a fresh start, but I didn't meet her for a couple of months because Mishy took ill and was in and out of hospital for a while.'

Cally looked up from her writing. 'What was she in hospital for?'

A flash of alarm whipped across Cleo's eyes, and she swallowed – her crinkled throat wobbling. She coughed and stared at Henry as though waiting for him to say something. After a long pause, Cleo leant towards the camera and lowered her voice. 'Barb wouldn't say. Misha's birth mother was a drug addict and I think it was something to do with that, but I don't know for certain. She had to have a lot of therapy.'

'What hospital?'

'St. Joseph's Medical Center.'

Cally jotted the name down. 'So, Cleo, tell me about when you first met Misha. What was she like and did she take long to settle in?'

Cleo clasped her hands together. 'Oh! She was a peach. Very quiet at first, but once she was settled in school and met some nice kids her own age, she blossomed. We all met up a couple of times a year during the holiday season and she and my kids got on brilliantly. We were so happy for Barb and Graham because they had wanted a child so badly. Mind you, I was surprised they adopted a teenager, but they were getting on a bit, and she was a cutey-pie and turns out they did the right thing – she was the perfect daughter.'

'So, when did they come back to the UK?'

'Graham is – *was* English and had been pining for the UK for a bit, God knows why, it's so grey and dreary over there, no offence, but when Misha wanted to go to stage school it just so happened to coincide with Graham retiring so it all worked out fine. They rented a place in Manchester for a couple of years. Misha acted and then she got that role in Downton, you know?' Cally gave an involuntary shudder then a nod. 'The rest, as they say, is history.'

'When did Graham and Barbara die?'

Cleo crossed herself again. 'It was about five years ago. They got trapped in the wildfires which destroyed almost all of their suburb. It was just awful,' she reached into her pocket for a tissue and dabbed her eyes. 'And now Misha...'

She started to sob.

'Aunty Cleo,' said Henry, leaning into the lens and obliterating Cally's view, 'don't give up hope. She's still alive and the police are doing everything they can to find her.' Cally gave his shoulder a gentle nudge so he sat back in his seat, and, once again, she could see the screen.

'Do you think it's a stalker?' asked Cleo. 'I mean, she's always had her fair share of whack jobs declaring their undying love for her.'

Cally stared into the lens. 'We don't know, but there's a possibility it's tied up with something which happened in her past life but we're not sure how far back to go. Do you know where in the UK Misha was originally from and what her name was before she was adopted?'

Cleo shook her head. 'Barb never said, but all their things were lost in the fire, so any paperwork to do with the adoption won't have survived.'

Cally clenched her hand in frustration. 'Does the name Jade or Jaden mean anything to you?'

Again, a firm shake of the head. 'Misha became their daughter and the moment she was legally theirs they never dwelt on the past – California was her fresh start.'

'OK. Thank you, Cleo, that's been very helpful. If you think of anything, anything which might be relevant you need to let me know. I'll send you my details.'

Cleo nodded. 'Sure, and Henry? Please, please keep me up to date with what's going on. I'll be waiting to hear from you.'

Henry hit the end call button and closed the laptop. They both sat back, but Henry's eyes had a glazed expression; he was still in shock, meanwhile, Cally's mind was racing. She pointed to the sideboard. 'The police will need to take any personal diaries or notebooks plus her laptop. Do you know her passwords?'

'Sure.' Henry got to his feet and moved over to the shelves, unplugging the other laptop. He opened a drawer and pulled out a bulging Filofax with a worn leather cover and coloured post-it notes poking out of the top. He wrote something down and tucked it inside the cover of the diary then took the bundle into the kitchen. 'Sure you don't want a top up?'

Cally shook her head. 'No. I need to get back home and figure out what to do next. But you, Henry, you need to see if you can get some rest whilst things are quiet. I'm sure, as I sift through the information you've given me so far, I'll have more questions, so I'll give you a call later.' She carried her glass through to the kitchen and saw the architects' plans and mock-ups for the flat laid out on the far end of the island. 'I can't resist this sort of thing,' she said, looking up at Henry who, she was relieved to see, was putting the wine back into the fridge. 'May I?'

Henry shrugged. 'Sure. I'm not going to do it anymore, though. First thing I'll do when I've got Misha back is sell up. Such a shame – the plans are great. I thought Misha would relish the prospect of doing a bit of interior design.' He shook his head and reached into a cupboard and pulled out a bag of dog food. 'Well, I say, such great plans, my pal, James, had the plans, I just bought them off him. He'd even sorted an architect too.'

Cally stared at a beautiful mock-up photo of a room with a dining section which led from a cosy seating area into a large kitchen lined with wall-to-wall units and a hidden pantry. She imagined herself leaning on the work surface and talking through her day, as Dan stir-fried something delicious on the gleaming hob. She put the glossy picture back onto a thick folder of floor plans and as she did so, something caught her eye. It was an ink stamp in the bottom right-hand corner which showed that the company who built the flat was none other than *Cambly Homes*.

Chapter 13
Mikey
2005

THE KNOCK at the door sounded like rapid gunfire, not that I'd ever heard it for real, only down at Pepper's Arcade; 20p a round and a bag of candyfloss if you hit the bullseye.

I don't know how I managed, but I forced myself over to the front door and opened it, not bothering to peer through the spyhole first. It wasn't a surprise to see the police officers standing there; one a grey-haired man with pockmarked skin partially hidden beneath a coating of salt and pepper stubble. He wore a crumpled silver-blue suit, and his beige tie was too thin for his shirt collar. The other was a slim Asian woman in a black and white uniform; she had on a pair of very ugly black shoes with smooth, shiny laces which I couldn't stop staring at. I almost held out my wrists to be cuffed, but at the last minute I tucked them behind my back.

'Can we come in, lad?' asked the man. He had a high-pitched voice which didn't match his gruff appearance.

In all the American crime programmes I'd watched, the police officers always flipped out shiny badges before anyone let them over the threshold.

'Can I see some ID first,' I said, pleased with how mature that sounded. They looked at each other; he raised an eyebrow and she smirked.

'Of course. Absolutely. I'm PC Stacey Bhatti and this is Sergeant Kenny Fuller. That scratch on your face looks nasty – how did you do it?' I ignored the question and instead made a big show of examining their photographs, but the writing underneath was all nonsense to me. They could have been a couple of axe murderers for all I cared – I knew what was coming.

My heart thumped against my skinny rib cage. Lucy was staring at the pair; her eyes flicking to them and then to me; eyeball tennis. Kenny closed the door behind him and stood with his hands behind his back and Stacey looked around the flat which I have to say, thanks to me, was looking much tidier than usual.

I was debating whether to offer them tea. I wasn't sure what the correct etiquette was when about to be arrested, but Stacey interrupted my train of thought. 'Would you like to come and sit at the table,' she asked – it was couched as a question, but it was an order.

'What's this about?' asked Lucy.

'It's alright,' I sighed, dragging my feet across the lino. 'So – what happens–'

'Be quiet,' said Lucy cutting me off. Stacey frowned, her dark eyebrows disappearing under the brim of her hat, the corners of her plump lips downturned.

Lucy raised her head but sat where she was, her arms folded. Meanwhile, I stood like a ninny in the middle of the kitchenette, staring at Stacey's ugly shoes.

'Are you Lucinda and Michael Jones?' asked Kenny.

We gave each other the side eye then nodded in unison.

Kenny took a deep breath. 'I'm afraid we have bad news.'

I pressed my lips together and hung my head, wondering if I'd look fetching in an orange jumpsuit. Although maybe UK prisons used a different material.

Kenny sighed. 'There's no easy way to say this, but your mum's been in an accident. I'm so sorry. She's dead.'

'Accident?' echoed Lucy.

'Yes,' said Stacey. 'No one's to blame.'

I shuffled back to the plastic chair and sank into it, almost toppling the flimsy frame backwards. This wasn't what I was expecting at all. In fact, it was so unexpected that I felt a bubble of laughter rise from the pit of my stomach. I coughed to disguise it, jumping up from my seat to fill the kettle as a distraction. The thing I'd wanted more than anything else had come true. Okay, so I'd never actually wanted Mum to die, but I'd always wanted her to leave us alone and even her absence this week had been a blessing. Life was so much better without her. Or so I'd thought.

Stacey came over and gently escorted me back to the chair and carried on making the tea, pulling open the tall cupboard to unearth the teabags. I didn't realise I was crying until I felt the snot run onto my lips. Kenny handed me a tissue and placed his palm around my shoulder, saying things like, 'there, there – it's alright son'. I couldn't tell either of them that they were tears of relief. Shielding my face with my hands, I looked at Lucy through a gap in my fingers. She was crying too, and I wondered if she was struggling with the same conflicting emotions. I closed my eyes and tried to block out the last image I had of her in my mind: a cheap tart, wearing an indecently short skirt, licking her crusty lips and leering at me, showing all her rotten teeth. I desperately tried to remember what she'd looked like a few years' ago, but that picture of Mum's face wouldn't appear. It had been such a long time since I'd had any proper contact with her and she'd spent the last year as a shadow, only visible in my peripheral vision.

The tea was hot and very sweet; I wanted to tell Stacey to go steady on the sugar as we were running out of our 'free' office supplies. I was only half listening as they told us how Mum had been under the influence when she stepped into the path of an oncoming lorry. That bit woke me up. Kenny said it would have been instant, but I couldn't help wondering if she'd felt any pain. Where was her soul now? Was she in a black hole – the same void I went to when I fainted in the bathroom? Then I moved on to thinking about what I was going to have for tea when the room fell silent. All eyes were focused on me.

'So, is that okay?'

'Huh?' I said, turning to Lucy.

She reached her hand across the table and squeezed mine. 'We each need to pack a bag of our stuff. We've got to go to an emergency foster place.'

'What? No? We can stay here – we can look after ourselves, can't we Luce?' The irony of what had just been happening here didn't register for one second although Lucy's hands slid to cover her stomach and her cheeks pinked.

'You aren't old enough to stay here on your own,' said Kenny. 'And, as you've got no family, we've got a duty of care.'

I pouted and shook my head.

'Come on, lad. It won't be forever. You'll get a nice warm bed and a cooked meal. Not bad hey?'

Lucy was already filling a bag with clothes. She handed me another one; it was one of our laundry bags and it smelt of the flower whose name I could never remember. I stood, hands on hips, regarding my cardboard box of clothes.

Stacey came forward and stooped so she was looking into my eyes; hers were the colour of a burnt hazelnut – our skin the same shade of olive-brown. 'You can come and get the rest of the stuff another time. Just take what you need for the next couple of days.'

I took out my jeans and a couple of jumpers and shirts, socks, pants and pyjamas, watching Lucy out of the corner of my eye.

'What happened to your coat?' asked Lucy, examining the

tears all over my jacket and trying to poke some of the white padding back into place.

'I dunno,' I said although I knew exactly where, why and how I had done it, but no one needed to hear about that now – it didn't matter.

'Don't forget your washbag,' said Stacey. I trotted off to the bathroom but when I emerged she was huddled up, talking in whispers to Lucy and the moment they saw me they went quiet. Lucy swallowed then gave me a sad smile and said, 'ready?'

I took her hand, and we went downstairs. As we left the building Mrs Slobberdown-yuck came rushing out of her flat and handed us one of her revolting sweets. I put mine in my pocket, as though it were a lucky charm. We crossed the grass-dust courtyard and the group of BMX boys, with the weird hybrid language, thought we'd been arrested and whistled at us and cheered.

Just under the arch which led onto the High Street, stood a woman, leaning against a pillar-box red minibus. She had a mass of wiry ginger hair, tied in a straggly ponytail. Her thin face was covered with large, greyish freckles and when she saw me, she smiled; her broad grin lighting up her dull green eyes.

She waved. 'Hello, Michael.' Her voice had a slight Scottish lilt to it. 'I'm Verity.' She banged the bonnet of the bus. 'Hop in – you're coming to stay with me for a bit.' She opened the door, and it slid back to reveal two faces, peeping over the back seat. There was giggling. 'Meet my twins; Callum and Connor,' she said. 'They're about the same age as you.' I stared at the two ginger boys with their bright marmalade hair – not the Seville kind – the cheap economy breakfast version.

I took a deep breath and turned to Lucy. She nodded her head in encouragement and I clambered in. 'Hi Callum, Connor,' I mumbled, hardly caring which was which. I shuffled to the far edge and put on my seat belt, patting the space next to me.

For a second it seemed as though time had frozen.

Lucy hung her head. 'I'm not coming with you. I've got to go to a different home.'

'No! No way! I'm not going without you,' I shouted and unclicked my belt, scooting back across to the door, my thighs sticking to the leather, but Kenny stepped into the breach, his arm stretched across the opening like a barrier. 'Son. This isn't easy for anyone, but, like I said – it's only temporary. We need to get you somewhere safe and then we can sort things out properly.'

'Lucy.' I could feel my throat tighten, her name sounding almost like a gargle. I had the sudden urge to pee.

Lucy couldn't look at me. She bowed her head. 'Mikey. It's just for a little bit. We'll be together again before you know it. Be brave. I love you.'

Kenny took her by the elbow and the door growled shut. I was mute with horror, my ears filling with the sound of the idiotic twins' giggles.

Verity climbed into the driver's seat and turned to look at me. 'Buckle up,' she said. 'I hope you're ready for life at the madhouse.' She turned the radio on, and classical music blared out, all strings and miserable wailing.

I pressed my palm to the window, staring at my ghostly reflection. Hatred towards my mother swarmed within me like bees abandoning a hive. She deserved everything she got, the silly, selfish bitch. Why was this happening? Of all the scenarios I'd envisaged, this wasn't one of them. There was a sharp slap followed by a sting both of which were accompanied by peals of laughter.

How I longed for the orange jumpsuit.

Chapter 14
Cally

CALLY SELECTED the flowers from her favourite florist, white roses and chrysanthemums for sorrow and loss. She wrote her name on a cream card and tucked it amongst the folds of the brown paper which wrapped the bouquet.

The Camblys' house was one of the lucky ones which backed onto Walkers' Common. Dan and Cally had walked along Mulberry Avenue, informally known as Millionaires' Row, many times imagining which house they'd buy if they won the lottery. Cally picked the penthouse in a luxury block of flats, whereas Dan opted for a vast Jacobean Manor house, never understanding her choice. Although Dan knew a bit about her family background, Cally hadn't gone into too much detail because it now seemed alien to her, but, in her early childhood, Cally and her parents had lived in the east wing of Carlton Castle. This was her dad's ancestral home, and her abiding memory of it was one of icy draughts; bigger, in her mind, was not always better but to say it out loud to Dan would sound like she was showing off. Val's house, Orchard Grove, was more difficult to assess from the pavement due to a drive which curved around to the left of a large privet hedge and obscured the view. As she crunched along the gravel, ducking out of the way of a rogue branch of violet buddleia, she was greeted by a grey brick building with crenelated turrets and mullioned windows. It resembled a shrunken Windsor Castle and she was genuinely surprised there wasn't a miniature, crimson-coated guardsman standing sentry outside the front door.

All was quiet as befitted a house in mourning and Cally decided to leave the flowers on the doorstep but as she stooped down, the front door opened and, straightening, she found herself gazing into Val's haggard face. Val who, in Cally's mind, was Amazonian in stature appeared to have aged twenty years, her cheekbones shrunken and hollow; her silver eyes bloodshot with a dull glaze as though dried out by all the crying. Even her usually sleek hair had lost its sheen.

'I'm so...sorry,' said Cally, her voice cracking with emotion.

Val stepped back from the door, holding it open and when she retreated into the shade, Cally could see her bony silhouette beneath the crumpled white linen trousers and pink shirt.

Cally shook her head. 'Oh – no. I don't want to disturb you. I just wanted to leave these.' Cally waved the bouquet and a loose rose petal drifted onto the gravel, but Val simply turned on her heels and went inside, leaving the door ajar. As Cally moved into the hall her gaze fell onto a circular table covered in vases of all different sizes, each brimming with flowers of every shape and colour. The sweet, honeyed perfume in the air was dizzying.

'Not very original,' said Cally, unwrapping her meagre offering and poking the stems into one of the wide-necked vases which had room for more.

Val took the paper from her and scrunched it into a ball. 'Not at all. It's very thoughtful of you to come in person. People are staying away to give me space, but I don't want to be left on my own so *please* come through and have a cup of tea with me.'

Cally swallowed. 'I'd like to. If you're sure.'

'I am.'

The circular entrance hall had a gently domed ceiling and a mosaic floor which was made up of cream tiles, interrupted by the occasional boggle-eyed turquoise fish. To the left of the front door was a spiral staircase with a corridor running behind and the passageway was lined by a teal carpet lit up by criss-crossed diamonds of light where the sun was shining in through the windows. Val ushered Cally through one of the adjacent doors into a small terracotta tiled kitchen. There was a small navy Aga to the left of the entrance and freestanding pale oak units lined the opposite wall. Straight ahead was a butler's sink and behind it a large sash window which offered glimpses of an immaculate lawn dotted with squat ornamental cherry trees. A crazy paving path curved towards a small iron gate in the middle of a hedge wall and Cally squinted, trying to see what was behind it. 'What a beautiful garden.'

Val filled the kettle and set it on the hotplate. 'Thank you. I remember when we were choosing the wedding flowers you said how much you liked gardening. You used to be a professional one, right?'

'Yes. For a couple of years, before I got into the hospitality industry.'

Val's lower lip trembled and she gave a loud sniff. 'Once I've made the tea, we can go and sit out there. We might as well make the most of the sunshine.'

There was silence apart from the ticking of the clock over the Aga which had *Don't Worry, Drink Gin* scrawled across it in pink italics. Cally had experienced the sucker punch of grief when her father died suddenly under suspicious circumstances ten years ago and she knew that the silences didn't need to be filled so she kept quiet whilst Val busied herself taking two polka dot mugs off the dresser and setting them on the table.

'Please sit down. Normal tea with milk.' Val opened the fridge door and set a striped jug onto the table.

Cally nodded although it was a statement not a question and perched on the stool nearest the window, frustrated she couldn't see what was on the other side of the garden gate. The kettle whistled and Val dropped the teabags into each mug then filled them three-quarters full. Cally rested her hands on the pine table then wished she hadn't as it was covered in patches of white granules and sticky rings and, in the centre, sat a plate piled high with shrivelled teabags and a bowl of crusty-topped sugar.

Val pulled out a stool and sat down. 'I'm awash with tea,' she said.

'It's something to do, isn't it?' Cally replied.

Val squished the teabags with a spoon and put them on the pyre in the middle then handed Cally a mug and a teaspoon. 'Do your own milk. There's sugar if you want.' Cally added a splosh of milk and gave it a stir, a film of tannin swirled then settled around the edges.

'Right. Let's head outside,' said Val beckoning Cally to follow her into a cluttered boot room with a stable door which opened out into the back garden. Cally's lungs filled with the scent of honeysuckle, and she closed her eyes, glad of the sun on her face whilst insects and birds chattered around her. Behind the kitchen was a patio area complete with wrought iron table, overflowing ashtray on top, and two matching chairs topped with pink and white striped cushions. Val set down her tea and reached into her back pocket, extracting a packet of cigarettes and a box of matches. Then she sat down, stretching her legs out in front of her; her cerise toenails, done especially for the wedding, peeping out from the ends of her wedges.

'I don't actually smoke,' said Val pulling a cigarette out of the carton and rotating it between her thumb and index finger; nails painted to match her feet although half the varnish was now missing.

'Something else to do,' said Cally, taking a sip of tea and wincing; she wished it was Earl Grey with a splash of lemon and not this tastebud-numbing builder's brew.

Val put the cigarette in her mouth, but her fingers trembled as she struck the match and after a couple more fruitless attempts Cally reached over and took the box from her, lighting the match and cupping the flame as Val inhaled and the end of the cigarette glowed. Val took deep drags letting the smoke funnel out of her nostrils whilst Cally focused her gaze on the dappled shade under the nearest tree.

After a few minutes, Val cleared her throat. 'I'm just so angry with him.' Her tone was both incredulous and yet she sounded tired. She flicked at the ash, spilling half of it onto the table which fell through the iron framework and disintegrated.

Cally turned to her and nodded, saying nothing.

'I needed him. I *really* needed him, you know, and he just took the coward's way out and abandoned me.' Fat tears spilled from her eyes and rolled down her cheeks, but she let them fall unchecked; it was as if she had become so used to the state of crying, she had stopped being aware whether she was or wasn't.

'Did he leave a note?' asked Cally, although she already knew he had.

Val swiped a hand across her face. 'Yes. He said he was to blame for Luella's death, whatever the fuck that means.'

'Why would he blame himself?' asked Cally, wrinkling her brow.

Val took another deep nicotine inhalation. She shrugged. 'Fuck knows. I mean, we were both devastated about Luella. So, what was he trying to prove – he loved her more than me and can't live without her?' She wiped her eyes with the heel of her hand.

Cally hesitated. She had formed a list of questions in her head but needed to be careful how she introduced them into the conversation. 'It must be more complicated than that. I mean –

was there anything in his past which might explain his guilt? Something which may have caught up with him.'

A flicker of something inexplicable passed across Val's eyes and then vanished. She hung her head. 'No.'

She was lying about something. Cally knew not to push; she'd come back to Bill's past via a different route. 'How's Sasha doing?'

Val gave a snort, a cross between a scoff and a laugh. 'I mean, I know she must be devastated and is dealing with things in her own way, but I just don't get the constant need to record absolutely everything. It's so bloody ridiculous.'

Cally nodded. 'Me neither, but it's what that generation do.'

'I've stopped her filming anywhere near me though,' said Val, turning to stare at Cally, 'I mean, I don't think this,' she circled her face with the remnants of her cigarette, 'is going to make good viewing, is it?' She gave a small smile; tears still tumbling down her cheeks.

'This is a beautiful house,' said Cally. 'Have you always lived here?'

Val stubbed out the cigarette and reached for another. 'We lived here when we first married. It was Bill's family home and then we moved away when I was pregnant with Luella, but we never sold it, just rented it out.'

Cally did a quick calculation. Luella was 19 when she died; that made her born around 2005. 'But it's so perfect. Why did you move?'

The strange look again. 'We needed a change.' She paused and bit her lower lip. What did that mean? 'Bill wanted to start up the yacht business and so it made sense to for us to be in Poole where the shipbuilding yard was.'

'What was his job before that?'

'He built designer flats and apartments here in The Village, but he sold that business yonks ago.'

Cally nodded.

Val pushed her tea to one side – she'd barely touched it. Her phone rang and she glanced at the screen then up at Cally. 'It's the funeral directors. Do you mind?' Cally shook her head and stood up, gesturing to the end of the garden. Taking her tea with her, she walked along the crazy paving, unable to help herself from stooping down to pluck at a stray dandelion poking up through the bricks.

She pulled her phone out of her pocket. Dan had left a couple of messages and she scrolled through them:

Weird soil taken from Mabel's claws. Unidentifiable animal faeces. It's going for further testing.

Going to go public with fact she's missing. Need to come home and change into my best suit.

Do you know where my smart navy tie is?

Cally sent him a four-leafed-clover emoji and ignored the comment about the tie which was, in reality, ugly and frayed plus it gave out a strange glow under the glare of certain lights. Now wasn't the time to tell him she had put it out for the charity collection along with his Hawaiian 'party' shirt. She was at the end of the paving and opened the gate onto another perfect patch of lawn but this time it was surrounded by wild meadow flower borders creating a messy rainbow of bright colours. Right in front of her was a large rectangular pond teeming with bright fish and a fountain at the centre spurted jets of water at intervals. At the far end was a fruit cage, bursting with strawberry plants and nectarines; crimson and yellow berries twinkling in the sunlight. She tipped the dregs of her tea onto the ground and took a step nearer to the cage, inhaling the mouth-watering sweet smell of the ripening fruit. As she went closer, she became aware of a loud whirring and humming sound coming from behind a large wooden screen on the far side of the cage, next to the fence which backed onto Walkers' Common.

'Hello,' came a voice. Cally startled and turned. A figure,

clutching an aluminium watering can, stepped out from the entrance to the cage.

Cally slapped her hand to her chest. 'Oh, bloody hell. You startled me.'

It was a woman in her late fifties with short, spiky salt and pepper hair. One of her ears was pierced from the lobe to the top of the cartilage, silver loops snaking down it like one of those slinky toys which should cascade down the stairs but, in Cally's case, always got tangled. She was wearing incredibly short denim cut-offs and a lilac linen shirt tied at the waist to reveal a washboard stomach. She was tanned and lithe with pointed features and grey eyes. She took the air pods out of each ear and put them into her pockets.

'Does Val know you're here?' she asked.

'What?' shouted Cally.

The woman beckoned her across the lawn. 'That bloody pond generator – it's so noisy.' She smiled. 'I said, does Val know you're here?'

'Yes. We're having tea. She's just taking a phone call. Do you work here?'

The woman smiled. 'I'm Di. Val's older sister and, yes, I suppose I do work here. I'm a sort of house *and* garden keeper.'

She could see the resemblance now; they had the same bone structure; the same large teeth set in small gums. 'So, do you live here too?'

She nodded.

Cally smacked her forehead. 'Gosh. How awfully thoughtless of me. I'm so sorry for both your losses.'

Di set the watering can down and plucked at a stray dogrose which was tangled in the folds of her shirt. 'Yes. Lou was a beautiful girl. Not half as foolish as she'd have you believe.' There was a pause and Cally waited for Di to move onto Bill, but she didn't.

'I was helping plan the wedding. Luella was a very easy client compared with a lot of the ones I've come across.'

'She said you were nice. Val, that is.'

'How do you think Val's coping?'

Di shrugged. 'It's not sunk in yet. Not properly – she's just going through the motions.'

'That's hardly surprising.' Cally took a step closer and lowered her voice. 'I met Bill too. Do you have any idea why he would kill himself?'

Di gave a sharp inhalation of breath.

'I mean – you lived here so you must have known him really well. He just didn't seem the type.'

Di raised an eyebrow. 'There's a type?'

Cally felt the colour flood her cheeks. 'Sorry. That was a dumb thing to say.'

Di flapped her hand. 'Don't worry. I know what you mean. I have a granny annexe. When Bill was around, I kept away.'

'You didn't get on?'

Di tilted her head to one side and her eyes narrowed. 'You could say that. He was a two-faced, womanising bastard.' She almost spat the words.

Cally opened her mouth then clamped it shut again.

Di's features had crinkled with bitterness. 'He chased anything in a skirt – fuck that, anything with a pulse. The younger the better.'

Cally could feel her heart thumping against her ribcage. 'Did Val know about the affairs?'

A firm nod. 'Though after a while she turned a blind eye.'

'Plenty of reasons why he might have been overcome with guilt, then.'

Di kicked the watering can with her foot and it toppled, water vanishing into the grass. 'Pah! That wouldn't have given him a guilty conscience – he was at it all the time. No. The only reason for him to kill himself was if something was about to come out of the woodwork and humiliate him.'

Cally froze – it took a few seconds for her brain to process what Di was saying. 'Wait – you don't think he murdered his own daughter because of something she had found out and then, racked by guilt, ended his life?'

Di held up her palms. 'Who knows what he'd do...' She jerked her hands up and gave an enthusiastic wave over Cally's head, dozens of leather bands slipping down her tanned forearm. Cally turned to see Val walking towards them and her eyes hopped from one to the other assessing the pair and finding Val to be a more refined, elongated version of her sister.

'Everything okay?' asked Di, her voice too bright.

'Yes. The funeral directors want to know when Bill's body is going to be released, but they haven't done the autopsy yet.' She looked around. 'Have you found the mystery intruder?'

Cally's ears prickled. 'What – someone's been breaking in?'

Di gave a dry laugh. 'Yes. A twitchy-nosed, long-eared, whiskered variety of trespasser. Beige fluff caught on the underside of the fence and a bit of burrowing around the gate to the park, but so far, they haven't managed to penetrate the fruit cage.'

Val sighed. 'All the world's fucked but as long as your nectarines can ripen in peace.'

'That's what you pay me for, Sis.'

Cally looked at her phone. Time was ticking by and she still hadn't addressed one of her queries. She'd have to resort to a bit of acting. She took a deep breath. 'Oh hell!'

'What?' asked the sisters in unison.

'One of our celebrity clients at The Nix has gone missing. *Shit!*'

'Who?' asked Di. They were standing side by side now and the shape of their jaws could have been moulded from the same piece of clay.

'Misha Carlton.' She said it – gauging each of their reactions. They both gasped in amazement, but it seemed a genuine response to a familiar name rather than to anything suspicious. 'I'd best get back. It's going to be all over the news.'

'Has she run off?' asked Di.

Cally shook her head. 'No. She's been kidnapped.'

'What? From The Nix?' Val shook her head in amazement.

'No. Apparently she was taken from Walkers' Common.'

'What? From here?' asked Val, waving her hand at the fence.

Di gave a low whistle. 'How awful. I always think of it as being such a safe place.'

'The garden gate's locked, though, right?' asked Val, her eyes wide with alarm.

'Of course,' replied Di. 'I don't think I've ever opened it – besides, the hedge behind it must be utterly impenetrable.'

Val fanned herself with her hand. 'Just awful, but at least Gloria Cavel will be thanking her lucky stars it's not more negative publicity for her. Misha's poor husband – what's his name…'

'Henry Carmichael,' said Cally. There was a pause as Val and Di let the news sink in then Cally clapped her hands together. 'Right. I've got to go.'

'I'll walk you out,' said Val, putting her arm around Cally's shoulder.

'No need. You stay here and soak up some sunshine. Call me, if you need anything.'

Cally walked back through the kitchen and put her mug in a dishwasher already choc-a-bloc with crockery. As she walked across the hall, Sasha came running down the stairs, for once minus the camera.

'Oh – hi, Sasha. How are you doing?' asked Cally.

Sasha didn't answer, but her face was pinched, mouth turned down at the edges.

'You look pissed off about something.'

Sasha's hair was tied up in a curated bird's nest on top of her head. She was wearing ballet pumps, black leggings and an oversized, grey crocheted smock which revealed most of the fitted black running top underneath. She balanced on the lower step, working her jaw from left to right, like a camel chewing its breakfast.

'You can try me,' said Cally.

Sasha let out a big puff of breath and put her hands on her hips. 'Luella was working on a deal with someone. That's why we were filming every section of the wedding. She told me...' she pressed an acrylic nail into her chest, '...she *absolutely* couldn't say anything about it, but that the moment she headed off on honeymoon all would be revealed, and she'd hand the project over to me. She said it was going to be huge.' Sasha made a circle with her arms. 'HUGE!'

'Surely you can trace back her messages and dig out the conversation.'

Sash wagged a finger at her. 'Duh! You'd have thought so, but I got her phone back from the police and there's nothing on it. I've gone way back through all the Insta DMs and there's fuck all there.'

'Forgive me for being obtuse...'

'Huh?'

'Thick. But why do you care about the deal now? I mean, your sister's dead and if the deal was for exclusive wedding footage, well... you haven't got it.'

Sasha pouted and shook her head as though Cally wasn't obtuse, but brain dead. 'Thanks to me, I've upped her following by about a bazillion and I think the funeral will be just as much of a publicity draw as the wedding would have been, but I still want to know about the project.'

The phone in her pocket went off and she answered it, squealing.

'Sorry about your dad,' said Cally, her voice lost amongst the peals of laughter. Cally shook her head and let herself out of the door, wondering how it was possible to be that shallow or whether Sasha was simply unable to differentiate between her real life and the image she projected onto the screen. Somewhere down the line, when she stopped living the drama, she was going to need a whole lot of therapy.

As Cally walked back onto the pavement, she realised she now had three things to pursue: what had caused Val and Bill to move away when Luella was born, and who was Luella's mystery work colleague and how had they been communicating?

Chapter 15
Mikey
14 months earlier

'JAY. JAY.'

'Huh?' I swung round to see my marketing assistant and on and off, mainly off, boyfriend, Max staring at me, phone squashed between ear and shoulder, his untidy black hair falling across his face. I'd been transfixed by my favourite orchid on the windowsill; amazed by how the light shining in through the glass turned the chocolate spots on the petals almost purple. There were cardboard boxes piled up everywhere; the majority containing free beauty samples which I hadn't got round to examining. The move into my new luxury apartment was only a few days away and I wasn't ready for it. I couldn't sleep without my pills but even they weren't able to shut out the increasing sense of dread which had been creeping up inside, leaving me exhausted. Every night before I drifted off I saw her face and she was the first image that I saw when I woke. A deep sense of unease filled my belly even though moving had always been part of my overall plan and I'd had my eye on the place for a long time; approaching a local agent to see if they could assist in my acquisition. I'd bided my time, then when the money was rolling in, I made an offer the owner couldn't refuse. Possessing the flat may have been one more worry off my mind, but living there was another matter altogether.

'They want to know if you'll give their mascara a shout out on your channel?' asked Max curling his fringe behind his ear.

'Who?'

'It's that brand of mascara which has the rose-gold, glitter tip – you're meant to apply it at the end of the day, before you hit the clubs.' He held one slender hand in a fist then spread out his fingers like an explosion, fluttering his eyelashes all the while.

I giggled. 'Oh – that one. It goes on like cement and makes you look like you've got pink eye.' I waggled my finger. 'It's a 'no' from me.'

Max nodded then spoke into the phone. 'I'm afraid JayDoll isn't prepared to promote it.' There was a high-pitched retort on the other end. 'Because –

'Because it's shit.' I shouted.

Max gave a hiccup of laughter and hit the red button on his phone.

I smacked my forehead with my palm. 'I shouldn't have said that. It was very unprofessional and bitchy.' I made claw marks in the air.

Max moved over to the kitchen table, where I was sitting, working through the designs for my own make-up range which my team were launching next year: *Dollymix*. 'What is up with you?' he purred, massaging my shoulders.

I was deliriously excited, but I couldn't begin to formulate a reply, plus Max wasn't to be trusted with the secrets I'd buried over the years. We were very close to A Lister status or, I should say, JayDoll was and that was all that mattered to Max; a beautiful, social butterfly who craved to be part of the in-tribe. I should also mention that Max was gay with a capital G and, although I preferred to date men, I also found women attractive too.

When I eventually finished beauty college and moved out of

the children's home, I started a YouTube channel to showcase my music, but I also used it as a way to express my talents as a hair and make-up artist too. It soon became apparent that my make-up tutorials were what most people tuned in to see and leave comments about. I did hacks and shared my tips so that anyone could transform themselves into a superstar in the comfort of their own bedroom. When I hit the golden number of followers, the sponsorships came flooding in and so did the money.

I knew Max had been drawn to me because of my creation and alter ego; JayDoll. It was one of the perks of the job of having a successful YouTube channel, getting to pick and choose who I hung out with. Max had made an appearance near to the beginning of JayDoll's career, but he had stayed in my life because he worked for a successful PR firm. His talents lay in marketing and, at the time, I was desperate for someone to help with the other side of success which I didn't really have, or want to make, time for. He was the one who recruited our small, eclectic army of workers and he was the one who kept the business running.

My inability to focus on anything was because I was about to force a reunion with Lucy who'd had a transformation of her own but now that an aspect of my past was about to enter my present, I couldn't guarantee that the extra fallout which might accompany it, wouldn't damage the brand. Max, as my marketing manager, would discourage me to leap in until I'd tested the waters first, but I couldn't do that, so had resolved to keep the whole thing quiet.

I never heard from Lucy again after we were taken to our different placements. I passed through various foster houses until I ended up living at a children's care home which I preferred. All I was able to discover from social services was that Lucy had been adopted and that her family had taken her to America to live. That's where the trail had run dry for me as they'd changed her name. A fresh start. It was as though she had vanished, but despite my grief, I always knew we would eventually find one another again – we had to; ours was a strong bond. As the beginnings of fame flapped its wings, I knew the platform I was creating would raise my profile. I wasn't sure how or when, but I knew Lucy would recognise me and come forward. In the meantime, I kept my past life a secret. I had to – if the truth about that came out, our lives would be ruined.

In actual fact, Lucy was the one whose stardom rose first. I had been watching an American show about a school for magical kids with hidden powers. The sort of show I binged on whilst holed up in the Cambly office. The main characters were all quite well-known but in one scene, the guy with the fireballs tucked up his sleeve, accidentally lost his temper and hit a girl, causing her to catch fire. The girl screamed then lay on the floor, unconscious. She'd got taller and her face was fuller, but it was definitely Lucy. My heart almost leapt out of my mouth. It turned out the film was a couple of years old, but I found out the actor's name was Misha Carlton.

I googled everything I could about Misha Carlton. It transpired that after her appearance in that show she'd attended a stage school in Manchester and her first job after that had been a role in *Downton Abbey*. Of course, I'd heard of the programme, but had never watched it. Now, I binged the entire season in which she featured – fast forwarding to get to her scenes. Her character was a chamber maid who'd fallen foul of the lord of the manor and suddenly found herself expecting a baby. *The irony!* Lucy or Misha, as she was now called, wore a long, curly black wig so, if I hadn't known it was her, and wasn't giving it my full attention, I doubt I would have recognised her. I also read that her current project was a UK film about The Duchess of Welford and that a year ago she married a TV actor called Henry Carmichael, but it was difficult to find out anything else about her as she kept her private life totally under wraps.

I had a contact, Laurie, who worked for the company which

was doing the hair and make-up on the film set so I phoned him on the pretext of telling him I was doing a feature on my channel and wanted him to talk to my audience about the perils of make-up for the big screen. It was a basic idea, but he was delighted and secured me and Max a morning on set with VIP guest passes.

There was, however, a niggle of doubt at the back of my mind. Misha was famous – she'd had the means to make contact with the wider world so why hadn't she come looking for me? I hadn't changed my name officially until a couple of years ago. Could it be there were too many Michael Joneses to sift through?

My physical appearance was different. I'd filled out. Got myself some Turkish teeth and acquired a gym-bod too. My hair was long and soft brown with blonde highlights – I liked it to fall about my shoulders, but I often tied it up when I worked. I'd already picked out what to wear for the reunion: jeans and a loose-fitting white linen shirt – and I'd decided to tone down my own make-up and accessories. I didn't want to freak her out with the more theatrical make-up with which I sometimes delighted my audiences.

I felt bad not telling Max the subplot of what he was filming, but I didn't want him to spoil anything as his excitement would be hard to contain. Of course, he was going to love being around all the actors so he'd be a starry-eyed flirt anyway but add my secret to the mix and he would be a hot mess.

The film was shooting on location at a stately home a fifty-minute cross-country walk from where Lucy and I both grew up and where I still lived. Max had booked us into a hotel in the centre of Market Bowden; a Regency townhouse which was next to a convent and opened out onto the square hosting lots of trendy bars and restaurants. The weather was beautiful for this time of year; May blossom and warm sunshine; and I pictured Lucy and I sitting out on a terrace bar, faces streaked with tears as we caught up on the intricacies of how our lives had unfurled so far. I'd already made up my mind that I wouldn't tell her I'd bought the flat in The Village. That could wait as I hadn't yet decided what I was going to do with it and how much to share with her.

The day arrived and Max drove us early to the set. We flashed our passes at the people on the gate and Max basked in the stolen glances and whispered excitement my presence was causing. The buzz of anticipation about what I was doing there added to the already effervescent atmosphere in my head.

A cream gravel drive bordered by tall redwoods meandered towards the Georgian mansion. To the left side, in front of the lawn, was a bank of lorries and vans; wires, lights and lifting equipment spilling from their open doors. Behind the vehicles sat a food truck; plastic tables and chairs spread out underneath a striped awning. Next to that were two canvas tents; one with 'wardrobe' scrawled above the entrance, the other said 'hair and make-up'.

Max and I headed over to the tents; Max filming all the while, and I texted Laurie. Within seconds he was outside the entrance, waving his foundation brush in the air. He was wearing dark jeans, white converse and a tee-shirt with a picture of a pineapple on the front. He'd had a buzz cut which accentuated his cheek bones, but also made him appear more neanderthal than usual.

'You look amazing,' he said, kissing me on both cheeks. He gave a little wave to Max who peeped his head from around the camera and fluttered his eyelashes.

'Laurie is heterosexual and married with two kids,' I said in a flat tone.

'Pity.' Max pouted and returned behind the lens.

I turned to Laurie. 'So – if it's okay with you. I'd like to film you talking us through how you prepare an actor for the camera. What needs to be done differently. I'll ask questions to prompt a dialogue, so it doesn't sound like a tutorial.'

'Sounds great,' said Laurie. 'I've done my first one already. Misha Carlton.'

I swallowed. *Damn!*

'But the thing about film make-up is, as you know, I'll have to keep touching up before each take, so there's a lot of traffic coming in and out.'

'That's such a good quote – you get that?' I turned to Max who gave a thumbs up.

We entered the marquee. Despite the promise of a hot day, it was chilly outside, but beneath the canvas the air was humid and filled with the smell of hairspray and the plasticene scent of the acres of foundation cream plastered on every actor's face. I scanned the row of swivel chairs, searching the mirrored partition wall for her reflection, but she wasn't there.

I had to use every ounce of resolve to focus on interviewing Laurie. He was having fun, but I was jumpy and glanced up at every person who walked in. When she did arrive, my heart leapt into my mouth. She came striding over to Laurie who was mid-sentence and cut him off – not seeming to care that he was being filmed.

'I'm on in a minute,' she said slumping into the nearest chair and pulling off her oversized sunglasses. My stomach was churning although now she was within touching distance, my immediate reaction was to run. She was wearing a white satin robe which covered her costume and I could see a flash of pink taffeta poking out underneath the hem. Her dark wig was cut into a sharp bob and the black eyeliner on the waterline made her blue eyes look small and mean. She placed a delicate tiara on the shelf in front of the mirror.

'Oh! Right you are. Misha, this is JayDoll – you've probably heard of him,' said Laurie.

Misha fanned herself with a thick script; large sections of

which were highlighted in green. She glanced at me then looked back down at her page. 'No.'

I stood frozen. My jaw hanging open.

'He's an online legend,' said Laurie, giving me an embarrassed smile. 'A very fine make-up artist and he's–'

Misha pointed a cream nail at the tiara. 'This needs to be fixed so I can dance without it flying off.'

A young woman, all in black, with a headpiece came rushing up to Laurie. 'They need to be on set in ten.' Thanks to my interview, Laurie was only halfway through styling the actor in the chair. He took a deep breath and then pressed his lips together.

'Let me, Laurie,' I said with a wink.

'Lifesaver,' he added, rustling in his make-up box and handing me a pack of hairpins.

I flexed my fingers making the joints click then reached over and picked up the tiara, placing it on Misha's head and shifting it around until it was in the correct position. I was staring right at her reflection and into her blue irises. I smiled but she shut her eyes. Max came over.

Max pointed the camera in my direction. 'Do you mind if I film this? It's for my channel.'

She kept her lids closed and the muscles in her jaw clenched. 'Actually, I do mind.'

'Oh – right.' I turned to Max and sliced the edge of my hand across my neck. He rolled his eyes and turned back towards Laurie whose brow was furrowed with concentration.

'So – you're from round here?' I asked.

One eye flicked open and her scarlet lips puckered, like she'd just bitten something sour. 'No. Where'd you hear that?'

I shrugged, focusing my attention on the hairclips. 'I thought you grew up locally.'

Her blue eyes narrowed. 'No – my dad was English, but my mum was American and we lived there for most of my childhood.

I came to Britain to go to drama school, but I'm certainly not from round here.' She shrugged. 'I think of myself as an American.'

I started, pushing a pin into her scalp.

'Ouch!'

'Sorry,' I said, removing the offending hairclip. I wasn't expecting that answer. 'So – wow – your family must be proud of you.'

'My parents are dead.'

'Oh! God. How awful.' My mouth was dry. I swallowed. 'Do you have any siblings?'

'No.' She folded her arms. 'I'm an only child.'

I dropped the hairbrush as though it was burning into my flesh. She tutted.

As I stooped, I tried to gain my composure, but I could feel the blood draining from my face. This wasn't how this conversation was meant to go. I needed to make her see me. 'Can you look right at me please,' I said, staring into the mirror, combing out the ends of her wig. I focused my gaze into her eyes and smiled. *Lucy! It's me.* She glared back. Not a flicker of recognition.

I opened my mouth to say something else, but she shook her head. 'Enough with the talking. I need to go through my lines.'

When the tiara was fixed, she shook her head from side to side, checking the miniature crown didn't wobble, then stood up. She let her robe slide to the floor, puddling at my feet, and stalked off in her salmon pink ball gown, without saying a word of thanks.

I wanted to call after her – shout out that I was Mikey, her long-lost brother and that I'd never stopped hoping I'd find her; that I'd never stopped loving her or wanting us to be together.

But then, like a kick in the gut, I realised Lucy hadn't felt the same. Blood whooshed around my ears and my cheeks flamed – I needed to escape the stifling heat of the tent. I stumbled out onto the lawn and went under the guy ropes and turned the corner, relieved to find an area with plenty of shade. I leant against the canvas, taking deep breaths through my nose, and releasing the air out of my mouth.

I smelt cigarette smoke. A voice on the other side of the tarpaulin cut through my thoughts. 'What is it with these freaks?' It was Misha.

'What's happened, gorgeous?' replied a man whose voice was gravelly and familiar. He was the main actor on set, playing her fiancé – Tom somebody or other.

'This random guy talking to me when I'm having my hair done. Excuse me – give me a break! I don't want to talk about my personal life to a complete stranger. A weird one at that. Kept grinning at me like some sort of freak.'

I dug my fingernails into my clenched palms, trying not to scream.

'He was probably just a bit stage struck,' said Tom.

'No – he's one of those egocentric make-up influencers – doesn't have a filter, asking me about my childhood, like it's any of his business.'

'Oh! Fuck – how rude.'

'Yes. God knows how much Mum spent on therapy for me to get over those years. People just don't think. There's nothing about my miserable childhood I want to remember. Nothing.'

Chapter 16
Cally

Cally walked into the bathroom, Rolly following her with his ever-balding tennis ball. Steam coated the mirror but, rather than the gentle aroma of rose or lavender, the air was heavy with the brutal smell of pine disinfectant – Dan's go to scent. He was outstretched in the bath, his torso coated with a mountainous heap of bubbles, his face pink and shiny.

'Saw you on the news,' she said, leaning over to kiss his shiny forehead. 'You scrub up nicely.'

'Autographs later,' he murmured holding up a hand, the skin on his fingertips pale and wrinkled. He opened one eye. 'What's happening?'

Cally sat on the loo and screwed the lid back onto Dan's bubble bath which was called 'Air of Alpine' and cost £1 from the local corner shop; in her opinion, he'd been robbed. Frankly, she wouldn't wash Rolly in it, even those times when he'd frolicked in fox poo.

'I've given her computer to the tech guys,' he said. 'It's going to be a long night.'

Rolly dropped the ball and nudged it with his snout onto her toes.

'You got anything else you can share?' she asked, kicking the rubber scrap so it went skidding across the floor, Rolly in hot pursuit, claws tapping against the linoleum.

'We've got Luella's phone records. A couple of the numbers were from burners which were dead when we rung them.'

Cally sat upright and gripped her knees. 'That's dodgy. I think someone was contacting Misha in secret on a burner – can I take down those numbers and see if any of them overlap?'

'Be my guest. We'll be checking them too. I've written them down in my notebook.' He rubbed his eyelids with his thumb and index finger. 'There'll be a media circus now. As we were leaving the park a tonne of lorries with broadcasting equipment arrived.' He sat up, causing a tsunami. 'I'm not sure going public was the right thing to do.'

Cally pulled his towel off the rail next to her. 'I don't think you had another option and, you never know, someone might have seen something relevant.'

'Oh yes. The phones are ringing off the hook with more tall tales than the Brothers Grimm.' He tutted. 'I'll have something to eat then go back in.'

Cally folded the towel and placed it on top of the loo seat. 'Tell you what, I'll go and get us some take-away – Rolly could do with a stroll. At least we can eat together before work takes over our lives completely.'

Dan went under the water, raising a thumb in the air.

Considering how sunny the day had been, it had turned into a rather dull and grey evening and the atmosphere was clammy. Thunder blighters dive-bombing her bare arms signalled that a downpour was on its way. Before she turned the corner onto the street which ran parallel with Walkers' Common, she was aware of a heightened volume of noise. Normally, at this time of an evening, the clashing of crockery and gentle hum of people talking and laughing as they dined al fresco, drifted into the air. What greeted her now was a cacophony of human noise and when she turned into Walkers' Boulevard, her view through the iron railings of the park was blocked by a row of stationary vans with satellite dishes on top. Extra tables lined the pavements with people crowding around them, drinking and eating whilst watching illuminated figures, microphones in the air above their heads, gesticulating and pointing to the entrance of the park. That view was uncluttered although the gates remained closed with a different police guard on sentry duty.

Cally's first thought was totally selfish; she was never going to get served anywhere, let alone procure two take-away gyros from her favourite Greek restaurant, *The Olive*. She picked up Rolly, cradling him in her arms; took a deep breath – as though heading into battle, and pushed her way through the wall of bodies. Someone knocked her elbow as they raised their Aperol Spritz and the orange liquid sploshed onto her shoe. No apology from the glassy-eyed woman, just a flicker of anger that Cally had got in her way, all the while bits of gossip flew around her ears.

'She's just run off with another fella. Don't blame her – that Henry what's-his-name is such a drip.'

'Batshit crazy, if you ask me – probably sat at home watching the whole thing and sucking it up. Great publicity for her new film.'

'Nah! She's dead – some psycho stalker's done it.'

Cally couldn't believe how horrible these people were being. She resisted the urge to stand on top of the bar and tell them the truth. Of course, it made sense for the police to release the statement that she had gone missing – too many details meant it became more difficult to sieve the truth from the nonsense, but if they'd seen that photo of Misha, gagged and bound in a cage, they wouldn't be saying such spiteful things, or then again, maybe they would...

The bar was just a couple of metres away. One final push. She felt something tugging her elbow. She looked down and found herself staring into familiar dark brown eyes. She did a double-take – it was a very underdressed Jay sporting a close-cropped hairstyle which suited him.

'I thought it was you.' Jay flashed her a neon smile and tickled Rolly's nose. 'Hello, gorgeous.' Rolly wagged his stumpy tail with delight. Jay was wearing faded jeans, ripped at the knees, white polo shirt and trainers. He wasn't wearing any make-up and Cally could see his eyelashes were naturally long and his olive skin was smooth; jawline defined without needing blusher. Out of costume, he was naturally good-looking and she could feel the colour spreading across her cheeks as he returned her gaze. 'Hey! Have a seat,' he said, kicking a stool out from under the table.

'Oh hi. Great to see you. I'd love to, but I've really got to get to the bar. I'm on a mission to order some food.'

'I've got a tab going – the waiter will be back over soon.' He rubbed his thumb and forefingers together. 'I've made it worth his while to be extra attentive, so you can order then.' He nodded to the bar which was three-people deep. 'I reckon it's your best chance anyway.'

Cally smiled. It would be good to sit down for a bit. She checked Rolly was tucked safely under her chair and watched as Jay poured her a glass of wine.

'You smell good,' he said.

'Thanks,' said Cally, 'I'm trying out a new scent called *Vanilla Dreams*, although I can't help thinking I smell a bit like cake batter.'

Jay laughed and pressed his thumb and index together, leaving a tiny gap between his fingertips. 'Maybe just a wee bit custardy.'

'Sorry,' said Cally registering the second glass. 'Are you expecting someone?'

'I've been stood up,' he said, sloshing the pale liquid into the glass. He checked the label. 'Phew! It's not a Chardonnay.'

Cally frowned.

A fraction of a pause. 'You told me you didn't like Chardonnay,' he said.

'Oh, right,' said Cally. 'Fussy bitch, aren't I?' She laughed.

'So why on earth did you arrange to meet your date here of all places.'

'Well, I didn't know all this would be going on.' He leant his head in. 'Have you heard anything?'

'No. Henry's frantic with worry though.'

'Poor guy. I take it you don't think she's just run off or staged an elaborate vanishing act?'

Cally shook her head. She opened her mouth to say something else then clamped it shut. This was a police investigation which she wasn't strictly part of, and if any information she passed on was leaked she could get Dan into serious trouble. Jay only knew Misha was missing because of her failure to turn up for his appointment this morning. It had to stay that way.

Jay leant back in his chair. 'It makes for interesting listening, sitting here. Some of the conspiracy theories for her disappearance defy the realms of the possible.'

'What? Like she metamorphosed into rabbit form and dug her way out of the park.'

He grinned. 'Something like that.'

Cally fiddled with the stem of her wine glass. 'Can we change the subject?'

'I'd like that.'

A waiter came over and gave Jay a salad piled high with chunks of feta, olives and ruby tomatoes and Cally took the opportunity to order her take-away. It was one of her favourite waiters', Carl, and she didn't have to tell him what she wanted, just that she wasn't dining in.

'Guess you come here often,' said Jay with a grin. He handed her the spare cutlery, but she shook her head.

She took a sip of wine. 'This is lovely. Thank you. So, did you used to live here – in The Village?'

'No way. We lived in a council block the other side of the park and almost never visited these parts – it was way too posh for us.'

'You mentioned a sister.'

He went quiet, taking his time to spear an olive on his fork. 'She died.'

Cally clasped his arm. 'I'm so sorry.'

Jay patted the back of her hand. 'It was a long time ago. She was...' he closed his eyes. 'She was a wonderful big sister. Always looking out for me, you know.'

'I'm an only child, so I can't even imagine how awful losing her must have been. I would have loved a sibling to do all that make-believe stuff with.'

He nodded and smiled. 'We were great with that. We'd come to the park and one of the big houses had a dog and we used to pretend it was a caged lion with a tangled mane. I'd take him scraps of food and poke it through the fence.' He sighed. 'Poor thing always seemed really sad. I think that's why I loved him so much – I could empathise with his neglect.'

Cally frowned. 'I used to hang round the park all the time but I don't remember seeing a lion dog – which house are you talking about?'

A quick flick of his tongue. 'One of the houses on the south side. It's long gone. It was probably a golden retriever or something.'

'Do you have any other family?'

He shook his head. 'Father unknown and as for my mother...' he whistled. 'She was a piece of work – to be honest, I was glad when she died.' He darted Cally a defiant look, the whites of his eyes flashing. 'She was an addict and to say she neglected us was a total understatement.'

'So, your sister dying must have been a double blow. How did you deal with it? When I lost my father, I went to pieces.'

Jay tilted his head; his eyes narrowing. 'What happened to him, if you don't mind me asking?'

Cally rubbed her temples. 'It was awful. No one really knows what happened, but someone broke into his offices whilst he was working there and tied him up. They ransacked the place – God knows what they were looking for and if they found it or not. He was a philosophy professor, for fuck's sake. Anyway, Dad died of a heart attack, no doubt brought on by the stress of the robbery.'

Jay shook his head. 'Jeez. How on earth did you process that?'

'Not well.' Cally took a gulp of wine. That was indeed an understatement. The truth was she had taken it very badly and when the police had allowed her, she brought home every single item from her father's office and transferred them to his home study. She then proceeded to pour over the contents; searching for clues – needing to find a reason for his death – the thieves didn't take his wallet or watch; in her head there had to be more to it than a straightforward robbery. After a few months, when Helen eventually intervened and told her she had to move on, Cally had reluctantly boxed the items up and there they sat; in Barrington Cranleigh-Simmonds' study at Graylands, gathering dust. Meanwhile, Cally was biding her time, waiting until she had more to go on; hoping a clue would eventually rise to the surface.

'Sorry. I didn't mean to pry.'

Cally blinked. 'How did I deal with it?' She smiled. 'I started up a relationship with a married man who was way too old for me.'

Jay tilted his head on one side. 'Ooh! Daddy complex issues. I suppose that's one way to get it out of your system.'

Cally started giggling.

'What?'

'The thing is, I'm still with him and we're getting married.'

Did she catch a slight flicker of disappointment? Jay threw back his head and laughed.

Cally wiped a tear from her eye. 'What about you?'

'I write music. It's always been my way to release the demons. It was why I started my channel – so I could share it. Off-load, if you like.'

'What sort of stuff do you write about?'

'The usual; love, hate, betrayal. It was a bit bleak to start with.' He laughed. 'I cringe when I listen to some of the early stuff – soooo pretentious and utterly dreadful.'

The waiter arrived with her gyros, foil poking over the top of a brown paper carrier bag. She pulled out her purse to pay, but Jay held up his hand. 'Add it to my account,' he said.

'No.'

'I insist,' said Jay. 'You kept me company,'

'And drank your wine,' Cally added.

'Indeed.' He paused. 'Maybe we could go for a dog walk next time.'

'That would be nice,' said Cally before picking up Rolly and launching herself back into the crowds. Once onto the pavement, she realised she'd left her cardigan hanging on the back of the chair – she sighed at the prospect of having to return for it, but although not expensive, it was one of her favourites so back she trudged. She stopped. Someone was now sitting in her seat. Cally squinted. It was a man wearing a baseball cap. *Was this his date?* Their heads were both bent in towards each other and they were talking animatedly. It was only when she took a step closer, she realised who the other person was: Bulag – the delivery thug from The Cobras. She darted behind the pillar, took a couple of photos then hurried back out, but not before she saw Jay reach into his jeans pocket and pull out his wallet, taking out a wedge of notes and handing them to Bulag. She took a few more photos and decided the cardigan could stay where it was.

Chapter 17
Mikey
14 months earlier

I SPENT the next few days in an alcoholic haze, unable to share what had happened with my sister. The level of my shock and misery was off the scale, akin to discovering she had died which I supposed was how she thought of me. Max took control of my YouTube channel – we had enough material for him to cover for me for a fortnight, so it didn't matter. He had no idea what had caused my intense grief, but cleared out my medicine cabinet before he departed and though he left me alone, he told me afterwards he had checked on me regularly – not that I was aware of his presence. I've never been a big drinker and the bingeing left me feeling washed out and with no energy to do anything; I was dirty and unkempt. My childhood memories had left me with insomnia and without my highly illegal, confiscated pills, if I wasn't passed out, I was unable to sleep and ended up staring at the wall.

I registered a knock at the door. 'Coo-ee.' Max poked his head around the frame. 'How are we feeling this morning? Jeez – it reeks in here.' Max went over to the curtains and opened the window, shaking his head in disgust. He had a paper bag spotted with grease marks tucked under his arm and the smell of warm pastry made my mouth water. I rolled over from my foetal position on the sofa and regarded him; only keeping one eye open as the rays from the morning sun shone onto me like a spotlight. My mouth was dry, tongue furry.

'Ah! Got your attention, have I?' he asked.

I sat up, hugging my knees and my stomach growled.

'I've come to ask if you want to push back the moving date?'

'No! What day is it today?'

'Thursday. Moving day's tomorrow.'

Max wafted the pastry bag under my nose but before I could grab hold, Max lifted it above my head, out of reach. 'Er – no way. You need to wash first – you smell like a tramp.'

He herded me into the cubicle and I stood under the dustbin-lid head, piping hot water drumming onto my scalp. The lemon and bergamot shower gel claimed to have some sort of organic grain in it which I worked into my skin like I was covered with itches. Slowly my hollow body came back to life; the numbness replaced with a tiny buzz of something I couldn't yet give a name to.

Max had made a fresh pot of coffee and was drinking out of one of the few mugs that hadn't been packed and was destined to end its days at the charity shop. He leapt up and took my croissant out of the warming oven and set it on the table behind the butter-dish and a miniature jar of raspberry jam. I pushed the jam away – I couldn't tolerate the stuff now – it left a bitter aftertaste.

'Want to talk?' asked Max.

I took a bite of croissant and swallowed it whole. 'No.' I gulped my coffee, smarting at how strong he'd made it. 'I can't sleep. Please can I have the Bonsai back.'

Max raised an eyebrow. 'Have you stopped drinking? You know you shouldn't ever mix the two.'

I kneaded my temples. 'Yes. I never ever want to drink again.'

He cocked his head on one side and grinned. 'Until tomorrow

when we toast your new flat with a rather delicious pink vintage champagne we've been given to test with a view to promoting it.'

I smiled.

'Better.'

I held out my palm. 'Pills?'

'Later – they're at my flat, but I'll drop them round this evening.'

I licked the tip of my finger and used it to transport the remaining croissant flakes into my mouth. Max folded his arms, his biceps bulging. 'Now are you ready to do some work?' I nodded and Max went to his satchel and pulled out his A5 snake-skin notebook into which he wrote everything in his illegible scrawl. We went through the immediate business which needed sorting and, as we finished, he reached out his hand and placed it on mine, giving it a squeeze. All his gaudy rings digging into my scrubbed skin.

'If it was someone dear to you and you lost them – well then, I'm so sorry – only time will heal. If it was someone who's done you wrong then all I can say is, it's true: revenge is a dish best served cold.'

He got up, tucking the book under his arm and left. My task for the rest of the day was to finish packing my belongings into the LV suitcases and bag up the charity stuff.

As I gathered the final bits and pieces together, what Max said ricocheted around my head. Being a hair and make-up artist instilled one with a sense of the theatrical and I did consider myself an actor of sorts, a chameleon. I felt my fingers itch with the need to put my thoughts into something tangible. I reached for my make-up case which I was never without and laid out the instruments needed to make my vision a reality. I turned the camera light on and started filming. First, I put my hair in a net then covered it with a bald cap which I glued down and blended onto my skull. I dusted my skin with white powder and then added a layer of foundation. Next, I cut bits of latex into jagged shapes which I moulded and affixed to my cheeks and jawline with glue. When this dried, I coated it with shades of grey, charcoal and brown. I was absorbed in my transformation and at the end of several hours, my face had become a jagged rock. I stopped filming and inserted sapphire contact lenses onto my irises and stuck tiny, coloured gems to a pair of long, black eyelashes which I glued to my lids. When I pressed play on the camera, I closed my eyes.

'Sometimes through no fault of your own, people will hurt you – crush you up and make you feel small, worthless and bland,' I said, my voice a gentle purr. I opened my eyes wide, staring straight into the lens. 'Rely on your inner strength to see you through. Stay strong.' I blew a kiss then stopped filming.

I was elated and after I'd checked the footage, I took off the make-up. I had to shower again, but once I was in my silk pjs, I made a cup of chamomile tea and started the editing; I was determined to post the video straight away while the muse was still at work. When I went over to the table, I saw Max had shoved my phenazepam through the letterbox and he'd left a note: 'Glad to see you're working again. See you tomorrow. Sweet dreams, Mxxx'.

The feeling I'd experienced in the shower was growing stronger. Was it resilience? I wasn't sure, but whatever it was, I felt a steeliness creeping through my veins, filling me with purpose. I went through the footage, frame by frame, cutting bits out and speeding the whole thing up. I needed to choose a soundtrack to go over the top and in the end I picked 'Your Time is Going to Come' by Thunder – it wasn't the exact sentiment I was after, but I didn't have the patience to find the perfect match.

Heart beating fast with adrenalin, I posted it and immediately comments and likes popped up on the screen. I normally let Max filter out a selection of the good ones to show me, but this time I stayed to watch the thread evolve.

Who hurt you babe? I'll sort them

Don't let anyone treat you bad

They went on in a similar vein; with the occasional negative post which I skimmed over. My fans' reaction made me feel good.

And righteous.

I had been wronged.

My earlier uncategorised feeling now revealed itself in its full glory – its name: Revenge.

Not only had Lucy denied my existence but throughout the following years she hadn't bothered to find out if her little brother was okay. I closed my eyes. I needed to go back to the beginning; who was to blame? Who should pay for the emotional damage which made me unable to form meaningful attachments? All the time I'd been working at a shitty hairdressers' to get myself through college, it had been the thought of reuniting with Lucy which had kept me going. Where was my purpose in life heading now?

What I needed to do struck me like a slap across the cheek. I would bring them down and make them miserable and sorry for what they had done, but I wouldn't forgive them. I would heap upon them the burden they'd placed on my shoulders; the one which I'd been carrying alone. I wouldn't hide in the shadows anymore – I didn't care what the consequences were.

Two people. A slow burn.

I reached for a notepad frantic with the need to formulate a plan. I googled Bill Cambly and his photo popped up straight away. A shiver ran down my spine. I'd spent so long trying to forget him, I was surprised at how normal he looked. His hair was greyer; his face fuller though his skin was still taut, perhaps thanks to some collagen assistance. He also looked less orange than I remembered, and his clothes were more conservative; the eighties medallion and curly chest hair had vanished. Wiki informed me that he, his wife and two daughters divided their time between homes in London, Leicestershire and Poole, and Bill was now CEO of a designer yacht company. I scrolled through the hundreds of images and Val's smiling face appeared. She was leaner with short hair and had that look which comes when a woman of a certain age overdoes it at the gym, a bit stringy. She had her arms around two young women and I felt tears prickle my eyes, so she'd got what she wanted: two girls. Ignoring the twinge of guilt at seeing Val, I zoomed in on the eldest one, Luella Cambly, and scrutinised her features. She was the spitting image of a young female version of Bill; tall and lean with a perma-tan, wavy dark hair and plastic features – that would definitely make things easier.

Luella was a TikTok and Instagram influencer-in-the-making who went by the name of LuellaBoo and I flicked onto her account. And what do you know? She'd even done a little homage to one of my make-up tutorials, tagging me, and showing how to rock the jewelled lip effect. Her grid was full of pouting posts and as I scrolled upwards I saw a brash, diamond engagement ring. From then on there were lots of teasers about wedding venues and flowers etc. and I gleaned that we were just over a year away from the big day. This was going to be easy. I'd found my route to Bill.

I had a selection of burner phones which I used to contact people I didn't want having my personal number. I turned one on, followed her account then sent her a DM.

Hi Girl – you look amazing. Want to collab? Top secret. No posting any spoilers... JayDoll xxx

Within seconds I had a reply. **Are you for real?**

I sent her a photo.

OMG! Absolutely.

Great. Send me your phone number and then delete this chat.

Within seconds I had all the details I needed.

I replied with a laughing emoji: **Hush Hush. I'll be in touch. Now delete.**

After a few minutes I went back onto her Instagram account and she'd already posted a selfie with her holding one hand across her open mouth; eyes wide. 'Something amazing just happened. I can't tell you about it yet, but it's going to be fabulous.' There followed a trail of whispering emojis and padlocks.

I googled Misha again. Nothing much going on there apart from her new film *Mother's Ruin* was coming out in a couple of months. She didn't seem to do social media, so I did a search on her husband, Henry Carmichael and found his Instagram page. I knew they'd relocated to a rental apartment between Leicester and Market Bowden while Misha was filming here and that he was taking some time out whilst there was a break from filming his TV show. There were a lot of photos of Henry; blonde tousled hair ruffled by the wind whilst walking a small tufty headed dog with a long body and short legs. I noted that, if Misha featured in any of the photos, it was only in the background, or so that her face was never in the shot. It's amazing how much a person can learn about someone from looking at photos alone. Although signage for The Phoenix Club wasn't in the shot, I recognised the exclusive boutique hotel with its extensive grounds, spa and gym. The General Manager had been pestering me to do some make-up tutorials as part of their exclusive bridal package and as a result I'd been sent a week's worth of free VIP passes of which Max and I had taken full advantage before I declined the work.

I zoomed in on Henry holding up a pint of Langton Caudle ale; his smile was lopsided which made him look a little goofy, but he had big, blue eyes, long eyelashes and cherubic cheeks and looked younger than his thirty years.

I felt a new best friend coming on...

Chapter 18
Cally

CALLY WAS SITTING in Gloria Cavel's luxurious office. Gloria, wearing a powder blue short-sleeved dress with cream cardigan draped around her shoulders, was staring at her computer screen, at the same time twirling a pen through her auburn ringlets. She hit the keyboard with a flourish and sat back in her chair.

'I've triple checked,' she said, pushing a piece of letter-headed paper across her desk. 'These are the dates we booked JayDoll for and, like I said, he wasn't available to do the make-up for the Cambly wedding. He had some big marketing event on in London.'

Cally stared at her. 'So, you're saying that there was no way he could have met Luella?'

She tipped her head back and stared at the ceiling, sapphire pendant earrings bobbing back and forth. 'I wouldn't say there was *no* way. In the early days he socialised a bit here in the VIP club, but–'

'With whom,' interrupted Cally, her pen poised.

A patch of colour spread across Gloria's freckled cheeks, and she swallowed. 'Er...Jay and I had what I suppose you might call a little fling.' She raised her head and stared at Cally, her hazel eyes wide and defiant.

Cally cleared her throat; a little twinge of disappointment prickled her scalp, the man obviously flirted with everyone, his interest in her last night had been nothing special. 'Oh. Right. Are you still seeing him?'

'God no,' said Gloria, her jaw clenching. 'He's an absolute tart. Gorgeous, but doesn't have a faithful bone in his body. To be honest, he used The Nix for a couple of weeks when I first signed the deal with him but that was it. He keeps his commitments to the VIP guests in his professional capacity, but I haven't seen him socialising here since then.'

Cally wrote down in her notebook: *Jay could certainly have met with Luella in secret.* 'Did he just hang out with you?'

Gloria shook her head, her marmalade curls swishing. 'No. If I recall, he made friends with Henry Carmichael. I think they went out drinking and to watch the rugby a couple of times.'

'What?' Cally dropped her biro and it clattered onto the parquet floor, rolling until it hit the clawed foot of Gloria's desk. She stooped to retrieve it then sat up like a jack-in-the-box, the sudden movement making her dizzy. She took a deep breath in through her nose. Her voice when she spoke was tight. 'Henry Carmichael? Are you telling me he was friends with Henry?'

Gloria shrugged. 'Yes. Before James did his vanishing act, Henry bought his flat off him.'

Cally could hear her jaw hinge open and shut again. She couldn't believe what she was hearing. '*James*?'

'Yes. JayDoll's real name is James. James Dollander.'

Cally's head was spinning with the amount of disjointed facts which had come bubbling to the surface. But surely this was a crucial piece of information; the flat Henry bought from Jay had once upon a time been a Cambly Home; one of the first properties Bill Cambly's construction company had built. Here was an important link. She shook her head as though trying to dislodge the tangled thoughts from the corners of her brain. She stood up and walked over to the window, staring at the river which meandered along the bottom of the meadow; a smattering of poppies mingling amongst a sea of buttercups.

'I don't get why Henry didn't mention the fact he knew Jay. I mean, the morning she disappeared, Misha was about to have a make-over by him and Henry seemed really pleased with himself that he'd managed to organise it. If he already knew Jay, I don't get what the big deal was.' She took a sharp intake of breath as she recalled the dirty garments and trainers in Jay's suitcase – could he have been in the park that very morning? She needed to get hold of those clothes.

Gloria interlocked her fingers. 'Henry met him when he was being James Dollander and, as you know, JayDoll is a very different creature altogether. I mean when he's being JayDoll he is utterly flamboyant – unrecognisable, but when he came to The Nix, as a guest, he always preferred to go by the name James.'

Cally turned to face the room, leaning against the window ledge. 'Hmmm. I suppose it might explain Henry's ignorance if he was hiding in plain sight.'

Gloria clicked her tongue. 'Also, and I speak from personal experience, Jay doesn't have a long attention span and collects friends and discards them at quite a high rate. I don't think he and Henry hung out together for long.' She gave a sideways glance and grinned. 'Mind you, being with him was such a blast. There was this one time he took me to a private fundraising function he was hosting at the zoo. I got to cuddle a baby lion cub. It was amazing.' She gazed into the distance as though viewing the scene, her expression dreamy then she suddenly seemed to remember where she was and the smile vanished. Her eyes narrowed. 'You know there is a very humble and generous side to Jay too. He wasn't doing the fundraiser for publicity – he wouldn't let anyone take photos of him because he didn't want to detract from the animals themselves.'

Cally frowned. 'That's odd for someone like him not to want to plaster such a great photo opportunity all over his social media pages.'

Gloria shook her head. 'Not really – he's one of the zoo's biggest donors, but he doesn't shout about it. In fact, the newest lion enclosure wasn't named after him but in memory of one of his friends. The governors of the zoo show him their appreciation by letting him visit out of hours – it's all rather adorable.'

Cally held up both palms. 'Fair play to him, cuddling a lion cub hands down beats the Tango Iceblast and bag of penguin food Dan bought me the last time we went there.'

Gloria stood up, pushed back her leather chair and walked over to Cally, her kitten heels clicking across the floor. She perched on the corner of her desk scrolling through her phone and then held it in front of Cally, her face beaming with delight. The screen showed a photo of a sleeping lion cub curled up against Gloria's chest.

'That's adorable,' said Cally.

'I know. There's more. Swipe right.'

Cally flicked through endless photos of tiny, sandy, clawed creatures tumbling around a square patch of lawn whilst well-dressed onlookers, sipping champagne and nibbling canapés, stood about pointing iPhones at them. Suddenly something registered at the back of her mind, and she swiped back, pausing on a group photo. She zoomed in. 'Wait! That's Diana Donohue.' She held the phone up.

'Who?' Gloria ducked in for a closer inspection and Cally inhaled the scent of citrus and freesia.

Cally tapped her finger against the screen. 'That's Val Cambly's sister. Did you meet her?'

Gloria folded her arms across her chest. 'Really? I had no idea who she was. I did meet her, and we spoke briefly but it was nothing more than a passing conversation about how cute the cubs were and how lucky we all were to be there.'

'Do you remember if Jay spoke to her at all?'

'Probably. He organised the whole thing so I guess he must have invited her, but I was far too absorbed in the cubs to notice.'

Cally's heart was thudding against her chest. She was growing more certain with every minute that Luella's murder, Bill's suicide and Misha's kidnapping were related and that somewhere along the line, Jay was involved. She closed her eyes and tried to get her thoughts in order; Jay worked at The Nix where the Cambly wedding was happening and there had to be more than a strong possibility that he was the one working on a deal with Luella – it would have been the perfect social media union. Now she could add an extra layer to that connection; Jay knew Di, Luella's aunt and Bill's sister-in-law. The final piece in the puzzle: Henry had bought his and, therefore, Misha's flat from Jay.

'Gloria, please can you send me all the photos from the lion cub party?' she asked.

'Sure.' She airdropped them and Cally saved them to her camera roll. She said goodbye to Gloria and went to the exit. She needed to talk to Dan about what she'd discovered. As she went to dial his number, she saw he had forwarded an email from the tech guys asking if she could shed any light on it for him. Intrigued, she sat down on one of the comfy armchairs in the entrance lobby and opened it. The message at the top said: *Hi Dan. We found one password encrypted folder on the laptop. Hope this will be of use to the investigation.*

Cally clicked on the file which was titled *Family Photos*. Cally gasped and the man behind the reception desk shot her a concerned look. She waved her hand in the air and smiled to gesture to him that it was nothing, but it wasn't. There, on the screen, was photo after photo of Luella – it looked as though

Misha had taken most of them from her Instagram account, but some had been torn out of magazines and scanned. There were lots of pictures of Bill too – old snaps of him holding Luella as a baby and then at various milestones of her life; school play, ballet performance, speech day etc. Father and daughter were like peas in a pod; same heart-shaped face and dark eyes. What struck Cally as odd was that there were no photos of Val and Sasha in amongst them.

She shut the folder then went outside, leaning against a pillar entwined with ivy to steady herself. Her fingers trembled as she dialled Dan.

He answered straight away. 'Hey, you. Alright?'

Cally realised her tongue was stuck to the roof of her mouth and she took a few seconds to answer. She could hear traffic. 'Dan – can you believe this was hidden on Misha's computer?'

She heard a car door slam and the traffic noise dulled. 'I know. Tell me what I'm looking at.'

'You've seen it, haven't you? It's full of photos of Luella and Bill.'

'I know *that*, but what does it mean?'

She took a deep breath. 'I don't know where to start. There are a few things which point me towards thinking that you should be looking at James Dollander AKA JayDoll as a person of interest in your murder investigation *and* the kidnapping. I think the two are related. Jay knew Henry Carmichael – he sold him his flat, and he also knows Diana Donohue, Val's sister.'

'Okay, so what do you want from me? We've got nothing concrete here to go on. Absolutely nothing.'

'I'm going back to see Val and Di. I definitely need to ask them some more questions. I think you should find out everything you can about Jay's background and where he was on the day of the murder. The General Manager seems to think he has an alibi which needs checking out. But there is one thing that's just struck me. I remember when he came into work the very same morning of Misha's disappearance, Jay had a bag of dirty clothes with him. He stashed them in his work locker so maybe you could see if they're still there? See if there's any DNA on them.'

'What do you think the connection is between Misha and Jay?'

'Maybe they're ex-lovers. Jay's from round here so there must be something about him on the system you can dig up.'

'I'm on it.'

They hung up. Cally went to her office in The Nix where she was keeping Luella's wedding clothes. She'd put Luella's dress into a suit carrier and boxed up her shoes and tiara which forensics had finished with on account of the fact they were still in their packaging when Luella's hotel room was searched. This would be a good excuse to go and visit Val again. She suddenly remembered as she carried the bundles through the car park that she had a photo on her phone of Dan outside the lion enclosure where they'd eaten their picnic. She searched and found it. There was Dan next to a lion pulling, of all things, a strong man pose. That wasn't what she was interested in. She zoomed in – there was the name on a plaque of the person Jay knew and for whom the new wing had been named: Jadis Jones. *Jadis!* Was that the name the journalist mentioned in the interview which caused Misha to storm out? If it was then who on earth was Jadis Jones and how did she fit into all of this?

Chapter 19
Mikey
5 months earlier

I FELT okay in my new apartment during the day, but the dark nights were impossible to manage without the pills. Now that the situation had changed with Lucy, I'd made a decision about what to do with the flat and had instructed an architect to draw up some wow factor designs to knock through a partition wall to make an open plan kitchen-diner. I was going to turn this apartment into something irresistible, worthy of a *HELLO!* Magazine shoot. Someone else's dream house.

I arrived at The Phoenix Club whose redbrick façade and small windows betrayed its former existence as a Victorian school for orphans – a stark contrast to the clientele who frequented it now. It had one foot in town, but being on the edge of Market Bowden, straddled the gentle pastureland which stretched towards the River Welland. It boasted plenty of valet parking for all the sports cars and SUVs, broken up by little pockets of frost-tipped green grass and flowerbeds full of pink and white cyclamen. Four tennis courts lined the back of the main building and a gravel path from the main bar and dining area swept up to an all-year-round open-air infinity pool with sun loungers, a smaller bar and a secret hot tub. Despite the biting cold wind people swaddled in fluffy white dressing gowns were sipping espressos at the edge of the pool, their ankles hidden by a layer of steam rising from the water. Underneath this floor were the various treatment rooms and a kidney-shaped indoor pool with comfy chairs, where one could relax after a hot pebble massage. The Phoenix Club had been awarded the silver medal in the UK's best wedding venues and, as a result of the publicity, the members' waiting list was huge.

I signed in at the reception desk and was directed through a side door and along a corridor lined with black and white Toile de Jouy wallpaper, towards the General Manager's office. I caught a glimpse of myself in the gilt-framed mirror which swallowed up the end wall, obliterating the nauseating pastoral scenes. I was taken aback – I almost didn't recognise myself. I cleared my throat then knocked on the mahogany door.

'Come in,' called out a sing-song voice.

As I opened the door, a woman with pearl earrings the size and shape of sugared almonds came rushing over from behind a tidy partners' desk. She was wearing a mint trouser suit, white cami, and vertiginous emerald heels with matching nail varnish. Her auburn hair was scraped back into a high donut bun which looked like it had been set in place with glue. Her skin was pale and freckled and the only make-up she had on was a nude lipstick and a flick of brown mascara to camouflage her white eyelashes. She had an enviable clear complexion. When she saw me, she stopped in her tracks and tilted her head on one side: the bun staying perfectly in place. 'JayDoll?'

I nodded and raised an eyebrow.

'You don't look how I expected,' she said, extending a graceful hand. She smelt of lemon and freesia. 'I'm Gloria Cavel.'

I smiled, smoothing down the lapels on my new blazer before reaching out to take her hand. 'I'm James Dollander but please call me Jay,' I added, giving her a firm handshake.

'I'm so glad we've managed to get you over here to The Nix,' she said, tottering back towards her desk.

'Tea or coffee?' she asked, picking up her phone; hazel eyes wide, waiting for a response.

'I'm great with a mineral water, please,' I said.

Gloria put the receiver down and took fairy steps towards the sideboard on which was a cut glass decanter of water, two matching glasses and a silver bucket, dripping with perspiration and draped with a towel. Her laboured movements and accompanying frown suggested that those exquisite heels were giving her grief and I wondered if she'd put them on purely for my benefit.

She lifted a set of silver tongs and plucked a golf ball sized ice cube from the bucket, depositing it in one of the tumblers. 'You're a local boy?' I didn't answer. She nodded her head towards a pair of wingback armchairs in front of a bookcase filled with a mix of hardback collectors' volumes with regency-coloured spines which I doubted had ever been read. The coffee table dividing the chairs had all the latest lifestyle magazines spread out in a fan with a posy of cornflowers at its centre.

Gloria handed me the water and I took a sip then placed it down, trailing my nail across the intricate glass indentations. She took a notebook from her desk and then sat opposite and crossed her legs, releasing one of her ankles from her shoe; the skin at the back of the heel was an angry red. 'God, these kill.'

'They're beautiful,' I said. 'The colour really suits you, but I guess you already know that.'

She took a sip of water, her eyes lowering to show a tiger stripe to her upper lashes – she really needed to take the mascara down to the base with a fine brush, but I wouldn't tell her that now. The slight pink tinge spreading across the top of her angular cheeks revealed I'd caught her off-guard; like most of my audience she'd assumed my outrageously camp on-screen persona was the real me. Sometimes it was rather lovely to play it straight and I felt a flicker of desire at the pit of my stomach; her porcelain skin and doll-like features were strangely attractive.

'What do you want from me, Gloria?'

She was totally taken aback by my question. She turned to a new page in her notebook, pulling out a ballpoint from the spiral binding.

'I want to offer you a deal, Jay. I know you're bringing a range of make-up out this summer.' She glanced at me for confirmation, and I nodded.

'I'll stock it and ensure our make-up artists use it when they do the wedding packages.'

I ran my fingers through my new, short hair. I'd dyed it a rich chestnut colour and over the past few weeks I'd curated a stubbled jaw. No jewellery and no make-up. I was an alpha. 'And?'

She took a breath in. 'And – I want you to come and do quarterly workshops for our guests. Pamper evenings are a real seller here – they'd pay even more to let you tutor them for an hour. Bridal parties, work weekends away...' She paused. 'I'll make it worth your while financially – the people who come here are quite happy to spend.'

I ran my tongue along my top teeth. 'As you can imagine, my diary's quite full at the moment...' I let the sentence hang in the air.

She handed me a print-out of the weddings coming up in the next two years. I ran my finger down the list and there it was, near the top: Luella Cambly and Jonty van der Kelt. I swallowed. It was fate – it was meant to be. I folded the paper and set it back on the desk.

Gloria was holding her breath. I clapped my hands together and smiled. 'Champagne, I think.'

She frowned.

'To toast our new relationship.' The words coming out of my

mouth were a bit cheesy, but they had the desired effect and she reached over and clasped my hands.

'Marvellous! Let's head to the bar. Of course – as part of the deal, you'll be given free VIP membership to use our facilities whenever you like.'

I gave a little bow. 'Perfect. Lead on.' I held the door open for her.

'Did I read that you're from round here?' she asked.

I gave a tight smile and I felt the skin around my cheeks stretch. I had done my best to keep the details of my childhood out of the public domain, but a few vague snippets had filtered through. 'Yes. I grew up not a million miles from Market Bowden, so when I do get time off – a bit of R&R away from prying eyes would be great. When I'm here working as JayDoll I'll be the character you're expecting, but as a guest – could you please just introduce me as James Dollander. I'd like to keep my identity under wraps.'

Gloria gave an earnest nod. 'We're the soul of discretion here.'

We walked along the corridor into the lobby, the bottom of her shoes click-clacking across the shiny tiles. A clear, rectangular vase bursting with hyacinth heads sat on the table in front of us; their celery stalks were hidden by a hoard of sparkling pebbles. I inhaled their perfume which always reminded me of home, and we side-stepped them, walking under an arch into a high-ceilinged room which opened out onto a terrace. The icy patio was broken up by half-barrel tubs bursting with orange crocuses and wide stone steps led down to a tennis court, the wire mesh partially hidden by a wall of russet ivy.

Gloria turned to place a palm on my forearm. 'So – this is the exclusive Members' Bar. If you're a guest at the hotel you can't drink here, we have a Visitors' Bar for that.'

Gloria ushered me towards a circular table and before I'd sat down, a young man in black trousers, white shirt and apron came over. He had a round face which was accentuated by his circular wire-framed glasses and his mousy hair was gelled into a deep side-parting which made his head appear lop-sided. 'Ms Cavel,' he said with a slight nod which made his glasses slide down the bridge of his nose.

'Champagne. Two glasses, Eric, thank you.'

Eric looked at me, but there was no glimmer of recognition as he slunk away. Just then, Gloria's phone rang, the chorus of an irritating pop song, and she glanced at the screen, then frowned, looking up at me.

'Take it,' I said, giving my hand a wave. She gave a smile of relief and went out of the doors into the hall, leaning against the hyacinth table, her back to me.

I gazed around at the artwork on the wood-panelled walls. They were full of portraits of people with long faces, round eyes, creamy skin and puffy red lips – beauties from history; uglies in the here and now. I was studious in my nonchalance, only flicking my gaze down towards the clusters of privileged people for a fleeting moment. There was no one I recognised although I wasn't into sport so wouldn't have known if there were any of the local rugby or football players there.

Then someone I did recognise walked through the door: Henry Carmichael. He was freshly showered, the tips of his blond curls wet, his round cheeks flushed and he had a small sports bag slung over his shoulder. He was accompanied by a slim man with long limbs, his dark hair slicked with too much gel. I turned my back and then, just as he was passing, pushed out my chair, knocking into him. He yelped, his bag thudding to the floor, and I leapt to my feet and spun around.

'Oh, my goodness, so sorry,' I said, patting him on the shoulder. 'I'm such a clumsy idiot – you okay?'

Eric was trundling over with the champagne.

Henry smiled, rubbing his shin. 'Yes, sure. It's nothing. Don't worry.'

I shook my head. 'Well, I'm sorry for almost kneecapping you. Let me make it up to you with a glass of champagne.' I turned to Eric. 'Can I get some more glasses, please.'

'No. No. There's no need for that,' said Henry, shaking his head.

The friend gave his upper arm a gentle punch. 'Don't listen to him. It's a yes from me.' He gave me a lopsided grin, showing slightly overlapping bottom teeth. 'What are we celebrating?'

I grinned. 'Life, my friend. Life.' I took the extra glasses from Eric and set them on the table, then pulled the bottle out of the bucket of ice. Eric hovered for a few seconds before retreating with a disgruntled snarl brought on by my audacity to take over his waitering duties.

I untwisted the wire cap, easing out the champagne cork which came away with a gentle pop. At that moment Gloria came back into the room. 'Ah! James – already making friends, I see,' she said. 'Have you introduced yourself?'

I shook my head, holding the flute at an angle and tipping in the pale liquid, bubbles tickling my fingertips. I filled all four glasses, back and forth, ensuring each had the same measure.

Gloria held her hands out like an airhostess showing where the emergency exits were. 'Henry Carmichael this is James Dollander.' I reached out and shook his hand, clamping it tight and looking him direct in his blue eyes before handing him a glass of champagne. Henry gave a little nod.

She turned to the friend. 'Sid Bhakra. James Dollander.' I turned to him, shook his hand and gave him a glass in exchange.

'James has agreed to help me out here,' said Gloria. I took her hand and put a finger to my lips and she gave a twitch of a smile.

'I'm sure Henry and Sid don't want to know what I'm up to – they're here to relax. We're all just part of The Nix family, hey?' I pulled up two more heavy chairs and when everyone was seated I raised my glass.

'Here's to not talking business for a change.' I went cross-eyed and my audience laughed and muttered their agreement.

Everyone clinked glasses and I took a sip of the champagne, letting the bubbles effervesce on my tongue before swallowing. It was sharp but not acidic and left an aftertaste of gooseberry sauce on my tongue. I crossed my legs and sat back in my chair. 'How about instead I bore you to death about my puppy which I'm picking up in a fortnight.'

'What breed?' asked Henry.

'You might not have heard of it because they're not that well known – in fact, they're kind of going extinct. It's a Dandie Dinmont Terrier.'

'No shit!' said Henry, reaching into his bag and pulling out his phone – scrolling through, an earnest and delighted expression on his face. 'My wife and I have got one called Mabel. They are just the most gorgeous creatures ever. Wonderful temperament.'

I clapped my hands together. 'Oh no way. Let me see.'

'Where are you getting yours from?' He handed me his phone and there was a picture of a small, long-bodied terrier with a topknot of fluffy white hair and big, chocolate eyes.

I grinned at the photo. 'A breeder in the Cotswolds,' I said, as though absorbed by the image in front of me when I was actually staring at Lucy's fingers entwined in the animal's fur.

'Not Amanda Parry?'

I turned to Henry, my jaw hanging open. '*No way*.'

Then I looked at Sid who had a bemused smile twitching across his lips. I shook my head. 'I'm so sorry – it's just I've never been a doggy daddy before and I'm so excited. Single parent too,' I added and saw Gloria give a slight gulp.

Sid tapped the champagne glass and took a large swig, a clump of dark hair falling across his forehead as he tilted his head back. 'I'm just happy drinking these bubbles,' he said; he had an Essex lilt to his voice. He looked a bit like what I would have looked like without the teeth job, the hair dye and the relentless gym routine. 'So – I want to know about you Sid – any obsessions, I mean pets?' Everyone laughed.

I topped up everyone's glass and ordered another bottle which I insisted on paying for and Gloria got some canapés sent over to the table; tiny little circles of oat biscuit with a dollop of pale pink salmon pâté on the top – they looked like Iced Gems. After quarter of an hour I looked at my watch then said; 'Ugh! I have to go. I've got an architect coming around to discuss plans for my flat.' I stood up. 'I hope we can do this again. I'll probably have picked up the puppy by then – you've been warned.'

Henry leapt up and reached for his wallet, fishing out a card. 'Look – here's my number when are you getting...uh?'

'Dolly.' I gave a goofy smile. 'Dolly Dollander. Predictable, I know!'

Henry slapped me on the shoulder. 'No. It's cool. Look, if you have any questions, just text. Anything, I mean it.'

I tucked his number into my back pocket and smiled. Gloria trotted out after me and grabbed hold of my arm, her fingernails resting on my shirt like a line of green beetles. 'So, Jay, can I get my lawyers to draw up an agreement?'

I nodded and stooped to kiss her cheek.

'Absolutely – you've got my details, although, I think we should probably have dinner at mine to finalise everything.' I winked and she flushed. 'I cook a mean Bolognese.'

As the taxi went through the gates, I marvelled at this new version of James – popular, charming, and fabulous with the ladies. Good job they didn't know his other new striking feature: wannabe murderer.

Chapter 20
Cally

CALLY RANG THE FRONT DOORBELL, but there was no answer. She heard the click of a latch and Di appeared from behind a painted white gate which was camouflaged by a pale pink clematis and tucked onto the side of the house. She smiled when she saw Cally.

'Hi there. Cally isn't it?'

Cally nodded. 'Hello Di. Is Val in?'

Di shook her head. 'No. She's gone into town. Not sure when she'll be back to be honest.'

Cally wasn't certain how best to play this; she wanted to talk to Di, but without Val there she didn't know the best way to launch into a conversation. 'Sorry to be a pain but I've got some of Luella's things here for her. Do you mind if I leave them with you? It's her wedding gown, shoes and tiara.'

Di gave a little shudder. 'Sure. I'll put them in my cottage until Val's strong enough to deal with them.' She ran her tongue across her lip. 'What on earth does one do with an unwanted made-to-measure bridal gown?'

Cally assumed the question was hypothetical and popped the boot of her sport's car and retrieved the bags. Di meanwhile held open the gate to her house and ushered Cally through into a small cobblestoned courtyard with an olive tree and vine basking in sunshine against the whitewashed wall. Cally, struggling under the weight of the voluminous bags, followed Di through a stable door into a small terracotta tiled kitchen with freestanding sink, stove and a pale blue dresser covered with a mish mash of chunky crockery. A small square table was pushed up against the wall and behind it towered a notice board smothered with photos, post-cards and tickets. Di turned to take the bags from her and disappeared through a door into a low-ceilinged sitting room. Cally peered at a card with embossed gold edges; it was for *Madame Butterfly* – one of her favourite operas and The Humming Chorus started up in her head.

Di returned, moving straight to a small machine next to the window ledge and flicked on the switch. 'Do you want a cup of coffee?'

'Were you about to head out? I don't want to hold you up although...' she sighed.

Di tipped her head to one side. 'That sounds ominous. My rendezvous at the garden centre can wait.' She pulled a kilner jar full of multi-coloured capsules from a cupboard and held it up. 'What do you want?'

'I'll have an espresso please,' said Cally.

Di pulled two small cups from the dresser and set one under the machine. 'So – what's up?' She gestured for her to sit down.

Cally tucked herself under one side of the table while the machine growled. 'I just wanted to know how Val is. I've grown close to her these past months and what you said about Bill...' She twisted her engagement ring around her finger. 'It worried me.'

Di placed a tiny pea-green cup in front of Cally and sat down, cradling a cerise one in her hands. 'I probably shouldn't have said what I did – it wasn't the right time. It's just...' she bit her lip. 'I can't stand it.'

'Can't stand what?'

She waved her hands in the air. 'Everyone saying what a wonderful man he was and what a tragedy his death is. He was a terrible husband.'

'If it was so bad then why did she stay with him?'

Di took a sip and smacked her lips. 'I don't know exactly what happened the first time he cheated on her.' She corrected herself, 'sorry, I mean the first time Val found out that he'd cheated on her. God knows how many times he'd done it before.'

Cally took a sip of her coffee, pleasantly surprised by the amaretto aftertaste. 'Go on.'

'Val took it bad, but she'd just found out she was pregnant–'

'With Luella?'

'Yes. They'd been trying for a while and Bill was so happy and swore he'd never do it again. He even went for therapy to prove how serious he was about the whole thing, but that's Bill for you.'

'What do you mean?'

'Bill was always a smooth talker. Good at reading the room and promising whatever you wanted to hear but never delivering. Instead, he just went on and did exactly what he wanted to.'

'Did he ever try it on with you?'

She laughed and shook her head. 'Oh no! I'm not his type.'

'He has a type?'

She pressed her lips together. 'Let's just say, he likes them young.'

'How young?'

'Legal, but only just.'

Cally wrinkled her nose.

'Whatever happened to make them leave must have been serious. It was like the Marie Celeste – there were still dirty plates on the table when I went round. You see, I'd got a call from Val asking me to move into the annexe. She knew I was looking for somewhere in the area to start my orchid business and she asked if

I would settle in and take care of the house for her. I just had to cover the bills.' She paused. 'Mind you I was pretty gutted she'd left so quickly. Especially as she'd only just told me she was pregnant. I was really looking forward to being an aunty.'

'Did she say why they'd left in such a hurry?'

'Val just said they were taking advantage of a great opportunity which had arisen or some sort of bullshit spiel like that.'

'But you said it was because of his infidelity.'

'Ah! But she only told me that much later when I went to visit her and baby Luella in Poole. I knew something wasn't right, but it only came out after we'd had a few glasses of wine together sitting on the balcony of their gorgeous flat overlooking the sea. I said to her something like, you're so lucky, you've got it all and she burst into tears. Told me that they'd had to move away because he'd cheated on her and that this was going to be their fresh start. But then she said she'd found out he was cheating on her again and she'd confronted him, and he'd promised to go back into therapy. Said it wasn't his fault; he had an illness.' She tutted and rolled her eyes. 'I told her to leave him immediately.'

'Why didn't she?'

She shrugged. 'I guess she wanted to believe him, then she got pregnant again with Sasha.' She made a circle in the air with her index finger. 'And so, it went on. Val finding out he was cheating on her, him apologising and her forgiving him. Round and round they went.'

'But...but they seemed so happy.'

'In a funny way, I think they were. Val did really love him, and things altered when they came back to Market Bowden.'

'How so?'

'Val had made peace with the fact he was never going to change so she did the next best thing which was to turn a blind eye. She got on with her life – pursued her own goals, threw herself into bringing up the girls and pretended to the whole world that she and Bill were happy. Like I said, against all odds, I think they were.'

'Do you think they were still, you know, sleeping with each other?'

She shook her head. 'No. They slept in separate rooms, but they did things together like going to the theatre or taking weekend breaks. They were more like good friends, but Bill's guilt enabled Val to live the life she wanted, and she set up her soft furnishing business and focused on making that a success.'

'When you put it like that, it doesn't sound so bad.'

Di shrugged. 'But what good is a marriage without love? I couldn't forgive him for making Val feel so unattractive and worthless – it was like he strayed because she wasn't good or young enough. And when they eventually came back to Market Bowden Val begged me not to leave. She needed someone to keep an eye on him when she wasn't there. It was pathetic. I used to have to ensure he wasn't left alone when the girls had their school friends over.'

'Ewww.'

Di pretended to put her fingers down her throat. 'Whenever Val and the girls were away, he'd get some tart over to stay the night. He thought he was being discrete, but I saw them come and go. If it weren't for Val, I'd have called the police – some of them looked way too young to be legal. He and I fought like cat and dog. He didn't want me there. He also insisted I paid rent, not that I minded in the slightest. My business was up and running and giving me a very good wage.' She clicked her tongue against the roof of her mouth. 'I loved it best when it was just Tommy and I, but of course, when the girls and Val were around it was wonderful. It was just him I loathed.'

Cally's ears prickled. 'Are you and *Tommy* still together?'

Di shook her head and laughed. 'No. No. It's not what you think. Tommy was my dog. Well, he was Bill's guard dog, but he treated him very badly. Val's scared of dogs so she never went near him, but I'm sure if she had, she'd have been horrified at his living conditions. I only had the privilege of being with Tommy for a couple of years, but I made sure they were the best he'd ever had. Bless him. I was devastated when he died. I could never have another one – I was heartbroken.'

Cally shivered as Rolly's whiskery face popped into her thoughts.

'Another coffee?'

Cally shook her head. 'Oh, by the way, I think we have a mutual friend,' she said, taking her empty cup over to the sink.

'Who's that then?'

'James Dollander. Jay.'

Di smiled. 'Jay. Yes. He's a client of mine.'

Cally didn't say anything, just nodded, hoping Di would elaborate further.

'He's an orchid fanatic and buys quite a bit from me.' She smiled and made a beckoning claw with her finger. Cally followed her out of the back door and into a glasshouse full of orchids squashed together on shelves, all different colours and shapes. The humidity of the room seemed to strip the moisture from the tip of her tongue and there was a strange sweet and fishy smell in the air like someone had mixed honey with a can of tuna and left it to ferment. She wrinkled her nose.

Di laughed. 'Sorry about the smell – you get used to it. I make my own fertilizer from powdered puffin guano.'

'Puffins?'

'Yes. It works miracles – it's full of the most wonderful nutrients. I get it shipped in from The Orkney Islands.' She tapped a long, violet stem covered with star-shaped flowers.

'They're beautiful,' said Cally.

'Thank you. I specialise in very rare ones like 'Praying Mantis' and 'Little Ballerina' – novelty ones too, but you name it, I can get it.'

'So, what was Jay after?'

She scratched her temple, 'a moth orchid, to start with.' She ran her finger along the wooden slats and stopped at a plant whose flowers were a dark chocolate colour with white spots on, and resembled moth wings.

'You knew him as Jay, not James or JayDoll?'

She laughed. 'Jay and certainly not JayDoll – he made me swear not to tell anyone who he was, especially not Luella.'

'That must have been a big ask.' She cocked her head on one side. 'Did you tell her?'

She laughed. 'No. My clients are very important to me and, bless Luella, but she'd have badgered him to death.'

'So, you made sure they never met.'

She narrowed her eyes.

Cally coughed. 'I mean, I'm giving you a compliment! I know Jay – he's fiercely private and once, accidentally, a friend burst into my office when he wasn't expecting it and they got all-star struck. I mean, he was very polite at the time, but he sulked for ages afterwards.'

She laughed. 'Yes. He's quite the man of mystery. He only came here a couple of times, but it was in secret. The girls aren't–' Di bit her lip and closed her eyes. 'Sasha and Luella weren't often here – they spent most of their time in the Chelsea flat.'

'I bet Jay loved this house,' said Cally – 'he's really into doing up property.'

'He only saw my cottage and the garden.'

Cally gave a knowing nod. 'Yes, he'd have insisted on a tour of the garden.'

Di smiled. 'Actually, he ended up touring it himself as I had another client drop by unannounced and so he scurried off for a bit whilst I dealt with them. He didn't mind – he's a lovely man. The best.'

They went back into the kitchen and Cally found herself standing next to the noticeboard again; her eyes scanning the various pieces of paper and photos. She did a double take and tapped her finger on a black and white cut out of a newspaper. 'Wow – is that who I think it is?'

She nodded. 'Yep. The King, well – he was the Prince of Wales at the time. He presented Bill with an award for industry donkey's years ago.' She laughed. 'Funny – you're so like Jay – he was fascinated with it – I even caught him photographing it. He said he has a thing for King Charles. Weird.'

Cally frowned. Why on earth would he take a photo of that. She took a closer look. She froze. In the photo right next to it there was a girl in the background whose face she recognised. It was Misha holding hands with a small boy. She gave a gasp. It was Jay. There was the proof she needed – James Dollander and Misha had known each other as children and holding hands at that age wasn't something you did unless you had a strong connection; they had to be related.

Chapter 21
Mikey
5 months earlier

PLANNING a murder isn't so easy. I had a lot of juggling to do – putting bits of my personality into different boxes and learning to keep them separate. I'd embraced my alter ego, James Dollander, and went on a date with Gloria where I'd cooked her a spag bol, as promised, and we'd ended up having sex on my new velvet couch which turned out to be less comfy and yielding than it looked. I wasn't sure what I was going to do with Gloria; I didn't want a relationship, but I knew she'd be useful, and the sex was a welcome distraction.

Gloria gave me a personal tour of The Nix to show me where I'd be doing my beauty classes and for that I came dressed as JayDoll in full war paint: blonde wig, pale face, orange lips and blue eyeshadow. I was meeting the other beauticians and I knew that this was the sort of look they were expecting. I handed out free *Dollymix* mascaras and eyeshadow palettes, took selfies and pretended to be interested in where they were going on their holidays. I had secretly hoped the flamboyant JayDoll would make Gloria feel a bit squirmy about us as a couple, but if anything, it had been a turn on and she'd locked the door of one of the treatment rooms and forced me onto the massage table. I didn't put up a fight, though I insisted on no kissing as she'd ruin my painstakingly applied make-up.

Gloria also took me to the less salubrious parts of the club – through the kitchens, cellars and housekeeping stores. I made a mental note of where the security cameras were placed, and which entrances were the most secluded. I felt reassured that, as long as I knew the code, it would be relatively easy to sneak in and out without being seen. When we stepped into the security office the pair on duty jumped to their feet as if they'd been electrocuted by a cattle prod. Lazy watchmen – perfect.

Meanwhile, the architect had drawn up some beautiful plans for my apartment and more importantly had created computer generated images of how spectacular the flat could look. I left the folder on my glass coffee table in front of the uncomfortable crimson sofa. I'd hung a black and white print of Lamorna Cove above it and in the corner was a large flat screen TV. I'd been acquiring some rugby knowledge – learning the Leicester Tigers players' names and their performance history. I'd a good memory and though the scrummage rules still wouldn't stick on account of the fact they were idiotic; I was confident of my ability to hold my own in a rugby-related conversation.

The one amazing thing in my life, however, was the arrival of Dolly my Dandy Dinmont Terrier. She was the most adorable thing I'd ever held, and I knew this part of me was real; I loved her unconditionally. Luckily for the purposes of toilet training, the floor of the apartment was a combination of wood and tiles throughout, broken up by a few decorative rugs which I had removed for the time being. I put newspaper by the front door and every half an hour, or when she woke or had just eaten, I'd take her out of the lobby and into the shared garden. We didn't always make it in time, but she was a quick learner and within a fortnight of being at home, would paw at the door if she needed to go out. I was proud of both of us.

You might have thought owning a small dependent creature would tamp down my need for revenge, but instead it had the opposite effect. I aligned myself with that helpless pup, totally reliant on others for my physical and emotional needs. I vowed never to neglect or abandon Dolly as I had been. Having a puppy was a great excuse to stay in the flat and carry on fine-tuning my plan although it wasn't so much the plan that was causing the problem, just the watertight alibi.

Max had been delighted with the added attraction Dolly would bring to the channel and didn't understand why I had resolved to keep her off my social media. I said it was because I was worried about her being dognapped, unable to explain that the dog was the property of the very conservative and social media shy James Dollander, not JayDoll.

One Thursday evening I got a text from Henry.

I'm passing. You in? I'm dying to meet Dolly.

Absolutely.

I cast my eye around the place; it was clean but a little bit messy. I'd dug deep with my investigation into Henry's life, dredging up every magazine article written about him; researching his school, family and friends but I was careful to hide these notes away when I wasn't studying them. I was creating a space Henry would envy, but in which he would also feel comfortable. Everything I had purchased was a subtle invitation to put him at his ease; a selection of hip, microbrewed IPA bottles were lined up on the kitchen counter. There was a framed, signed photo of his screen idol, Paul Newman, on the wall in the loo and in the sitting room a huge flat screen TV was tucked into an alcove with play station attached, the latest COD game resting on the top – I'd read that Misha had banned it from their home because she deemed it too violent.

I kept my work in the third bedroom where I'd set up a permanent filming station with a green screen. Max had bought an incredibly expensive package which enabled us to create wonderful backdrops to my tutorials; my favourite so far was a very realistic café terrace with the Eiffel Tower in the background which changed its aspect in conjunction with the seasons. The far wall of the room was filled by one large wardrobe, bursting with make-up and clothes. Stacking boxes in rainbow columns contained my wigs, jewellery, and other accessories. One of the violet cubes now contained a locked metal box which hid the notes of my drug experimentation. So far, I hadn't got further than grinding up my phenazepam tablets and trying to conceal them in various baked goods. Unfortunately, they had an unpalatable bitter taste and cooking them also destroyed the chemical compound. It was frustrating – the other part of the equation, which involved getting the victim to drink the accompanying alcohol was easy, but the two had to be combined to be lethal.

I checked I didn't have on a trace of make-up and changed from my silk robe into a pair of jeans, polo shirt and crew-necked jumper. I put on my puffer jacket and took Dolly out for a quick pee and just as I kicked off my loafers, there was a buzz on the intercom. I scooped up Dolly and tucked her under my arm then opened the door, barefoot.

'Henry. Hi. Come in.'

Henry was dressed for an expedition to the North Pole; a tartan scarf hid the lower half of his face whilst a woolly hat rammed down over his ears camouflaged the top section and when he took it off, his hair fizzled with static electricity. The moment he saw Dolly he squealed with delight and wrestled her from me, showering her with kisses.

'She's gorgeous. Oh! Jeez, my wife would love her. May I take a photo?'

'Sure. Can I get you a lager or a beer? I'm drinking a local ale which is rather delicious.'

'What is it?' Henry scrunched up his eyes and giggled as Dolly licked his face.

'It's from a brewery near here in Langton – this one's called Inclined Plane.'

'Oh! No way. I love that stuff,' said Henry. *No shit!* I reached into a cupboard and pulled out two beers, taking their tops off with a bottle opener which was shaped like a rugby ball.

I handed him the beer in exchange for his phone and took a photo of him with Dolly.

'Thanks.' He put the phone in his back pocket. 'You've just got to come over and meet Mabel. These two can be pals.' I went to the cupboard and pulled out a several bags of roast beef Monster Munch and emptied them into a large melamine bowl. Henry put Dolly into her basket and looked around. 'Wow – this is a nice place you've got here.' He grabbed a crisp and took a bite. 'I love these,' he said.

'Not my favourite flavour,' I said with a shrug, 'but they'd sold out of pickled onion.'

He chinked my beer bottle. 'I'm totally with you on that.'

I pointed to the sofa. 'Have a seat.'

Dolly came hurtling over with a balled-up sock she'd discovered.

'Adorable,' he said, reaching down to tickle her under the chin. 'That reminds me – I must send Misha the piccy.' He pulled out his phone and sent a text, sticking his tongue out whilst he tapped at the screen. Before he sat down his eye caught on the photo above the sofa. He shook his head. 'You're never going to believe this, but I grew up there. We moved away when I was five, but always went back for the holidays.'

I took a swig of beer and smiled. 'It's where I go when I need space – it's just so...'

'So?'

I laughed and rubbed my temples. 'I was going to say magical, but I thought you'd take the piss.'

Henry chuckled. 'No mate. I know exactly what you mean.'

I laid one arm across the back of the sofa and stared at Henry's profile; he had a cute button nose and such a boyish face – he was no more than an eager little puppy himself. 'So, – busy week?' As I set my beer down, I moved the portfolio of pictures closer to Henry's side of the table. 'I know we're not meant to talk business, but do you mind me asking what kind of work you're in?'

Henry grinned showing white, even teeth, and his smooth cheeks dimpled. 'I'm an actor.'

'Oh!' I sounded surprised. 'Er...brilliant. Would I have seen you in anything?'

He shrugged, pulling at the edge of the soggy label. 'I play a detective in The Lantern Mysteries.'

I looked at him and frowned. Then I slapped my palm across my forehead, my mouth falling open. 'Oh wow! It's you. I thought your face was familiar. That's cool.'

He grinned. 'How about you, as we're sharing?'

I took a swig of beer. 'I'm in marketing and product placement – mainly for cosmetics. Dull, but as you can see, it pays the bills.' I swept my hand around the apartment. Dolly had crashed out on her sparkly princess cushion, the sock next to her head like a lumbar support pillow.

'Well – you're certainly doing something right,' he said his fingers alighting on the plans. 'Are these the architect's drawings you mentioned? May I?'

I nodded. 'Yes. Do have a look – I'd love to know what you think.'

He opened the folder and went through the bundle of glossy photos one by one. 'This looks incredible,' he said. 'I'm so jealous.'

I pulled a sad face.

'What?'

'I don't know for sure, but I might have to move.'

Henry patted me on the shoulder. 'Man, that sucks. Why?'

'Work. I mean I'm hoping it's not going to happen, but...' I pressed my back into the sofa, the button at the centre of one of the folds digging into my spine.

'You've got a great home,' said Henry, chinking the tip of my beer bottle. A little too enthusiastically as some of the ale came fizzing over the rim and I had to take a large gulp to stop the overflow.

'You're very kind, but with enough money anyone can tart up a place. It's more the location I'm most pleased with. I mean, it's just a short walk to the station and then 45 minutes to London. Plus, you're right next to the open countryside so you get the best of both worlds.' I paused. '*And* I'm close to the rugby – I mean, what more could a guy ask for?' I gave his upper arm a punch; it was very firm.

Henry circled the mouth of the bottle with his finger. He gave a coy smile. 'Misha and I are looking to buy somewhere. She wants London but I want somewhere like this. Actually – I want this.' He laughed.

I tipped my head on one side. 'Oh! so, you don't live around here?'

He shook his head. 'No. She's filming at the moment.' He looked at me with his big blue eyes. 'She's an actor too. Misha Carlton?'

I did a double take. 'No offence to you, but I have *definitely* heard of her,' I said, and he laughed. I picked up his beer bottle and shook the dregs. 'Another?'

He nodded. 'That would be great, thank you.'

I wandered over to the kitchen, tiptoeing past Dolly who had rolled onto her back, her round, pink tummy on display, tiny paws in the air. 'So, are you just visiting?'

'Yes. I'm taking a bit of time out between shooting the next in the series and she's here filming for two months, so we thought we'd rent somewhere nearby and try and keep things as normal as possible, but I'm longing to have a place of our own. I'd like more Mabels and maybe a few kids eventually. Maybe she should come over and meet you and Dolly – that might make her change her mind – about where we should buy, I mean.'

My heart skipped a beat. That was definitely not what I wanted – Misha couldn't come anywhere near the flat – it would ruin everything. I cleared my throat. 'You need to keep your powder dry, mate,' I said. 'The builders are coming in very soon. There's hardly anything structural to be done apart from knocking down the wall – it's all the fixtures and fittings which will make it. She should come round when it's done then I reckon she won't need much persuading.' I brought the beers over. 'But I tell you what – if I do decide to sell and I'll find out very soon, you can have first refusal.'

'You're a thoroughly splendid fellow,' said Henry, taking the beer and raising it to toast me. 'I need a pee.'

I pointed to the room off the hall, congratulating myself on my acting and the restraint I'd shown, even though my inner voice had been screaming at me to hand the flat over to him there and then. He'd left his phone on the table and I picked it up. Misha had replied to his text, but I couldn't see what it said.

Henry came back. 'I see you're into the rugby. Have you got tickets for Saturday's game?'

I shook my head. 'I didn't think I was going to be around and then it was too late – it's sold out.'

'Want to come with me then? I've been given two tickets in one of the boxes and Misha wants to stay at home and play with Mabel.'

'Yes, I'd love that.'

Dolly shifted in her basket then hopped out and went towards the door. I grabbed my keys and slipped my puffer jacket and shoes on.

'Her turn for a pee break,' I said connecting her lead onto the loop on her collar.

'I'm right behind you,' said Henry, picking up his coat and our beers. We went into the garden and Dolly performed, earning herself a little biscuit treat shaped like a heart. The orange street-lamps behind the wall lit up the bodies of the skeletal trees in the park and gave the inky-black sky a soft glow. There was a chill in the air which made the hairs on the backs of my hands stand upright and we sat huddled on the bench, our breath turning into little clouds, whilst Dolly had a sniff around the bare flowerbeds. The chatter of people enjoying their Friday evening drinks and the smell of cigarettes floated over the mossy boundary wall which separated the garden from the main street. The twinkling lights from the entrance to the park looked like fireflies or fallen stars and the various smells emanating from the restaurants made my mouth water.

'This is such a cool area – a bit like Notting Hill,' said Henry.

'Yes. It's certainly got London vibes to it,' I replied. 'Want to get some take-away?'

He glanced at his phone. 'You know what, I'd love to, but I'd better get home. I've got to pick up Misha on my way back.'

We went back into the flat and made plans to meet for beers before the game. If I wasn't careful my stomach was going to balloon – I was usually a wine or G&T guy. I went into the bedroom and got on my treadmill. The beer and crisps joggled uncomfortably in my stomach. An hour later, I showered and put on a white tee, a bit of light make-up and a baseball cap. I scrolled through my phone to see what LuellaBoo was up to and saw that she was at a friends' party in Woking – perfect. I had bought another handset with a pay-as-you-go sim, and I sat back in front of the green screen, G&T in my hand, and texted LuellaBoo.

It's JD. Sorry I haven't been in touch for a while, but do you have ten minutes now for a private video chat?

The reply was immediate – as though her phone was glued to her hand.

Yes. Give me five to find somewhere quiet. Will call when I'm ready.

In less than five minutes my phone rang. I answered and there was LuellaBoo sitting on a bed in front of a ruched pink headboard with a hideous fringed bedside lamp to her left. She was wearing a tight pvc red dress which looked like she'd been shrink-wrapped into it, her orange flesh oozing over the edges and I found myself holding my breath in sympathy for her discomfort.

'So good to talk to you,' she said, her voice husky and gushing. Her crimson talons were wrapped around a huge glass of white wine which appeared to be missing a lily pad and goldfish.

'And you, darling,' I drawled. 'Where are you? Looks...quaint.'

'Just a friend's house party. Nothing special.'

'Now then darling. Let's see those eyes.' I clicked my fingers and she held the phone so that her face filled the screen. She had good skin, but the make-up was very drag – she looked as though she was about to go on stage and burst into a rendition of *I Will Survive*. That aside, she was a pretty girl with a heart-shaped face and big dark eyes, like Bill's. Her teeth were slightly too big, so she needed to soften her lip line to divert focus towards the eyes which she'd not made a bad job of, although I disapproved of the Daisy the Cow eyelashes.

'Beautiful.'

'What's this all about?' asked Luella, taking a sip of wine and leaving an oily red smudge on the side of the glass.

I tapped the side of my nose. 'It just so happens that I've got a little secret venture starting at a very exclusive celebrity wedding venue.'

'Where?' asked Luella, pulling at one of her hooped earrings which had become tangled in her hair.

'Guess.' I wagged my index finger in the air.

'Not The Nix?'

I pursed my lips and winked. 'A certain number of the more exclusive bridal parties are going to be invited for a hair and make-over consultation with me. The team at The Nix will make notes and mimic the designs on the big day, if wanted, but you probably won't need that because I know you are more than capable of doing it yourself.'

Luella fanned her face with her free hand. 'That's just super amazing. I'm such a big fan. I don't know what to say. What do you want me to do? A live feed?'

'Actually darling,' I crooned. 'I'm dying to get my hands on your pretty little face, but I'd really love it if you would just keep this to ourselves at the moment. The venture's a new one and I want it to coincide with the launch of my make-up brand which is the day of your wedding. You could say, you'll be the first face of *Dollymix*.'

Her eyes were on stalks, the tips of the lashes almost touching the top of her forehead. 'What? No way!'

I pressed my fingers to my lips. 'But, darling, it's all a bit hush hush at the mo. We're talking proper NDAs and if word gets out, my business manager will make me cancel because it has to be a total surprise for my viewers.'

'Totally. Totally.' She nodded, tilting her wineglass and creating a tsunami.

'But if you agree, then the plan is for me to take lots of exclusive footage at our private tutorial and then upload it onto my channel at the same time as the launch of *Dollymix*, obviously giving you a massive plug at the same time.'

'Wow! Just wow!' Her crimson mouth opened wide showing her tombstone teeth, and I could almost hear her mind whirring as she calculated how many new followers this would get her. 'I mean that would be amazing.' She paused. 'So, I can post something myself at the same time you post?'

He wagged a finger at her. 'Patience, darling. You can post on day one of your honeymoon. My footage only, though I'll ensure some of it is exclusive to you.' I tilted my head on one side. 'Say, where are you two lovebirds going?'

'Maldives.'

'Gorgeous.' *Predictable.* 'So, the next step, if you're happy for this to go ahead, is for us to arrange a session. I'll send over all the dates I'm available. The sooner the better darling, so I can make sure you get exactly what you need from me. Oh, and by the way, you need to get yourself a burner phone to be used only when communicating with me. You wouldn't believe how often I get hacked. Send me the number to this phone the moment you've got it sorted. Cheaper the device the better.'

'OMG – I can't wait,' said Luella, wriggling her fingers with the huge engagement ring flashing its diamond at me.

'Adieu,' I said blowing a kiss. The screen went blank. That was the first time I'd spoken to her, and I felt strangely calm. I thought I'd feel weird about killing her – that something within me would curdle and change my mind, but if anything, I felt elated and excited. I couldn't distinguish if it was the deceit I was enjoying or the thrill that the plan was about to get off the ground. I picked up Dolly and cuddled her, some of my foundation rubbing off onto her curly sandy coat. And then it came to me in a flash. I knew exactly how to get the Bonsai into her system without her realising. A special range of make-up. I giggled to myself: *Dollymix for the Dead.*

Chapter 22
Cally

It was late and Cally, and Rolly, were ready to drop straight into bed, but as she hurried into the bedroom, she noticed the light in Dan's study was on. It had once been her bedroom, and seeing the pink glow from the lampshade spreading under the door gave her a prickle of nostalgia. She could almost hear her father's footsteps padding along the corridor, ready to tuck her in for the night; she pretending to have lost her teddy bear to prolong his presence in the room. Dan, trying to be sensitive, claimed he didn't want to change anything about the room, but she knew she ought to encourage him to re-decorate; even eight-year-old Cally hadn't liked the rainbow and unicorn wallpaper. She should have let him use her dad's old study, which was far more appropriate, but since his death she couldn't bear for anyone to go in there, nor was she ready to clear it of his belongings, so poor Dan was stuck with the unicorns.

Dan was gazing at a computer screen, his face spliced by a large yucca leaf. The reflection of the monitor gave his skin a pistachio hue and accentuated the dark bags under his eyes. As she approached his desk, she stumbled into the wastepaper bin, knocking it over, the contents spilling onto the floor. She hoped the numerous Wotsits and Cadbury's Flake wrappers, by some miracle, weren't his, but the orange and brown speckles clinging to the front of his shirt were a dead give-away. He was stress eating. She swiped the files and his crumpled jacket off the chair opposite and sat down.

He looked up and smiled. 'What are you looking so excited about?'

Cally leant forwards. 'Jay and Misha are connected. I'm almost certain they're related; maybe brother and sister.' She pushed her phone across the desk and Dan stared at the photo of the young girl in her waitressing outfit. 'If you zoom in on the little boy she's holding hands with, you'll see it's Jay.'

Dan removed his glasses from the top of his head and peered at the phone screen. He gave a low whistle and tapped his finger on the table. 'That fits with what I've dug up.' He reached for his notepad and dragged the tip of his biro down the margin. 'Yes. Here it is: James Dollander's real name is Michael Jones and he was born and raised, along with his sister, Lucy, on the *Hazleton Estate* – you know, the one the council are about to pull down. When he was ten, and Lucy was fourteen they were both taken into care. Michael spent the rest of his time moving between foster homes, but Lucy was adopted.'

Jones – she'd heard that surname recently, but she couldn't remember where. She swept the thought to one side – it was a common enough name. Cally steepled her fingers together. 'Let me guess, she moved to America?'

Dan's eyes narrowed. 'Yes. How did you know that?'

She grinned. 'I've spoken to Misha's Auntie Cleo from Boston and she told me about Misha's parents, Barb and Geoff Hamble, but sadly –'

'They were killed in a wildfire. I know.'

'Yes. Cleo said all their belongings were destroyed so I'm

guessing the paper trail runs dry after that, but it makes sense to conclude that Lucy Jones is Misha Carlton.'

Dan clapped his hands together and stood up, knocking over an empty coke can. 'Right – I'll go and bring Jay in for questioning.'

Cally shook her head and gestured for him to sit down. Dan frowned but lowered himself back onto his seat.

Cally cleared her throat. 'I think that's a bad idea. If he clams up, we're going to lose Misha.'

Dan clicked the end of his biro in rapid succession. 'But, on the other hand, if we arrest him, he'll see that the game is over and might come clean.'

'I don't think so,' said Cally. She held up her right hand and hooked back her index finger with her left one. 'Let's think about this logically; first, this isn't about money, so I reckon it's a weird sibling thing.'

Dan nodded.

'This is something he wants Misha to pay for emotionally.' She pushed back her middle finger. 'Second, we've got to find a way to put Bill Cambly into the equation because I think Jay targeted Luella to punish Bill.'

'Why?'

'According to Val's sister, Di, Bill chased anything in a skirt – the younger the better.' She tapped her phone. 'We've got a photograph of a teenaged Misha working for Bill so what are the odds he tried it on with her – a pretty, young thing.'

Dan rubbed his chin with his hand, making a noise like someone was sand-papering a brick. 'Okay. I get why Jay – Michael, or whatever we're calling him, would punish Bill but not Misha and Luella. That doesn't make sense.'

Cally closed her eyes. 'Yes. I know. There's some big connection we're missing, but I can't fathom what it is.' She paused. 'By the way, did you check Jay's whereabouts on the morning of Luella's death?'

'Yes.' Dan ran his finger down his messy writing, only legible to him hence why last weekend Cally came back from the shops with a pineapple instead of a jar of pine nuts and ruined Dan's plans for making pesto pasta. 'He was making a special appearance in Trafalgar Square. Caught the 7.26 am train to London, St. Pancras. We have witnesses and CCTV footage of him getting on and off the train.'

Cally tapped her finger against her left temple. 'He can't have been at The Nix at the same time Luella died.'

Something buzzed at the back of Cally's mind. She slapped her hand across her forehead. 'Unless. *Yes!* Bloody Bulag. That's it!'

'Bulag. What's that dirty great oaf got to do with it.'

Cally felt the blood whoosh around her ears, and she stood up, grinding her fist into her other palm. 'Where are the evidence tapes from the smuggling at The Nix? The one's you found in Bulag's bedsit.'

Dan rolled his chair across the pink, fluffy carpet to the filing cabinet behind him and returned spinning a disc on the tip of his finger. 'This is a copy but they're all on here.'

Cally swiped the disc and ran round to Dan's computer, kicking the bin further across the floor. She knelt next to Dan and popped open the disc drive then clicked on the drop-down menu to reveal the contents. After a few seconds the screen filled with video attachments and a date printed below each one. Cally moved the cursor to the date of Luella's wedding day and clicked play on the video. The time on the screen showed midday. She paused then hit the rewind button.

'What are you looking for?'

After half a minute she paused the footage and tapped the screen with her finger, then enlarged a shadowy figure, wearing a dark hoody and tracksuit, who was standing by the tradesman's entrance. The person's head was angled away from the camera. 'I'll bet you anything that's Jay.'

'But how can you tell? Their face isn't visible.'

She zoomed in some more. 'Whoever it is, they're wearing gloves to type the code into the keypad.' Cally shifted from one knee to the other as she sped through the footage and sure enough, about half an hour later, the hooded figure disappeared via the same route. 'The timings of Luella's death fit in with this person's movements, but...' She pulled at her hair.

'Nice try, Cally.' Dan squeezed her shoulder. 'How come you remembered about the recorded security footage?'

Cally got to her feet and moved a few more empty coke cans to one side before leaning on the edge of the desk. 'We'd forgotten that on the day of Luella's wedding, the delightful Steve and Paula were busy recording who came in and out of the back entrance of The Nix. Some of it was legitimate, so that anyone checking wouldn't think anything was amiss, but some of it was for Bulag's eyes only.'

'Er...okay.'

'You were looking at footage of who was going into the hotel assuming what you saw was right and that they only fiddled with it when Bulag arrived with the crates of wine.'

Dan pressed his fingers to his temples. 'Yes.'

'But what if Bulag was using those tapes for his own purpose. I wouldn't put it past him to have a little blackmail business going on. One which those high up in The Cobras didn't know about.'

Dan nodded. 'Clever. The Nix prides itself on a no camera policy, except, understandably, for those overlooking the swimming pools. Privacy for their celebrities is one of its main selling points.'

'But no insurance company on earth would allow that, so they had to install very discrete cameras at both entrances but which only the GM and security staff are able to access.'

'And Bulag.'

Cally laughed. 'Exactly. And it just so happens that the other night, when I went out for our gyros...' she paused and Dan absent-mindedly patted his stomach, '... I happened to see Bulag come into *The Olive* and sit down at Jay's table. They were having quite an intense conversation and then I saw Jay pulling out a fistful of notes and handing them to Bulag. I took a photo of the transaction.'

Dan wrinkled his brow. 'What was he paying him for? Drugs?'

'That's exactly what I thought at the time, but in light of this footage, I think Jay was being blackmailed. What if Bulag saw him in the flesh on the day of Luella's death? Then, when he went through his unedited version of the tapes, he realised that he had captured on film someone entering The Nix at roughly the same time a murder took place. It doesn't take a genius to figure out it was Jay.'

'Right. So, you think Bulag knew Jay was there on the day of Luella's murder and put two and two together then decided he could profit quite nicely from it.'

'Yes. Like you said, there aren't cameras inside The Nix for privacy reasons and Jay is the master of disguise. He could easily have got to Luella's room without being seen especially if Luella was in on the secret.'

'What secret?'

'The sister, Sasha Cambly, said Luella was very excited about some exclusive material which was only going to be released after the wedding. I think Jay had told her he was going to make her an overnight star by using footage of him doing her wedding make-up with his new brand, *Dollymix*, which was going to launch that very day. In fact, he was going to London that morning to kick off the promotion.'

'Bloody hell. He's got some nerve. But we still don't have enough to make an arrest. Bulag won't squeal, that's for sure.'

Cally reached out and grabbed Dan's arm and squeezed it. 'You need more proof. Something watertight. He's got an alibi for the train – you said it yourself; he can't be in two places at once so we need to figure out how he did it.'

'But what about Misha. We've not seen or heard anything of her since the first photo. She's running out of time.'

Cally swallowed, trying to quell the uncomfortable fluttering in her stomach as she pictured Misha in the dark; alone and frightened. Was she still alive? 'Just give me a bit longer. I'm going to go and see Val again. She's hiding something about Bill, I'm certain of it, so let me see if I can prise it from her. If I can't, then you should bring Jay in. I've got a lead about a superfan and I'm going to see if I can get Miriam's tech girl to track them down. Maybe they can shed some light on what he's been up to.'

'That's a great shout. In the meantime, I'm going to keep looking into Jay and Misha's past and tell the nightshift to get out there and shadow Jay's every move – with a bit of luck he might even lead us back to his sister.'

'Yes,' said Cally. 'We know Jay grew up around here, so he'll have plenty of places he used to escape to as a little boy. I'll bet you anything, where he's hiding her is somewhere personal to both of them.'

Cally sat in her car under a tree which was shedding so many tiny yellow, furled petals she had to turn the wipers on every five minutes in order to see out of the windscreen. She was a couple of doors down from Val's house, waiting for her to return, and her head fizzed with information. Her phone rang and she glanced at the screen; it was a number from outside the UK and a code Cally didn't recognise.

'Hello. This is Cally Simmonds.'

'Hi there, Cally,' came a familiar female voice with a strong American twang. 'This is Barb's sister, Cleo.'

'Aunty Cleo!' Cally's heart sunk at the lack of good news concerning her niece. 'Hi. I'm so sorry but I can't update you on the case other than to say the police and I are doing absolutely everything we can to find Misha.'

There was silence on the other end of the line.

'I think I'm getting closer though. Much closer.'

Cleo gave a sigh. 'That's not why I'm calling.'

Cally pressed her lips together. 'Right. Well. Fire away.'

Cleo clicked her tongue. 'Look I don't know if this is the right thing for me to do.' She paused again and Cally could hear a faint rattle to her breathing. 'You see, it's not my business and, besides, Barb swore me to secrecy on pain of death. That sister of mine always was so melodramatic!' Her voice caught in the back of her throat. 'But she's not here to make the decisions anymore...'

Cally's ears prickled. 'Swore you to secrecy about what?'

'About why Misha had to spend so long in hospital.'

'I thought you said it was for mental health problems.'

'I lied.'

'Why would you lie about something like that?'

Cleo tutted. 'I was waiting for Henry to pipe up and say something but when he didn't it got me thinking that it was because he didn't know.'

Cally tapped her finger on the steering wheel – this wasn't making sense. 'Didn't know what?'

'That Misha had given birth in September 2005, a few months before she left the UK. It turns out the birth had caused a lot of internal damage and she had to have a hysterectomy. She can't have kids.'

It took a few seconds for Cally to process what Cleo was saying. 'Wait. You're telling me that Misha had given birth?'

'Yes. And she was only a little girl herself at the time. It was awful.'

'What...what happened to the baby?'

'Misha said the father had taken custody of her. He was an older man apparently.'

'*Her?*'

'Yes. It was a little girl, but Misha wouldn't say anything else about the father, or if she did, Barb never told me about it. In my opinion they should have pursued it further and arrested him, but I think after Misha recovered they just decided to put the whole thing behind them and move on.'

Cally's heart was thumping against her ribcage. *Luella* – she was Bill and Misha's baby. She had to be. Suddenly, everything was clicking into place. Her tongue stuck to the roof of her mouth and she could barely get her words out. 'Thank you, Cleo. Thank you so much. That's very, very helpful.'

Out of the corner of her eye she saw Val's silver Mercedes shoot past. Cally said a mumbled goodbye to Cleo and leapt out of her car, rushing up the drive just in time to catch Val turning her key in the lock.

'Val,' she hollered and Val spun around; her knee-length denim dress hung off her frame and her hair was a mess. When she saw it was Cally she gave a little wave and pushed her Jackie-O sunglasses to the top of her head.

'You, again.'

Cally smiled. 'Yes. Me again.'

Val beckoned her into the house, and they stood in the entrance hall which smelt of Cally's compost bin – the flowers on the central table were in dire need of attention. Cally's fingers itched to pull out her secateurs and snip off the dead heads; at the very least she could replace the cloudy water in the vases.

Val waggled a finger at her. 'Let me guess, you're here for

more tea?' She smiled, showing her small teeth. 'Or perhaps this time I can tempt you with something stronger.'

Cally swallowed. 'Val. There's something I need to tell you.'

Val raised a neatly plucked eyebrow.

'I'm a private investigator.'

Val froze for a second then flopped down onto the nearest chair; a high-backed, velvet throne pushed against the wall. Above it hung a huge oil portrait of Bill and there was a small smile curled into the corner of his mouth which made him look as though he was leering at her.

Val threw her sunglasses onto the vase table. 'So, you lied to me. You aren't my friend, after all.'

Cally pulled up a footstool covered with a tapestry of a hunting scene and perched on it, her head parallel with Val's bony knees. 'I am your friend.'

Val leant down and reached into her purse, pulling out a battered packet of cigarettes and a lighter. 'Who were you investigating? Bill?'

Cally shook her head. 'No. I started off working undercover for the hotel. Valuable stock was going missing, and because I discovered there was a local criminal gang involved, the police asked if I would dig a bit deeper.' She ran her hands through her hair. 'I want you to know the work I did on Luella's wedding was completely legitimate and I loved every minute of it.'

Val lit a cigarette and took a long drag, blowing the smoke upwards so that for a few seconds it obliterated Bill's smirking face. She waved her cigarette at Cally. 'I don't understand.'

'After Luella was killed, my boss thought it would be a good idea for me to stay undercover to look after Misha Carlton who was having some sort of breakdown. At the time of her kidnapping, I thought Luella's death was a totally separate incident, but then after a bit of digging it became clear the two things were connected.' She shrugged. 'I stayed in character so I could look at what happened from a different angle.'

Val snorted. 'You mean spy on my family.' She flicked ash into the nearest vase and Cally winced.

'I thought you asked too many questions. I'd like you to leave please.'

'No, Val. Whatever you think, I *am* your friend and all I've ever wanted to do was to find out who did this to Luella... and Bill, but you're keeping something from me. I know you are.'

Val exhaled a cloud of smoke from her nostrils. Her voice when she spoke was sharp. 'I can assure you; I want nothing more than to find out who killed my daughter.' A pause. 'And husband.'

'Then tell me the real reason you moved away to Poole.'

Val threw the cigarette butt into the vase and there was a hissing noise. 'I told you. Bill wanted to build boats and Leicestershire's about as far away from the sea as is possible. We could hardly sell them for the rich and famous to cruise around Rutland Water.'

'Di's told me about Bill's predilection for young women.'

Val opened her mouth then snapped it shut, grazing the flint on the lighter with her chipped fingernail. After a few minutes of silence, she took a deep breath and her voice, when she spoke, was soft as though she were recounting a dream. 'Once upon a time, I adored him. He was my world, and we were going to set the whole bloody place on fire.' She gave a hollow laugh. 'I was so naïve.' She stared at Cally; the whites of her eyes were bloodshot. 'There was this girl. She was a poor little thing – had a horrible home life and so I tried to help them –'

'Them?' interrupted Cally.

'Yes. She had a kid brother. Mind you, she was barely an adult herself – just turned 17.' She pulled out another cigarette and rolled it between her thumb and index finger. 'That's why it was so appalling. I was trying to find a way to help them get out of the hole they lived in and he...' She stood up and the cigarette fell to the floor and rolled under Cally's stool. Cally ducked down to retrieve it whilst Val walked over to a small white cabinet, flinging open its double doors which were covered with little gold fleur-de-lys. She pulled out a whisky bottle and two tumblers and set them on the central table. She unscrewed the lid from the bottle and poured a generous helping into a glass which she proceeded to knock back in one go. She held aloft the other glass and waved it at Cally who shook her head.

'Working, I suppose,' said Val before topping up her glass again. She took a step backwards and stared at the painting of her husband. 'Stupid, stupid man.'

'How did you find out about the affair?'

Val continued to stare at her husband's image. 'I don't suppose you could really call it an affair. More an abuse of power.' She arched an eyebrow. 'He liked to take photos but wasn't so great at keeping them hidden.'

Cally bit her lip but then blurted out; 'I'm sorry but...but you actually *forgave* him?' She paused. 'And, if you don't mind me saying, Di said he strayed more times than she could count. Why the hell stick with him?'

Val ran her finger around the rim of her glass. 'The first time – the girl –'

'Do you remember her name?'

'Yes. She was called Lucy.' She sat back on the throne and cradled her glass in both hands. 'I'd just discovered I was pregnant. We'd been trying for several years and suddenly there I was expecting Luella. At the same time, I found out about Lucy and so I confronted him. He broke down, said it would never happen again – said he'd go and have therapy to cure his addiction.' Her voice had grown husky. 'I wanted to believe him and that's why we moved so suddenly. I suppose it was our way of pretending it had never happened.'

Cally held out her phone which had the picture of Michael and Lucy she'd photographed from the notice board in Di's kitchen. 'That's Lucy.' She pointed and Val nodded. 'She was fourteen in that photo.'

Val gave a strangled gasp. 'No.'

Cally moved the focus onto Michael. 'That's her brother, Michael?'

'Mikey.' Val's eyes were brimming with tears. 'Sweetest little thing. He adored his sister so much. Would have done anything for her.' She stared into the distance for a few seconds. 'Mikey Jones; Nine; Flat 439, *Hazelton Towers*.'

'Do you know what happened to them after you left?'

Val shook her head and gazed down at her empty glass.

'It's interesting because at exactly the same time you left, Lucy gave birth to a baby. A little girl.'

The colour drained from Val's face and her hand started to shake. She put down the whisky glass and cradled her knees. 'A baby? Oh, for fuck's sake. Are you telling me the baby was Bill's?'

When would she stop lying? Val was convincing, Cally had to hand it to her. The surprise on her face looked genuine – worthy of an Oscar. 'Here's the thing; Lucy, who after her horrendous ordeal of giving birth in secret, wouldn't talk about who the father was, apart from to say that the baby was being cared for by him.' Cally raised an eyebrow. 'You moved away suddenly...'

Val frowned then suddenly the creases across her brow smoothed. She threw back her head and laughed; a horrible, tinny cackling sound. 'Oh – I'm so stupid. I see where this is going.' She wiped the tears from her eyes and sniffed. 'Fucking hell, Cally. Do you seriously think that I faked a pregnancy?' She shook her head then jumped to her feet and marched out of the room and down the corridor. Cally heard clanking sounds and doors opening and closing then Val returned with a large chocolate-moleskine bound album. She thumped it onto Cally's lap and opened the cover, tapping a photo with her index finger, now devoid of the pretty magenta varnish and bitten to the quick.

'I told you Bill liked to take photos. Well – look. That's me in the hospital giving birth to Luella.' It took a few seconds for Cally to register she was looking at a blow-by-blow visual record of a baby being born. There were dozens of photos of Val at each stage of labour – Cally winced at the graphic shots of the delivery but there was no way they had been staged. And in amongst the hospital gowns, Val's tired and exhilarated face and all the blood and gore, was the close up of a swaddled infant, bearing a wrist tag with Louise Ella Cambly and the exact time and date of birth written on it. Cally ground her teeth. *Damn!* It was seven months after Cleo said Lucy had given birth to her daughter.

Cally closed the book and set it on the floor. 'You can see why I had to ask.'

Val gave a small nod.

'You know,' Cally continued, 'Lucy's real name is Misha Carlton.'

Val's eyes widened. 'Who? The actor?'

'Yes. The one who's gone missing.'

Val pressed her lips together.

'And Lucy's brother, Mike – *Mikey*, now goes by the name JayDoll – he's a big YouTube star.' She scrolled to a couple of photos of him on her phone and held them in front of Val's face – one of him in drag and the one as James Dollander.

Val was frowning and shaking her head at the same time. 'I've never met either of them. I mean, as adults.'

'Are you sure? It would seem that they both have good reason to despise Bill.'

Val folded her arms across her chest. 'No. I've never spoken to or had anything to do with either of them.' She stared at Cally and held her hand over her heart. 'I promise.'

Cally took a deep breath then stood up and moved towards the front door.

'Cally.'

She turned. Val was flicking through the photo album, tears now streaming down her face.

'What do you suppose became of Bill's other daughter?'

Cally's stomach felt heavy. 'I don't know.' She had been so sure Luella was Misha's child but instead of putting the jigsaw together, she'd accumulated more pieces, none of which fitted into the puzzle.

Chapter 23
Mikey
A week earlier

As I WENT UP to the penthouse floor, my stomach disappearing for a milli-second with the speed of the elevator, it struck me how easy it was to be invisible. Here I was, looking out of a glass box attached to a skyscraper, the sun's rays bouncing off the pea-green sea beneath my feet; dozens of white-hulled yachts bobbing around like toy boats in a bath. The building oozed success and wealth; it should have been a fortress and yet no one at the main desk had questioned me as I'd waltzed in wearing a navy jacket and chinos with a bouquet of flowers for Mr Cambly. I was being careful – there were still plenty of loose ends I needed to tie up, but I knew I was running out of time. The rather sweet private investigator who I might have screwed in another life, was onto me. It wouldn't be long before she'd piece everything together and, besides, the Bulag situation was growing more difficult and expensive by the day.

The lift opened and ahead was a glass, wrap-around desk with Cambly Yachts written across it in blue letters; a stripy lifebuoy hanging off the Y at a jaunty angle. Behind the desk sat a jowly-faced woman with greying hair scraped into a bun – presumably someone hired by Val to make sure Bill, the little perv, kept his mind on the job. Her watery blue gaze fell onto the flowers. 'I don't suppose those are for me?' Her voice was high-pitched and very soft.

'I'm here to see Bill Cambly.'

She swallowed and the flesh beneath her chin shook. 'He's not here. There's been a family bereavement.'

I waved the cream roses at her, then leant one elbow on the desk. 'But I know he is here, and I need to see him. I'm family.'

She gave a slow owl-like blink then lifted the phone and pressed a button. I heard a loud buzz coming from a nearby glass box; the inside shielded by striped blue and white slatted blinds. Bill Cambly was written across the door in blue italic letters which matched those on the desk.

'Pat – what is it?' came the gruff voice.

'Mr Cambly,' she gushed, 'I'm so sorry to disturb you but you have a visitor. A family member –' She looked at me for enlightenment, but I pressed a finger to my lips and went to the door. I opened it and there he was standing behind a pale desk. The window behind his head revealing acres of cerulean sky. Bill's mouth gaped open as I entered, the receiver glued to his ear.

He was smaller than I remembered. Less shiny and brash – like he'd been through the wash too many times and had faded and shrunk.

He slammed down the phone and his dark eyes widened. He looked so like Luella, the hairs on the back of my neck stood to attention.

'You're not family,' he said, his voice hoarse and gravelly.

I pulled out the upright chair in front of his desk and threw down the flowers which caused a few of the petals to dislodge and stick to the newton's cradle as though some of the silver balls were wearing miniature bonnets. I flicked them away before setting the spheres crashing into each other. The noise and movement were so satisfying.

'You're not family,' he repeated; the growling undertone increasing.

'Please sit down Mr Cambly. Or should I say, Bill. I mean we aren't technically family, but we could have been.' I reached inside my pocket for the envelope of photos I'd brought with me and placed them next to me on the desk.

Bill's glance went back to the phone and his pinky finger, adorned with a brash gold signet ring, twitched.

I tutted. 'I wouldn't call security.'

There was a knock at the door. I pushed a photo across the desk; it was of his daughter, Sasha, standing outside their Chelsea home. His front teeth fell like a guillotine onto his lower lip.

The knock sounded again, and Pat popped her fat head around the door frame.

'Do you want tea?' she trilled.

'No, thank you,' I said before Bill had time to open his jaw. Pat ignored me and stared at Bill who shook his head and flapped his hand towards the door until she got the hint and disappeared. Bill slumped in his leather chair and ran his fingers through his hair which was a more sensible foxy shade for his age than the inky-blue black he used to dye it.

'What's this about? Why do you have a photo of my daughter, Sasha, outside our flat?'

I crossed my legs and sat upright in the chair. 'Because she's going to be next.'

He blanched and leapt to his feet, but I whipped open my jacket pocket and tapped the butt of my revolver. It wasn't real, but it was a very good fake – from a distance. 'Sit back down please, Bill.'

He opened and closed his mouth a couple of times before the words came out. 'You...you killed Luella?'

I drummed my fingers on my kneecap. 'Yes.'

Bill let out a dry sob then buried his head in his hands. 'But I don't understand.' He looked at me. 'Why?' A globule of spit flew into the air.

The emotion on his face deepened the grooves in his leathery skin; the orange pallor sliding to grey and puffing up the bags under his eyes. His dark irises flashed with rage, and he clenched his large hands into fists, the blood visibly running away from the knuckles.

I wagged a finger at him. 'If you want me to explain what happened then I'm going to have to ask you to be quiet.' I was starting to feel a little prickle of annoyance at his indignation; after all, this whole thing was his fault.

'Where to begin, I wonder.' I sorted through the photos until I found a faded one of Lucy and me – Fat Eddie had taken it of us eating a Mr Whippy next to the fountain in Walkers' Common. I slid it across the polished surface. Bill stared at it, screwing up his eyes. He looked up at me – his forehead furrowed in confusion.

I closed my eyes and took a deep breath. 'No.' I spat the words. 'She meant nothing to you, did she?' I snatched it back from him and gazed at the muted sepia tones which had developed over the years.

He swallowed and his large adam's apple bobbed down and up his throat.

'Happy days. This here is a picture of me, Mikey, and my sister, Lucy, only she doesn't call herself that anymore.'

Something registered in Bill's mind which seemed to turn off the elasticity in his body, causing him to crumple into his leather chair.

'She now goes by the name of Misha Carlton. Have you heard of her?'

Bill nodded. 'She's a film star.'

I leant forwards. 'Do you want me to let you into a little secret?' I didn't wait for him to answer. I held up a photo of

Tommy's metal cage. 'In a couple of days' time she's going to be spending a bit of time in there.'

He gasped. There was a bottle of water next to his monitor and he reached for it, fumbling as he twisted the lid. 'But...but why? She's your sister.' He took a large swig and the water dribbled down his chin.

I rolled my eyes. 'Families, hey?' I shrugged – a big grin spreading across my face. 'I'm going to teach her a lesson in manners. You see, I did so much for her, and yet she was so ungrateful. I think she could do with a bit of time out to reflect on everything.'

Bill took another swig of water. 'I don't understand.'

'*I don't understand,*' I said in a nasal whine. 'If you just stop with the interruptions all will be revealed. You see a long time ago – nineteen years ago to be precise, Lucy, who you raped repeatedly, gave birth to a child. A girl.'

Bill's lower jaw clenched and I clicked my fingers together in quick succession. 'Come on Bill. You do the maths.'

'The baby was mine?'

'Oh yes. A very sweet little thing.'

'But why didn't she say anything to me about it?'

I slapped my forehead. 'Duh! Because she was terrified out of her wits.'

'But I would have helped her.' He twisted his signet ring back and forth; eyes darting from side to side.

'What? And gone to prison. She was fifteen at the time.'

Bill made a sound as though he was going to vomit.

'Anyway, we were both taken into care and –' I gave an exaggerated yawn. 'Really it's so tragic and *so* predictable. She moved abroad and I was left here bla bla bla.'

'I...I'm so sorry about Lucy, but what has this got to do with Luella?'

'Don't you fucking even try to say you're sorry.' I said the words through clenched teeth.

Bill held up his palms.

'I had a... what's the word, a revelation. You see, I'd just got to a stage in my life when I realised that everything I'd done to protect my sister had been for nothing and quite frankly, I felt used. You see, I'd been the one who'd suffered. I'd had to bear the emotional scarring of what happened to Jadis.'

Bill raised a bushy eyebrow.

'Jadis. DUH! *Your* daughter.'

He swallowed again and I realised his whole body was trembling and he was picking at the skin around his thumbnail.

'And yet you and Misha hadn't given one thought as to how my life was left in tatters.'

'But I didn't know about it,' said Bill, his voice had now morphed into a mewl.

'But that doesn't mean you aren't responsible. You were the one who groomed my sister, got her pregnant and then abandoned her.'

'But I didn't know she was pregnant.' Blood trickled down the side of his thumb.

I made fists and rubbed my eyes. 'Boo! Hoo! So that's alright then – poor little you didn't know. Pah! You shouldn't have fucking done it in the first place. It's disgusting. And from what I've gathered – you didn't learn your lesson. Poor Val – she deserved better. I always did like her.'

'But Luella?' He started snivelling and reached into his pocket for a hanky which he pounded against his eye sockets as if he could force the tears to return. 'Think of how much this has destroyed Val.'

I shrugged. 'Collateral damage, I'm afraid. I needed you to share some of the pain I'd experienced, Bill, when Lucy and Jadis were both taken away from me.'

'But what about – er...Jadis? Surely, it's not too late to get in touch with her now?'

I snorted. 'That's impossible, I'm afraid. She's dead.'

He gave a sharp intake of breath and his face concertinaed. 'How?'

'That doesn't concern you.'

'Please, please don't take my other daughter from me. Please, I'll do anything – give you all the money you want. Just don't hurt her.'

I stroked my chin, my eyes darting from left to right in the pretence that I was giving his request some consideration. 'I don't know. It seems wrong to profit financially from this situation, so I still think I'm going need some more physical reparation.'

He held the hanky, now speckled with blood, to his chin. His face was mottled. 'No. Take me instead.'

I clapped my hands together and grinned. 'So, there is a decent human inside there after all.' I held my palms flat out and pretended they were weighing scales. 'Okay. So, here's how it's going to work. You're going to go home, back to good old London and you're going to leave a suicide note saying Luella's death was all your fault. No need for details – less is more and all that. Then you can kill yourself – don't care how you do it, and we'll call it quits.'

Bill was breathing fast and the film of perspiration above his lip glistened.

'If you don't, or if you try to alert the police, Sasha will be next, then – I hate to say it, Val plus I'll also release all the details about you and Misha Carlton to the press – it's such a wonderfully sleazy story. Then they'll probably look into your past a bit more and see how many other children you've slept with. I hear paedophiles don't have much fun in prison.'

I stood up and brushed some imaginary fluff from my chinos.

'How did you kill Luella?' Although he was still trembling, Bill's voice had become clear. Matter-of-fact – resigned to his fate.

'Alcohol and phenazepam are a lethal combination, but it wasn't a bad way to go. Plus, she had no idea it was happening. She simply slid out of consciousness and then drowned in her own bathwater.'

He hung his head – the realisation there was no way out had taken away all the fight from him. Suddenly he looked like an old man.

'The sins of the fathers.'

'What about Misha? Are you going to kill her too?'

'I haven't decided,' I said, drumming my fingers against my lips. 'She won't last long in there without water, but I'm kind of intrigued to see whether or not someone will figure out the clues for finding her which I'm going to leave behind. It's not too difficult and to be honest, and this will make you laugh, really it will, because it's somewhere *very* close to your beloved sister-in-law's heart.'

Chapter 24
Cally

Miriam's resident computer whizz had found out the identity of Jay's superfan: real name Clive Worsley. Cally had phoned him under the guise of being a journalist writing an article on superfans and their relationship with the object of their adoration. Clive was only too happy for Cally to pop around to discuss everything *JayDoll* saying he had an abundance of information to share.

Cally had never met a superfan before and was intrigued, wondering whether he was the sort who rifled through the rubbish bins which, for her current case, could turn out to be quite useful. Clive's postcode led her down a wide, tree-lined road, two streets away from Walkers' Common. It was a Victorian brick mid-terrace. An estate agent would say it was 'bijoux' – i.e. posh but not too fancy as there were no views of the park. Cally opened the latch gate of No. 24 and walked up the paved path, somewhat peeved that Clive's sweet pea tower was twice the size of hers. It was a neat garden; the wheelie bins had their own slatted enclosure and the flower beds which were on either side of the path were full of pink and white violas and the patches of soil between them were weed free. So, Clive had green fingers and that meant if the conversation was stilted Cally could mix it up with some gardening chat, for example, just how come his sweet peas resembled something out of Jack and the Beanstalk.

She knocked on the black lacquered door and a tiny woman wearing a coral velour tracksuit opened it. The sound of electronic pop music came drifting down the stairwell along with a strange whirring and clunking. The woman who was in her sixties had short white hair with a Tintin quiff at the front and curranty eyes; her half-moon glasses dangled from a silver chain around her neck. She had an apron around her waist and the top half was dusted with flour. There was a delicious smell of baking bread and a hint of sweetness mingled with the underlying yeasty aroma which made Cally's mouth water.

'Hello?' said the woman, clawing at the chain around her neck.

Of course, Clive still lived with his parents. He probably couldn't tell the difference between a dahlia and a delphinium either. 'Are you Mrs Worsley?' asked Cally.

She nodded.

'I'm here to see Clive.'

Mrs Worsley pursed her lips and tutted. 'Yes – Clive's told me all about the article. Right. Yes.' She wiped her hands down the skirt of her apron and stepped aside, beckoning Cally into the narrow hall. Cally squeezed through, grazing her thigh on the console table complete with cream telephone and a jam jar bursting with sweet peas; their vanilla scent filled the cramped space and made Cally's nose tingle. Mrs Worsley shut the door then stood on the bottom step looking up towards an arched window which overlooked the first turn of the staircase.

'Cliiiiiive.'

The whirring stopped and a few seconds afterwards the music lowered in volume.

'What is it Mum? Are the scones ready?' came a high-pitched male voice.

'The journalist is here.'

'Oh! Okay. Send her up will you.'

Mrs Worsley turned and faced Cally, her eyes level with Cally's chin. 'Will you be wanting tea?'

Cally shook her head. 'That's very kind of you to offer, but no thanks.'

Mrs Worsley swept her hand upwards through the air. 'Go on. Nothing Clive likes more than talking about *JayDoll*.' She said JayDoll's name with a sneer and wrinkled her nose.

'Don't you approve?' asked Cally, her hand resting on the newel post, one foot on the stairs.

'It's unhealthy,' she said, lowering her voice to a whisper. 'Clive's vulnerable. He'd do anything if JayDoll asked him – jump off a cliff.'

'Do you think JayDoll would ask him to jump off a cliff?'

Mrs Worsley put her hands on her hips. 'I'm just saying...'

'Muuuuum!'

'You'd better go on up,' said Mrs Worsley with a sigh. 'You'll see straightaway which room is his.'

Cally's scalp prickled; it was weird meeting an adult in their bedroom – it didn't feel right. The staircase turned back on itself at the arched window and ascended half a flight more to a square landing with silver-green carpet and four rooms leading off it. To the immediate right was a door, an inch ajar, with a full-sized poster of JayDoll stuck to it. She could hear tinny music coming from within.

Tentatively she knocked.

'Come on in,' came a sing-song voice.

She entered and her gaze was met by hundreds of eyes pasted to the wall; Jay's face was staring at her from every angle; each one a different colour palette. The rectangular room which overlooked the front of the house contained a single bed, topped with a garish patchwork quilt, tucked under the eaves. The opposite wall was swallowed by a huge built-in wardrobe made of white pine which didn't match the rest of the dark oak furniture. The door to the wardrobe was shut although it would seem a pair of stonewashed jeggings was trying to escape. Clive was standing at the far end of the room by the window, leaning on a table covered by a sewing machine. Next to it stood a dress-maker's dummy, half swaddled in a Little-Red-Riding-Hood cape with an ermine trim.

Clive wore denim dungarees with no tee-shirt on underneath, so a vast quantity of his bronzed flesh was visible; gold sequinned trainers peeping out from the hem of the flares. His wavy hair was a milk-chocolate colour with caramel highlights and he had it piled on top of his head in a messy bun. Clive fluttered his heavy eyelashes and smiled; his lips were puffy and glistened with candy-pink gloss. It was like looking at an inferior, slightly smaller version of Jay.

'Wow!' said Cally, crossing her fingers behind her back. 'You and Jay could pass for twins.'

'I know,' he said, mumbling the words, before shaping his hands into a picture frame around his face. 'It's uncanny, isn't it?'

'So, Clive, I really need your help – I want to know everything about you and, of course, your relationship with Jay.'

A grin split his face to reveal a top set of teeth which jutted out over the lower ones and though they were equally as bleached as Jay's he obviously hadn't gone to Turkey to get them fixed. Clive pulled a chair on casters out from under his sewing table and pointed to it whilst he went to the end of his bed and as he sat down his trouser legs rose to reveal that the shoes had at least a six-inch platform.

'So – you're a super fan? Is that right?' Cally pulled her note-book out from her handbag.

He wagged a finger and gave a little pout. 'I mean – I don't like the label superfan *per se*. It makes it seem one-sided.'

'How would you describe it?'

He stroked his stubble free chin. 'We're friends – soul mates.'

'Right. Right.'

'I mean, I'm not lying when I say I'd do anything for him.'

Cally nodded. 'And you follow him closely on social media.'

'I do more than that. I follow him physically whenever I can. I work shifts at the local supermarket to help with my board and lodging. Mum insists.' He tutted and rolled his eyes and the tips of one of his fake lashes caught under his eyebrow so he had to flick it free. 'When I'm not doing that, I try and get out to see him. He's such an inspiration. Always lets me take a selfie and we DM. He used not to respond – in fact he blocked me for a while, but he said it was a silly mistake. Now he responds all the time – sometimes it's just an emoji but often he sends a photo for my eyes only.' Clive gave a coy smile.

'Why do you think he's been responding more recently?'

Clive leant back on his bed and reached into his bedside drawer which was covered with faded stickers – the sort they award at primary school for good behaviour. He pulled out a folded piece of pale blue paper and handed it to Cally.

Dear Clive, I was so sad to learn about your struggles with depression. I know how that feels, truly I do. It's such an honour to hear that I inspire you and that being able to express yourself through make-up and clothes is helping you lead your best life. I enclose a VIP ticket for you to come to the launch of Dollymix – it would be great to see you although I'm going to be tired as I have to catch the 7.26am train from Market Bowden!! YAWN! I hope you can make it. Yours, Jay xxx PS. I know you like to be matching – I'll be wearing what I wore to the opening of Foxy's Nightclub.

'How lovely of him,' said Cally, her pulse quickening with the realisation Jay had been spoon-feeding Clive information.

Clive pressed his hand to his heart. 'I know, right.'

'By the way, I'm sorry to hear about your depression.' She

tilted her head on one side and smiled. 'So, spill then. What did you wear?'

He plucked the letter out of Cally's hand, kissed it and put it back in his drawer then went over to his wardrobe and slid back the doors on either side to reveal a mass of sparkling brightly coloured garments. There was a floor-to-ceiling shoe-rack; a shelf dedicated to hats, a shelf for wigs and, in the centre, a table with a light-up mirror and a pull-out stool underneath. Cally recoiled, about to run out of the bedroom, until she realised that the army of parachuting spiders hanging down from the mirror was a strip of fake eyelashes. Clive walked his fingers along the garments before pulling out a scarlet jumpsuit with electric orange collars. Cally supposed one might as well go out naked rather than put that outfit on, as it left nothing to the imagination.

'You made it yourself?' she asked, trying to look enthusiastic.

'Yes.' He jabbed a thumb at the sewing machine. 'I'm self-taught.'

'Amazing. I wish I could sew.' She paused; she really did wish she could sew. 'And, let me guess, the morning of the launch, you caught the same train as Jay?'

'Oh yes. He was in first class but only five minutes into the journey he came down the aisle and sat down next to me for a bit of a catch up. He didn't want a selfie, but he promised me one later on, once the event had kicked off – you see, he was very nervous. He also said I had to wear his hat and coat for good luck. He made me promise not to take them off at all.'

That's how he did it!

'Then I somehow lost him.' Clive paused, 'but here's the funny thing – I was sitting there, at *Le Pain Quotidien* killing time having my superfood granola bowl and skinny latte and he came running past a couple of hours later, wearing a completely different outfit.' He folded his arms. 'At first I was a bit put out, but I asked him at the event why he'd changed into something else and he was *so* sorry. In fact, I could have cried at how apologetic he was – said he'd changed at the St. Pancras Hotel where he'd been having breakfast.'

Cally frowned. That didn't make sense – the hotel was in the opposite direction – he wouldn't have been going past the café unless he was getting off a later train. 'How fascinating. Please go on. Did he tell you why he'd changed his clothes?'

Clive nodded and reached behind to the shelves and pulled off a framed photo. 'His publicity team wanted a more multi-coloured outfit to mirror the broad palette of the range.' He shrugged. 'He did say how pleased he was I'd kept the hat and jacket on.' He handed the frame to Cally. She stared at Jay, dressed head to toe in black, his arms around Clive who had squeezed into the jumpsuit, diamante encrusted cap glued to his head, leather jacket hanging off his shoulders.

'That makes complete sense now.'

'What does?'

Cally hadn't realised she'd said that last sentence out loud. 'Oh! Just why you like him so much. He's so considerate. Just remind me what time you saw him coming past the café – it helps my prose if I can have a timeframe to hang everything on.'

'It must have been 10.30am. We didn't speak until I got to the event but by way of apology he gave me loads of free *Dollymix* make-up and he let me keep the hat.' He closed his eyes, his eyelashes trembling. 'It was one of the best days of my life.'

'Could I borrow the cap?' asked Cally.

Clive frowned.

'You see, if you'll let me, I want to take a photo of you in it, and then I'm going to speak to Jay after this and I want it to look as though you've just passed it to him. You know what I mean? I'll return it straight away. I promise.'

Clive beamed showing those wonky gnashers again. 'That's so cool. Sure, you can.' He put the cap on and tilted the peak to the left then pouted. Cally captured the image. Then Clive held the cap in his hand and stretched out his arm. Cally took another shot.

'Fabulous.' Cally stood up. 'Right. I'd best go.'

Clive's mouth did a downturn. 'But...but you've asked me hardly anything.'

Cally cleared her throat and lowered herself back into the chair. 'What specifically do you love about Jay?'

Clive gazed up at the ceiling as though the artexed swirls would give him inspiration. 'He's just so talented. His make-up is outstanding and brave – his creations are as though he's wearing himself inside out. Each metamorphosis bares a part of his soul.' Clive's eyes narrowed as he noticed Cally's idle hand and she coughed and started scribbling into her notepad – she'd remembered she needed to buy Rolly some more dog food so she started a shopping list. Clive stood up and went over to the window, threading the hem of the voile curtains through his fingers. 'But yet he's grounded. He said whenever he feels his world is spiralling out of control, he goes back to his roots – back to where he grew up because it reminds him how far he's come in life.'

'That's humbling.'

'Yes, he–' Clive cut short his own speech and held a finger to his lips. 'Listen.' He turned up the volume on his stereo; it was an old-fashioned CD player just like the one Cally had owned when she was a kid.

Cally tilted her head taking in the twanging of an electric guitar and the sound of someone wailing – a high pitched mewling like a cat caught outside in the rain. She tried to make a facial expression to indicate awe but was worried that it was coming across as *woman in pain*.

'You know who this is, right?' asked Clive.

'Er...no.'

He tapped his foot on the carpet and tutted. 'Why, it's JayDoll, of course. Isn't it amazing? It's one of his early songs. You see that's how much of a fan I am – I was there for the music at first – before he got into make-up. I went to a live gig of his at *The Swan* in Kibworth and bought this with my pocket money. You can't get hold of his early stuff anymore – which, if you ask me, is his best. It's so full of...'

Shit? Cally raised an eyebrow.

He clasped his hands together. 'Angst. Genuine angst and torment.' He stared at his fingers. 'Look. I don't normally do this, but if you promise to take care, you can borrow it along with the hat.' He pulled the CD out of the stereo and slipped it back into the cover which he then thrust into her hands. 'He did the artwork himself too,' said Clive, shaking his head with wonder. Cally looked down at the cover. *Bark Like a Lion* was the title and there, beneath her fingertips, was a sketch of a lion's goofy face peeping out of a cartoon shaped dog kennel.

'Er. Thanks.'

'My favourite – promise me you'll listen to it first, is *Crying Inside* – man, it's dark. It's about a person trapped inside the walls of a house, but it's so relatable. I think we all feel trapped by constraints like that sometimes.'

Cally opened her mouth and closed it again, unable to summon an answer. She put it into her bag and noticed a message from Dan on her phone.

Can't find Jay anywhere. He's disappeared. BTW I have more news. I'm waiting for you outside.

Cally cleared her throat. 'Clive. I don't suppose you know where JayDoll is right now do you. I'm supposed to be meeting him to get his side of things but he's not answering.'

Clive clapped his hands together and giggled. 'I do. Yes. I was dying to tell you earlier, but he made me promise not to say, but now I've got to know you better I can't see the harm in it – after all you're doing the interview with both of us. He's gone to Paris for some *me* time.' He made air quotes when he said the words *me time*.

Cally froze. 'You're certain?'

Clive held up his phone and showed her the DM with a picture of Jay holding up a croissant – the Eiffel Tower in the background. 'Ooh! Lucky man,' she said, taking a photo of Clive's screen, her heart sinking.

Cally bid Clive a hasty farewell, giving him the impression that she'd be calling again soon. She ran down the road to her car and saw a familiar figure leaning on the bonnet. Dan. She sped up and as she approached, he turned and threw his arms around her, kissing the side of her head.

With reluctance, she pulled herself out of his grip. 'The good news is I know how Jay tricked the CCTV cameras at the station. The bad news is that Clive – the superfan, says he's gone to Paris – I've just seen a holiday snap.'

Dan gave the front wheel of her car a half-hearted kick. 'Fuck! If he's gone then that's it for Misha. We're no closer to finding her and he's stopped giving us any more information. I'll get onto Interpol.'

Cally's mouth went dry.

Dan ran his fingers through his messy hair. 'It's him Cally. We've got the forensics back on his clothes from his work locker and the mud on his trainers matches the weird stuff we found in the dog's claws. It's laced with some sort of seabird faeces – I mean we couldn't be further from the sea here. We also found drugs stashed in a box in his closet – the same brand of phenazepam which was in Luella's bloodstream.'

Cally stared again at the photo of Jay in Paris. She frowned. 'Wait a minute.' She zoomed in on a tree next to the table at which Jay was sitting. 'Yes! I knew it! The plane trees in the background are in full leaf and if you take a closer look you can see the foliage is covered in hairs and the fruits are tiny.' Cally clapped her hands together. 'But by this time of year the leaves should be smooth and the fruits at least four times the size.' She pulled at Dan's cheek. 'Don't you see, Dan. This is good news, the photo's a fake. Jay's been using Clive all along to spread a false trail and to ensure he has an alibi. Jay told Clive what he was going to wear on the day of the murder and so, of course, Clive mirrored his outfit.'

'But the footage shows Jay getting off the train at 8.30am.'

Cally wagged her finger. 'No. It shows someone who looks like Jay getting off the train. Because the moment Jay got on the train at Market Bowden, he went to find Clive and gave him his baseball cap and jacket to wear. Immediately after that little exchange Jay went into the loos, switched outfits and hopped off at the next stop. I'll bet you anything there's footage of a man in a dark hoody getting into a taxi at Kettering station.'

'So – what does that mean for us?'

'I'm saying, I reckon this means Jay wants us to think he's out of the country when in fact he's here somewhere, close-by, and, as long as he's sticking around, I think it means Misha's still alive.'

Chapter 25
Mikey

I'd watched my *once* beloved sister climb into the cab. I'd overheard her arguing with Henry about his plan to decamp to The Nix which he deemed to be a place of safety. At that particular time, I hadn't realised Cally was a PI, not that it made any difference when I did find out as the first time I met her in The Nix, I didn't give anything away. I had to hand it to her, she was a good liar and attractive too, although I disliked her perfume – it was far too sweet and – well, *vanilla* but, in another life, we could have been friends – maybe even more than friends. I'd got hold of Lucy's phone number – Henry carelessly copied me into a WhatsApp group titled: *I love Dandy Dinmonts* which had her details on it. And, with Di's help, albeit unknowingly, I'd been able to get everything ready. It was easy to access the garden using the side gate adjoining her cottage and over the weeks I'd sneaked in several times to make alterations to Lucy's prison. I also knew Di's movements; she worked at a garden centre every weekday morning and, apart from her, no one else in the family ever set foot in the very end stretch of the garden. The generator for the pond was noisy enough to mask any sound a gagged and bound Lucy would be able to muster. It was perfect.

I used a burner to ring Lucy. At first, she didn't respond but I persisted, and she answered with an angry *who is this?*

'Mikey Jones. Your brother.'

There was silence. I thought she had hung up but then I heard Mabel panting and the distant hum of a radio in the background.

'We need to talk,' I said.

'I…I can't. Mikey – I don't…I've put that part of me behind. It's too hard. It's been too long.'

I couldn't figure out the emotion in her voice. She sounded panicked and cross at the same time, but also resigned; as though she had been expecting me to call. After all, I'd left her enough hints that I was still out there, alive and kicking.

'I don't understand your reluctance, but I must insist we meet. There's something important I need to tell you.'

'No, Mikey. Whatever it is, I don't want to know.' Her voice was thick, and she was making snuffling noises. I imagined her flawless creamy skin probably stayed unmottled when she cried. Her tears didn't soften my resolve and I gave my voice a steely edge.

'You owe me, Lucy. I've never asked for anything from you, but now you're going to hear what I've got to say and then you can carry on pretending I don't exist.'

'It isn't like that.'

'Isn't it?'

She blew her nose. 'Where do you want to meet? I can't be seen with you.'

I gave a reflex snort of laughter at her callousness; it was such a hurtful thing to say and yet her need for anonymity played straight into my hands. 'That suits me too. I don't want to be seen either. Go into Walkers' Common – take the route through to the dog walking field then double back along the farm track which leads down the rear of Millionaires' Row. We'll meet by the hedge just beyond the entrance to Aslan's cage.'

At the mention of his name she gave a sharp intake of breath – was the nostalgia causing her icy heart to melt? I wanted to ask her when she'd last thought about that place or whether she'd simply blanked it from her memory the moment she left me to fend for myself.

The hedge along the back of the track was thicker than I remembered, but that was a good thing as the blackthorn gave it a natural barbed wire effect. I'd spent some time cultivating then concealing a little break in the undergrowth so I could open the gate in the fence without any difficulty.

Lucy arrived, Mabel trotting behind her attached to a pink gingham lead with matching bandana. She wasn't as cute as Dolly, but they'd have been good playmates, I was sure of it. I stooped to chuck her under the chin although she was far too busy trying to scrabble underneath a small gap at the base of the gate, hoovering up rabbit droppings as though they were dog treats. As I stood, I found myself face to face with my sister. She was painfully thin; her skin in need of a good moisturizer and her irises were dull, but she was still beautiful.

She stared at me for a few seconds then wrinkled her brow. '*You!* But you're the make-up guy,' she said. I could smell stale coffee on her breath.

I took a bow, my sleeve becoming hooked on a stray bramble, and it took a few seconds for me to untangle myself. 'That's me.'

She tugged at Mabel's lead; the little dog had managed to get her head through the gap into the Camblys' garden, unaware that her chubby torso wasn't going to follow suit. 'Why didn't you say anything to me when you were on set?'

I tilted my nose upwards a fraction. 'I heard what you said about me to your co-star. If you recall, it wasn't very polite.'

The tips of Lucy's cheeks grew pink, and she gulped.

'That was also after you denied having any siblings.'

'You don't understand.' Her hands were trembling. I had to tone things down – I didn't want to frighten her off.

Before Mabel wedged herself into a position of no return, I gently lifted her out of the way and opened the gate into the garden. It was an Alice in Wonderland moment, and despite her struggle to remain in control of her emotions, I could see a spark of excitement in Lucy's cornflower eyes.

'Aslan died ages ago,' I said, pushing the gate shut behind her. As she took in her surroundings, I locked it and slipped the key into my pocket.

Lucy turned to me. 'How come you have access?'

I tapped the side of my nose. 'I know the owner and I also happen to know that, for the last few years of his life, Aslan was extremely well looked after and very, very loved.'

Lucy smiled and reached down to straighten Mabel's gingham bandana, giving her an affectionate tickle under the chin.

'As you can see, it's a fruit cage now. He'd have loved that, wouldn't he?' It was a clumsy thing to say – I hadn't a clue whether dogs liked fruit and I also had a hazy recollection that peach stones were toxic.

She didn't answer.

I walked towards the cage, beckoning her to join me. She darted a glance over her shoulder at the locked gate then, after a pause, followed.

I unhooked the latch to the entrance, and we went inside, breathing in the jumble of sweet fragrances and the unusual briny and sweet smell of Di's homemade compost. Some of her precious orchids were standing in earthenware pots between the strawberry plants giving the illusion we were in some sort of tropical paradise. Mabel sniffed and licked at an unripe nectarine which had fallen onto the gravel path between the rows of slatted shelves. Lucy pulled her away and shortened her leash, wrapping it around her hand. With her other hand she ran the back of her finger over a fat, red berry which was defying the laws of gravity.

'Mikey.'

'It's Jay now.' I stood opposite her, on the other side of the central aisle.

'Jay. I like that name. But Jay, I don't know what you want me to say.'

I shrugged. 'Maybe sorry would be a good place to start.'

She gave a huff of annoyance. 'I was also a child when we went into care.'

'Me too, but I never stopped thinking about you or wondering where you were.'

Mabel had spotted another fallen berry and lunged towards it, causing Lucy to buckle at the knees. She steadied herself, tapped Mabel on the nose then set the dog between her legs, clamping her in situ with her skinny ankles. 'I was the same. To start with and then...'

'Then?'

'I was ill. *Really* ill. I had to go into hospital, and I had an operation.' She pulled at a jaundiced leaf and rolled it between her thumb and index finger. 'I can't have kids anymore.'

'That's a blow. All the more reason to stay in touch with family. Blood ties.'

She shook her head. 'My adopted parents – they wanted me to let go of my past.'

I waved my hand. 'Just like that.'

'There was so much hurt there and once I began to look forward, I never wanted to go back.'

I tapped my index finger against my chin. 'I wonder if you'd have been so quick to forget your childhood if you hadn't become famous.'

Her eyes narrowed. 'I don't want people knowing about my

childhood. Can you blame me? Surely you don't want your followers hearing about how Mum earnt a living.'

'I don't care about her. What about us, Lucy?'

'Misha. I'm Misha now.'

'Are you telling me you never loved me.'

Her shoulders drooped and her voice grew softer. 'Of course I loved you, but I'm a different person now. So are you. All we have in common is an awful childhood and a terrible mother. I find no comfort in dragging that part of my life out into the open again.'

'And what about Jadis?'

Lucy gave a shiver and set her mouth in a flat line.

'Have you managed to forget about your daughter too?'

Lucy's eyes filled with tears. 'No, but I do know she had parents who loved her. Before...'

My hand shot up, like I was a school kid asking the teacher for permission to speak. 'Wait!' I swallowed. 'Are you telling me you know where she is?'

Lucy frowned. 'Yes. I thought you did too.'

I shook my head, smacking my ear, unable to comprehend what I was hearing.

'She *was* called Louise Ella but everyone called her Luella.' A tear ran down her cheek and sploshed onto the gravel. 'She died on the morning of her wedding day.'

I was stunned at her stupidity and gave out a guffaw of laughter. I shook my head several times and gave her a withering look of pity mixed with condescension. 'Sorry to burst your bubble, sister dear, but Luella wasn't your daughter.'

The tears were falling fast, dropping onto the gravel path like raindrops. She tried to ebb their flow with the back of her hand whilst a trail of snot streamed from her nose.

'What?' She swallowed. 'She's still alive?' The tone of her voice had changed from despair to one of hope.

'No. Your daughter died a long time ago.'

Her jaw sagged open. 'But...but you took her so she could live with Bill.'

'He never showed up, so Jadis died and I had to deal with it on my own.'

'I didn't know.' She pressed her hand against her heart – she was sobbing. I was wrong – her face did go red and blotchy when she cried.

I pointed a finger at her. 'And why didn't you know? Because you buried your head in the sand and let me deal with everything. After you'd recovered you should've come back to find me – find out what happened to Jadis – your daughter. But you were too selfish. No one gave me a fresh start in America.'

'But...' she flapped a hand at me. 'Look at you. You're doing fine now.'

I opened my eyes wide – a look of mock horror on my face. 'Am I? What do you know about me? Do you know how much medication I'm on just to get through the day, dragging your guilt around with me. It became my burden when it should have been yours and Bill's.' I gritted my teeth. 'Not mine.'

I saw her body grow rigid as a slow trickle of realisation started filtering through, changing her expression to one of fear.

'Did you...did you have anything to do with Luella's death?'

She started edging sideways, towards the entrance of the fruit cage. Mabel growled, sensing her anxiety.

I blocked her path. 'I never thought you'd abandon me.'

She cleared her throat. 'Mikey. I mean Jay. I tell you what. Let's meet somewhere else. Somewhere we can sit down and talk properly.' She couldn't keep her eyes off the door, and I held up my hands and took a step away.

She ran. Whilst she reached up to unlatch it, I pulled the syringe filled with a sedative out of my pocket and jabbed it into the soft flesh on the back of her arm. She yelped, then turned, rubbing her arm before thudding to the ground, bringing down a ballerina orchid with her. The cane holding it upright snapped in half, sending a few dancers pirouetting onto the gravel. Meanwhile, Mabel was yapping and nudging her unconscious mistress with her big wet nose. The noise was grating, and I reached hold of her, tying her by her lead to the underside of one of the shelves where she strained and scrabbled around, kicking over a trug of fertilizer and sending clouds of chalky dust into the air.

I crawled under the first set of shelves until I reached the metal handle – an ornate iron wheel which resembled that of an old paddle ship. In Aslan's day, there had been a mechanical system in place which rotated the chains at the press of a button, but that no longer worked, and I had to operate it by my strength alone. I kept twisting the handle until the cage was at ground level. I bound Lucy's hands and feet with the plastic ties I'd already placed inside, ready for her, then I gagged her and dragged her inside the cage, arranging her in a foetal position. I lowered the cage which, thanks to gravity, was a bit easier than I was expecting with her dead weight inside. Then I took a photo, before covering it up with a mat weaved from twigs and leaves. All the time, the generator next to it clanked and whirred.

Mabel had grown quiet and was whimpering, every few seconds little ripples of fear ricocheted across her body. I picked her up and took her back through the gate, once more locking it behind me. My hood up, I hurried along the overgrown track and took a right into the wood which lined the dog walking field. I waited for five minutes, trying to regulate my breathing and, when I was sure no one was about, I let Mabel loose. She bolted as far away from me as she could and, using the trees as cover, I slipped out of one of the unofficial side entrances onto the road and headed back into town to set the rest of my plan into action.

Chapter 26
Cally

CALLY'S STOMACH bubbled with anticipation – it was the calm before the storm. She and Dan had pulled up outside an artisan coffee shop to re-fuel on much needed caffeine and blueberry muffins. Both were tired and aware this snatched moment of time together was going to be brief. Cally had so much stuff whirring around her head, she didn't think she could vocalise any of it, even if she wanted to. Dan's old BMW had a CD player and Cally pulled out Jay's album from her handbag and inserted the disc.

'Shall we listen to some wedding marches for you to waltz down the aisle to?' asked Dan.

Cally shook her head. 'Sorry – this is work related. Superfan Clive said I absolutely had to listen to *Crying in the Walls* – apparently JayDoll's best one.'

Cally hit the 'on' button, and the sound of a twanging guitar followed by a reedy voice filled the air. Dan, whose mouth was full of muffin, wobbled his head from side to side.

'You, know, I actually like it,' he said, crumbs spilling onto his lap. 'It kind of reminds me of a really bad Morrissey. One who's had his balls trapped in a vice.'

Cally snorted and her coffee sprayed across the front of the glove compartment. If it were her car, she'd have been cross, but Dan's footwell was littered with empty sandwich boxes and squashed coke cans so she didn't much care.

Dan stopped at the lights and tilted his face to look at her. 'So, you think bringing Henry back to the park for the appeal will work?'

Cally took a sip of coffee. 'I don't know, but there's a possibility it might prick Jay's conscience. I'm sure he's watching us.'

Dan tapped his fingers on the steering wheel, glancing up at the traffic lights. 'Sick bastard. Getting his kicks from someone else's suffering.' The lights changed and he sped forward, flying past the entrance of Walkers' Common. The vans and TV crews, although still there, had thinned in numbers – off chasing the latest scoop somewhere else.

Dan hit the brakes again as they reached the row of restaurants and boutiques. He knocked on his side window. 'Hey! Look at the dress in that shop over there. I can imagine you'd look stunning in it.' Cally peered across his torso and saw an ivory bodiced, puff-skirted wedding dress which filled a bay window – tissue paper balls in pastel yellow, blue and pink, dangling above it.

She gave a sudden shiver and opened the window, taking in a few gulps of air. The overwhelming sensation of claustrophobia was making her feel nauseous.

'What?' asked Dan. 'It's lovely.' He gave her a quick sideways glance. 'You know, you haven't mentioned the wedding for ages now. You're not having cold feet are you?'

'No. No. I'm super excited about it.' She blurted the words out. Now wasn't the time to tell him she was having Arctic feet about the wedding, but not about marrying him. Her stomach sank. He seemed so enthusiastic about the whole thing; she didn't know how to tell him she couldn't go through with it. She squeezed his thigh. 'I'm just not looking forward to talking to Henry.'

'Yes. It sucks we don't have anything positive about Misha's whereabouts.'

'It's not just that. I can't help thinking about the fact he didn't know about Misha's baby or that she can't have kids. They're pretty big secrets to keep from your husband.'

Dan pressed his lips together. 'I wouldn't overthink it. At the moment, all he wants is for us to find her – the other stuff is all background noise.' He paused. 'I promise I won't keep any secrets from you.'

Cally grunted; aware she was already keeping a massive secret from her fiancé; that she no longer wished to be his bride.

They pulled up outside the apartment block and Henry buzzed them in. When they got to his door, he was standing there, waiting for them. He looked like he hadn't slept for a week and his curly hair was greasy and stuck to the sides of his head. Everything about him looked puffy – as though a packet of ham past its sell by date and about to burst. As she stepped into the flat, she gagged – the air smelt rancid and the poor dog, rather than jumping up to meet her, stayed on her blanket, looking forlorn – eyes following her on stalks.

Dan marched through and opened all the windows. 'Coffee?' he said, more to himself than anyone else. He went into the kitchen, opening and slamming shut cupboard doors.

'Maybe see if you can get some food for Mabel?' called out Cally.

He nodded over his shoulder at Cally and widened his eyes, signalling for her to get on with the update.

'Can you sit down a minute?' said Cally.

'Christ. Have you found her? Is she dead?'

'No and therefore, we're fairly confident, no.'

The coffee machine buzzed into action and a rich burnt hazelnut smell wafted through – a welcome relief from the other stale odours. The wind ruffled the curtains.

'But there haven't been any more photos of her, have there?'

'No, but we know who kidnapped Misha and we've got all our available team out looking for him.'

'Who is it?'

'James Dollander.'

He shook his head. 'James? No, surely you're mistaken.' He shook his head again as though there was water in his ears. His eyes opened wide. 'But why?'

'Did Misha ever go into detail about her past?'

'No. She said her mum died of a drug overdose and she was adopted.'

'So, there's nothing relating to her past life here in the flat? No photo albums or school reports lying around?'

He shook his head. 'I never pushed her for information. I knew it was traumatic for her – I suppose I thought eventually she might tell me about it.'

'She used to live round here, Henry.'

He mouthed -o. 'Probably explains why she wasn't keen to move to this neck of the woods.'

'She also had a younger brother called Mikey who wasn't adopted and stayed in various foster placements.'

'A brother.' He whistled. Dan brought over the coffee and sat down next to Mabel, giving her a handful of kibble before setting a plastic bowl full of it next to her. Mabel started to lick the biscuits and then crunched into them with gusto.

'This brother changed his name to James Dollander.'

Henry screwed up his eyes. 'What? So, James is Misha's brother?'

'Half-brother.'

Henry scratched his head. 'So, he used me to get to her, but all the time we were hanging out they never met and...and why kidnap her, for God's sake?'

'We're not sure of the motive. Although...' Cally bit her lip and looked to Dan who gave a nod. 'Before Misha left for the USA she gave birth to a baby.'

Henry slammed down his coffee causing Mabel to give a low growl. 'What? No.'

'Yes. A little girl and we think that whatever happened during that period of time has led to James feeling he needed to punish all those involved. We believe the father of the child was Bill Cambly who recently committed suicide. It looks as though he was having sex with her – a minor, and when his wife found out, he made a swift exit. Bill's daughter, Luella, was murdered on her wedding day and we believe James was responsible.'

'*Shit! Shit!*' Henry pressed his fingertips against his brow. 'What about the baby?'

'We don't know – there doesn't seem to be any register of her birth anywhere.'

'Poor Misha,' said Henry. 'No wonder she doesn't want children. What a terrible thing to happen.' Cally didn't say about the hysterectomy – it wasn't relevant; that was a private matter for them to discuss.

'So,' said Dan, 'we think James is running again, lying low, but we don't think he wants Misha to die.'

Cally reached out and touched Henry's arm. 'I believe he just wants an apology from her for whatever that ten-year-old boy felt wronged by. I think if you make a television appeal, saying how sorry you are for any hurt he has experienced it might open the channels of communication.'

Dan put an arm around his shoulder. 'But you need a shower first buddy. Come on, let's go and find some appropriate clothes too.' He pushed a dazed-looking Henry out of the room and five minutes later Cally heard the sound of running water. Dan returned with a dog lead around his neck. 'I'll take this one outside for a bit. Give her a run around.' Cally smiled at him – he was such a softie.

Through the French doors, Cally watched her fiancé patrol the garden with Mabel trotting at his heels. She felt a pang of disappointment run down her spine. She sighed – she loved him so much and he'd made it clear that their wedding was an important way for him to show all his family, friends and colleagues that they were a team, but she couldn't go through with it. How was she going to make him see that it didn't matter what other people thought; that all they needed was each other? The overwhelming burden of the case and the panic about her future felt like weights upon her shoulders, pressing her down to the floor. She staggered over to the sofa and closed her eyes. She didn't have time to think about her and Dan – she needed to focus on Misha. What was she missing? She couldn't concentrate with JayDoll's silly song going round and round her head. She glanced at the array of empty wine bottles on the table and saw one was a Chardonnay. *Wait!* She remembered when she bumped into Jay at *The Olive*, he had known she didn't like Chardonnay, but she hadn't told him. She hadn't. So how did he know?

Dan came in and the dog skipped over to her water bowl and took a few laps.

She held a finger to her lips then pulled Dan over to her by his collar then whispered in his ear. 'I think Jay has been bugging the place.' Dan immediately shot his head up and looked all around, pointing for her to take one side of the room. Cally moved one of the dining room chairs up against the shelves situated above the alcove. Gloves on she began to sweep each one and then there it was – a tiny camera sitting between the legs of a small lion statue.

Henry came back into the room, wearing nothing but boxers and rubbing a towel behind his head.

'Is this yours?' asked Cally holding up the lion.

He shook his head. 'No – I've never seen it before.' She pulled off the small camera and handed it to Dan who put it straight into a plastic evidence bag.

'He's been spying on you, Henry.' She looked at Dan then back to Henry. 'Did you move this at all? Maybe if you were cleaning.' Although the thick layer of dust which lay across the shelf pointed that no one had been near the shelf for weeks.

Henry shook his head.

Cally rubbed her temples. 'It's a strange place to put the camera. Why have it angled at an empty wall? Why not at the sofa so he can see you both and also have a view through to the kitchen.' She paused. 'Also, he's known I'm a PI for a while which is weird – you'd have thought it would make him react in some way. Up the ante or at least send Henry another warning to back off.'

Dan shrugged. 'It feels like he's not sure what to do with Misha. Almost as though he wants to be caught.'

Henry was pacing up and down. 'This whole situation is fucking weird! It really doesn't make sense at all. He engineered me buying the flat. He was so insistent it was the right place for me. Surely you wouldn't go to all that bother just to spy on someone – he could have planted the device anywhere.'

'Yes. Why the flat?' Cally froze. 'Those plans. I need to see them. Now.' She ran into the kitchen where the architects' drawings were still open on the end of the island. 'He sold you this flat. His flat. He was grooming you to take it over and change it just as he wanted.'

She paced up and down. 'Why would anyone *do* that?'

Dan peered at the plans, pulling out his reading glasses. 'Tell me, Henry, what specifically did he want to change about the layout.'

Henry walked over and stood side by side, pointing his finger to a line indicating the wall between the dining room and the sitting room.

Dan looked at Cally, shaking his head in confusion. 'It's the place the camera was pointing at.'

The tune was screaming at her. *Crying, crying, crying inside the walls.*

Cally's body went cold and her knees buckled. Dan leapt over to prop her up. 'What is it?' he said, almost lifting her by her shoulders and setting her down on the sofa. 'You've gone really pale.' He went into the kitchen and came back with a large glass of water. Cally was still struggling to find her voice when he set the water in front of her. She downed the whole thing in one and wiped her mouth with the back of her hand. Both men were standing in front of her, staring.

'He wants us to find something in the walls. Something he buried there.'

Dan gasped. 'We need forensics. I'll call them now.'

Cally felt the blood whoosh around her ears – the dizziness had passed. 'Call them, Dan, but we need to make a start. If he's been watching us all this time, it might be too late.'

Dan nodded. 'Henry, do you have a saw?'

Henry went to a cupboard by the front door and brought out a tool kit. Dan rummaged around, seized a drill and fixed a cutting attachment to it. He went over to the wall and made a series of small holes just above the skirting board then set it down and started smashing the weakened plasterboard with a hammer. When there was a hole the size of a tennis ball, Cally turned on her torch and peered inside.

'I think I can see something under the insulation. You need to make the hole bigger.'

Five minutes later Cally, latex gloves on, reached in to pull out a small, lidded box. Her heart was pounding against her rib cage and her tongue was glued to the roof of her mouth.

She set the box down, dusting the layers off the surface. They all stared at it for a few seconds then Dan nodded for her to open it. She picked off the lid and the three of them drew a sharp collective breath of horror.

Wrapped in a pink towel with a pompom nestled next to its head and a note by its feet was the skeleton of a tiny baby.

Chapter 27
Mikey

MY WORK WAS DONE. They'd found her. Misha would have to bear the collective guilt of what happened now; I was a runner, my own lap complete, now passing on the baton. My body flooded with relief, and I felt light; weightless. Jadis, at last, would be given a funeral – there would be a tangible event to mark the fact she'd once lived and breathed. I hoped they would cremate her as she'd already spent so long alone and in the dark; they could scatter her ashes where there were lots of trees and flowers. Somewhere like Walkers' Common – the place where Lucy, despite what she now said, and I had found our own happiness.

The angry painted sign telling the general public to keep out of *Hazleton Towers* was covered with swear words and poorly drawn phalluses. Rolls of barbed wire and meshed fencing surrounded the complex but now there were plenty of places where the metal barriers had been peeled away. In fact, I'd made one of the entrances myself when I'd felt the need to reconnect with my childhood. Walking across the concrete paths, watching out for the broken glass, reminded me of the time, nineteen years ago, I stole into the Cambly Homes block of flats – carrying Jadis over the rubble, past the parked diggers and staring up in the night sky at the hollow buildings with windows like jack o'lantern teeth.

I crossed the once bald patch of turf outside the entrance to our block; the grass was now almost at waist height; jaundiced and whiskery – the odd poppy illuminating the blandness.

The council were destroying my home. The whole thing was going to be demolished and it felt right that when it was reduced to a shattered pile of concrete, my corpse would be hidden within. My whole body quivered with excitement – I'd never felt so alive which was the ultimate irony as I was about to die. My stomach turned somersaults and my tongue felt heavy in my mouth. Of course, I was terrified – I didn't know whether I believed in an afterlife, and I assumed that if there was such a thing as heaven, I certainly wasn't going to be sitting on a golden throne – I'd be cast straight into the pit of fire. But I was excited, and it was the satisfaction of completion which was filling my body with adrenalin. I was about to finish what I'd started. Misha wouldn't die – I'd left it up to fate to decide her destiny and I was glad of the outcome because her punishment was to be haunted forever by Jadis. And me. Although, ultimately it didn't matter what happened to Misha because she wasn't Lucy – my sister had died the moment we'd left this block of flats and so had I – so had Mikey.

I stepped over puddles of tarry water into the entrance area and stood in front of the lifts with the stairwell off to my right. The entrance doors, now off their hinges, meant the air should have smelt better, but the aroma of stale piss lingered and now had top notes of decay instead of bleach. I couldn't help but grin; the status of the lift which had the sign saying 'out of order' was exactly the same, along with the graffiti scrawled over every surface available. Some things never changed.

I was home. I'd been here before when I needed space to think, but this felt different. Wasn't that what salmon did? Returned to their place of birth to die. I remembered reading about it and thinking how weird it was, but now it made sense. I belonged here – no matter the journey I'd made, I needed to come home.

As I approached the stairwell, I heard the patter of running feet and from out of the shadows emerged a hooded figure. The estate had been taken over by dealers, prostitutes, squatters and junkies although, once again, arguably this sordid mix of residents hadn't changed much over the years.

'What you want?' hissed a man's voice and I caught the glint of silver in his hand.

I took a step closer and stared into the gaunt, acne ridden face. 'I want you to fuck off,' I said, in my poshest King's English.

There were steps behind me and the skin on the back of my neck prickled. I was surrounded.

The man snarled, showing his bleached teeth. 'No one speaks to me like that and lives.'

Without thinking, I pulled out my gun and pointed it at Acne-face. 'That so?'

My heart was thumping in my chest – if they found out it was a fake I'd be killed there and then or at least given such a pasting I'd be hospitalised and then the police would come, and my plan would be ruined. I could feel sweat pool at the base of my spine and the bubbles in my stomach started sinking. This wasn't supposed to be how it ended.

Acne-face's mouth twitched as though he was going to try his luck, but he must have had second thoughts because, all of a sudden, he spun around and bolted straight out of the building – his fellow gang members following suit; spotless high-top trainers gleaming in the half-light. When they were clear and undercover of the neighbouring block, one of them, not Acne-face, shouted that they would be waiting for me.

I wanted to reply that they could wait for me all they liked as I wasn't ever coming out again, but I kept quiet and took my time, climbing the worn stone stairs to the ninth floor. I crawled on my hands and knees along the corridor to the flat so they wouldn't be able to see where I was heading. The door to Number 439 was no longer there so I went straight inside and found myself in the living room where Lucy and I had spent most of our childhood. The first time I came back I was struck by how much smaller it was than the picture of it in my head, but it was just as shadowy. It was completely stripped of furniture – even the kitchen cupboards had been removed leaving a sketchy imprint of where they'd been. I closed my eyes and I could almost taste the jam upon my tongue. I went over to the window and looked out at the familiar view of suburban Leicestershire. I gripped the windowsill as the thought hit me – how I'd always had to push a chair or upturned box of my clothes up against the wall to see out. I turned and leant against the ledge, and, as I tilted my head upwards, I smiled. It was still there – the stain shaped like a hippo emerging from a swamp.

I took my bag from over my shoulder and sat down, cross-legged on the floor.

I undid the cord and pulled out the small vial of ground up phenazepam and the bottle of vodka. Max always said my pills would be the death of me and he was right. I wasn't sure how long it would take to slip into unconsciousness. Luella's demise had been quick but I, unfortunately, didn't have the added surety of drowning. I closed my eyes and recalled how it happened. She'd laid back in the bathtub, sipping her champagne, her burner phone safe in my pocket, and I'd dabbed away at her face, grinding the drugs into her pores with my brush. I pictured her slipping under the water, waiting until the bubbles from her nostrils ceased to rise to the surface – that's when I had a little quiver of panic as it struck me that no one bathes in their bikini. It had been surprisingly difficult to remove her two-piece and I threw it into the sink as though it was a dirty dishcloth. As I manhandled her naked body back into place, her glazed eyes staring up at me, it worried me how little remorse I felt, but she was the third death I was responsible for – add Bill's into the mix and that made four. Did that make me a serial killer?

I heard another commotion – the sound of broken glass and more shouting. My heart pounded against my ribcage. I worried I wouldn't be dead before any of the gang got high and with added chemical-based bravado decided to come and find me. Not that they would go running to the police or call for an ambulance to resuscitate me. Instead they'd be pissed off to discover I had no wallet or valuables on me, although, hopefully Acne-face would lose his status within the gang when they realised my gun was a fake.

I tipped the rest of the contents of my bag onto the floor; a book and a photo. I picked up the snapshot of Dolly and gave her beautiful face a kiss. Saying goodbye to her had been the hardest thing I'd had to do in a long while. I'd given her back to the breeder telling her I was terminally ill, a fact closer to the truth than a lie. The poor woman was terribly upset on my behalf and made it her business to consult with me on who I would like to become her new owner – something which I found very cathartic. Now Dolly was with a couple who live near the sea on the Dorset coast and who have two children – a teenage girl and a young boy. She's got a great life ahead of her.

I opened the pill bottle and tipped the contents onto my tongue then washed the powder down with the vodka. It was done.

The other thing in my bag...*The Lion the Witch and the Wardrobe*. I opened the worn cover and stared at the first page.

Chapter 28
Cally

Cally stared at the note resting on the baby's tiny feet; the writing was childish and had been done with a green felt-tipped pen which had faded over the years. Dan put one arm around her shoulders and handed her a tissue with the other. She hadn't realised she was crying.

You are my daddy. Please look after me. My name is Jadis Jones. When I'm older please take me for a walk around the park to see Aslan – it is Mummy's best thing to do.

On top of Jadis' body which had been swaddled in a pink towel, was a multi-coloured woollen pompom. Someone had loved this baby.

There was a loud buzz from the intercom and within minutes forensics had burst through the door along with a couple of Dan's team. Cally put her arm around Henry and ushered him into the kitchen. Henry went straight over to the sink and turned on the tap, splashing water over his face. He dried his skin with a dirty tea towel then picked up Mabel and cradling her, sat down at the island, his knee unable to stop jiggling up and down. An overhead spotlight shone down onto his crown, turning his skin almost translucent and lighting up the film of sweat now covering his face. Cally handed Henry one of the mugs of coffee Dan had made earlier – it was still warm.

'Fucking hell,' said Dan, coming into the room and he put both hands on the island and pushed against it. 'The kid buried the baby in the wall.'

Cally shook her head and moved along the line of cupboards, opening and closing them until she found a jar of sugar. 'It was an accident. You wouldn't ask someone to look after a baby and suggest they take her for a walk in the park if you were going to kill them. You'd say sorry.' She took a deep breath. 'I think Jay tried to solve a situation which had backfired. He caused the baby's death, but it wasn't on purpose.'

Dan opened a drawer and handed her a spoon. 'It explains the build-up of grief and resentment.'

'Yes.' Her mind was spinning. She put several spoonfuls of sugar into Henry's mug and stirred. Jay had a real obsession for lions – he'd even donated a new enclosure which he'd named in memory of Jadis. Had this interest stemmed from when he was a young boy and used to walk in the park to feed a neglected dog which looked to him like a lion? It was one of the first things he'd told her about himself. For some strange reason, she had a very clear picture of it in her head. She placed the mug in front of Henry. 'Drink it up.'

Dan leant against the fridge and fiddled with the magnet holding up an empty shopping list. 'What is it? You've got that look on your face which means you're onto something.'

'Aslan,' she murmured. She turned to look at him. 'That's the name of a famous lion isn't it and once when I was talking to Jay he mentioned a lion he used to visit in the park, but it wasn't really a lion – it was a dog and for some reason a vivid picture of it keeps bursting into my head.'

'I don't understand.'

She closed her eyes and tapped her temple. Then she started. 'That's because I *have* seen a photo of it. The dog was Di's dog – Tommy, but it used to belong to Bill Cambly.' She grabbed Dan's arm. 'We need to go. Right now. I think I know where she is.'

Henry leapt to his feet, knocking over his coffee and almost dropping Mabel. 'I'm coming with you.' Brown liquid pooled across the granite surface and started trickling onto the floor.

'No mate,' said Dan, laying a hand on his shoulder. 'This is a matter for the police, and I can't have you in there contaminating the scene. Do you understand?'

Henry tore a fistful of kitchen towel from a roll by the sink and started dabbing hard at the puddle of coffee. He shook his head and pursed his lips. 'No way. I'm coming. I'll wait outside if I have to.' He dropped the ball of soggy paper onto the floor and his face crumpled.

Cally went over and took his hands in hers. 'Look Henry, I could be wrong. I hope I'm not, but I could be, so I think it's best if you wait here. You're my client and I'll be there acting on your behalf and afterwards I'll be able to relay everything back to you immediately.' She squeezed Henry's palms. 'Jay might already have let her go and you need to be here in case of that. You need to be here for her. Someone from Dan's team is coming in right now to talk to you and they'll stay here with you until we've checked it out.'

He stared at her, his eyes full of tears. 'You'll call me straight away. Good or bad?'

'Good or bad. I promise,' said Cally.

They sprinted to Dan's car, and he turned on the blue light and they went speeding to Val's house. Cally loved how the traffic disintegrated around them like a knife through butter. As a PI her work was always under the radar, so she liked it when some of Dan's official status rubbed off on her.

'I've already called for back-up and paramedics to meet us

there,' said Dan, his fingers gripping around the steering wheel. 'Do you have anything else to go on apart from Jay's throwaway comment and a photo?'

'Yes. That strange soil on Jay's trainers and Mabel's claws. I think it's from the fertilizer Di makes for her orchids – she sends off for powdered guano–'

'What?' He gave her a sideways glance.

'She uses puffin poo sent to her from a remote Scottish island.'

They arrived at the house, having beaten the squad car and the ambulance. As Dan was still parking, Cally was already out of the vehicle, through the gate and hammering on Di's stable door. She opened it, took one look at Cally's face and her jaw dropped open. 'What is it? Has something happened to Val?'

'We need to get into the garden.' She could hear Dan behind her, his breathing heavy.

Di pointed to the side gate. 'It's not locked. What's going on? Is Val okay?'

Cally had no time for answers and went tearing over the lawn towards the hedge at the far end with the gated archway. She hurtled through the gap, sidestepping the rectangular pond, and stopping in front of the fruit cage. Wasps and bees buzzed around her head. She turned to Di who had followed.

'Di. Is this where you used to keep Tommy?' she could barely get the words out of her mouth.

Di frowned. 'No. He lived with me.'

'Yes, but you said he was a guard dog, treated badly by Bill and ignored by Val. Is this where Bill used to keep him?'

'Oh, I see. Yes, but I dismantled his kennel ages ago and turned the space into a fruit cage.'

Dan was beside her at the door to the cage and they went in. Cally's heart sank. There was nothing there apart from an abundance of plants. Cally dropped to her hands and knees and crawled along the gravel path; she could feel the sticky wetness of the fallen berries sinking into her trousers. The generator was whirring and clunking, getting into her thoughts and frazzling her nerves. Her eye caught a large wheel under one of the shelves. She looked up at Dan and Di, who were staring at her. Di had a look of bemusement on her face, but Dan's was sombre – he clearly thought she'd made a mistake – one which he was going to be made to look a fool over.

'There's a wheel under here. What's it for?'

Di frowned then her expression softened. 'Oh – that. Well, when they bothered to clean out Tommy's pen they used to put him in a cage to stop him from attacking them – it was so cruel. He wouldn't have hurt a fly.'

'Cally where've you gone?' asked Dan. Cally was already at the far wall, upturning the surrounding shelves.

'My orchids,' shrieked Di as the colourful pots started to tumble. She darted around picking them up and placing them on the ground out of Cally's way.

The area cleared, Cally started to turn the wheel. 'Bloody hell, this is heavy.'

In the next second Dan's hands were on top of hers and they rotated it together.

Up to the surface came the crate – a lid coated with gravel and weeds fell off and Cally peered inside. There, bound and gagged, with her eyes closed was Misha Carlton.

'Oh my God! Di go to the drive and tell the paramedics where we are.'

'What is it?' asked Di. 'What have you found?'

'It's Misha Carlton. We've found her. Go! Go!'

Dan reached in to touch Misha's neck and her eyelashes flickered. 'There's a faint pulse,' he said. Cally sat down on the gravel and put her head between her knees, taking in deep breaths through her nose.

A few minutes later Misha was on a stretcher being carried to the ambulance. Cally phoned Henry to tell him the news and that she would fill him in on everything when they were at the hospital.

As Cally and Dan went back to the car, her phone rang. She glanced at the screen – the number wasn't in her contacts.

'Hello?'

There was a pause. 'Hello Cally. It's Clive.' His voice sounded subdued.

'Hello, Clive. Is everything okay?'

He gulped.

'You phoned to tell me something?'

'I lied to you.'

Cally's mind started whirring. 'Oh. Well. Hey! It's great that you're coming clean. That's a brave thing to do.'

He gave out a big puff of breath which crackled through the receiver. 'Mum said if I didn't tell you then she would.'

'Right.' Cally coughed. 'So...'

'JayDoll told me to tell anyone who asked, that he was in Paris and to show them the photo he sent me a couple of months ago.'

'I know,' said Cally.

'Oh?' Clive sounded annoyed.

'Yes – the foliage on the trees wasn't right for the season. But never mind that. Do you have any idea where he is right now?'

'Sorry. I really don't know where he is.' He paused.

'Clive? What is it? We really need to find him.'

Dan drew a flattened hand across his throat.

'His life – it's in danger.'

'Well, before, when he's gone under the radar, it's because he's gone back to *Hazleton Towers*, where he grew up. You know those flats that are going to be demolished next month. He goes there sometimes to think and have time out – he calls it exorcising the demons.'

Chapter 29
Mikey

RIGHT BEFORE MY eyes the words jumble, spin and then they shuffle across and slip right off the edge of the book. I look for them, but I am too slow and they slide between the floorboards. I claw at them with my fingers, but it is too late – they have vanished. I turn back to the empty page, and the rectangle turns from cream to black and I am looking into a hole filled with dark water, but suddenly, from the deep, a picture floats to the surface. The wavy image steadies itself and I see myself as a young boy. I'm inside the chemist behind the back of the estate. It's the one which stays open until late and the entire shop is lit up with neon tube lights running across the grey ceiling tiles and their harsh glare bounces off the huge windows casting white rectangles onto the pavement. There are a couple of orange plastic chairs backed against the glass and an old man in a beige anorak and flat cap sits in one, two gnarly hands holding onto his stick, his wrinkled forehead presses against the curve of the handle. As I wonder what medicine he's waiting for, he coughs and his whole body shakes with the effort. Afterwards he takes a hanky and dabs it against his shiny wet lips.

I'm wandering up and down the aisles, swinging a wire-meshed basket in one hand; it contains a purple box of sanitary towels for super-heavy flow. My fingertips run along the shelves, picking items up to look at them before setting them back down again. My shoulders are pushed back, and I have an earnest expression on my face. I'm doing important business. I'm thin, my cheeks are gaunt, and it makes my dark eyes seem huge – I look like an alien from outer space; the Roswell one. My legs are like a couple of denim matchsticks and my charcoal hair is wild and unkempt. I kneel on the floor of the well-being section, holding up white tubes of vitamins and squinting at the labels as I decide which will work best to get Lucy pink-cheeked and bursting with energy.

It is two days after my tenth birthday and one day after Jadis' birth.

I go out of sight and then re-appear. The security guard is watching me, hovering at the end of each aisle I walk down. He thinks I'm going to try and shove something inside my coat and do a runner. I smile at him, but he doesn't smile back. I'm walking up the section with all the baby things; my brown eyes are wide with curiosity and something else – the way I linger over each item makes my heart ache. I am sad – I can see my eyes are shining with tears. I pick up a fat-bottomed baby's bottle and stare at it then trail my fingers along the huge wall of nappies. I touch the tins of powdered milk. After a while, I shake my head then go to the till and pay for things with cash from my wallet, hard-earned wages from my weekly paper round. I check the receipt then put the things into my backpack and hoist it onto my scrawny shoulders. The old man has another coughing fit and, before I leave, I offer him a Polo mint from my pocket which he takes, giving me a gummy smile in return. I feel very grown up, like Mrs Slobber-down-yuck only my mints are way nicer than hers.

The automatic doors open, and I shiver as I step outside. The air is biting and I'm about to throw the receipt into the rubbish bin, but instead I roll it up and suck the paper tube, blowing out a cloud of breath as though I'm puffing on a cigarette. My coat is thin and after a few seconds I stop pretending to smoke, throw the paper to the ground and tuck my hands into the folds of material to keep them warm.

Now what? I've stopped and am staring at something. The full moon is low in the sky; it is fat and glows orange; it is what Lucy says is called a blood moon, and though it looks marmalade, it gives everything it shines on a snowy tinge. I am squinting into the distance – staring across the industrial estate towards the bridge. I have a strange angry expression on my face and my nose is turned upwards, as though I've seen something I don't like the look of. I should turn left to cross the road then go under the arch towards our flat, but, instead, I'm turning right. I pull my hood down over my ears, scurry over to the pavement on the other side and move down the zig-zag slope towards the industrial estate with its concrete sheds and metal roofs. My face is set; determined. There are dozens of leaflets blowing across the paving slabs, offering to exchange cash for gold, and a black bag of rubbish sits amongst them; its bottom has torn open spilling plastic cups and squished teabags into my path.

What am I doing?

I march down the slope, heading towards a chip van. Its rectangular window is like a light-house beacon, warning me to stay away from danger, but I keep going. Inside the van, the white-coated ladies with their netted hair tucked into caps, are wrapping cod and chips in paper and handing them out of the window like Santa handing out gifts to good children. But I don't stop. I don't wave hello or stop to speak to the women, not even to try to charm a bag of hot scraps from them.

The businesses on the estate appear to be closed – their metal shutters are padlocked for the night, but with a certain signal or special knock a side entrance will fly open to let a shadowy figure in. There's plenty of trading here to be done under cover of darkness where there are no cameras to be seen and cars cruise in and out; their headlights switched off. The air is filled with the stink of skank which is so powerful it is making my nose twitch and my eyes stream with tears.

I'm moving away from the streetlights into the shadows. As I approach this area, women, like zombies of the apocalypse, come out of the darkness. They are dressed as though they are teenage girls going off to a nightclub, but a closer look at their haggard faces shows they are much older than that. I wince at all the flesh on display. They whistle and call out to me, but I lift the neck of my jumper over my chin and pull my hood down even further. I press myself into the wire fence and follow its curve towards the tunnel which loops back towards the slip road and onto the busy bypass.

There is a woman, propped against the slimy walls of the tunnel, holding a large can of Special Brew in one hand. She is wearing a short, faux-leather skirt and her pale legs give off a white glare – they are thin and streaked with bulging blue veins. Her leopard print handbag dangles from her elbow; it is cheap and stained and there is a small pink pom pom tied onto the zip. There is a body lying next to her scuffed stilettoes; the figure is flat on its back using a large piece of cardboard as a mattress. It could be a man or a woman – their eyes are shut and their mouth gapes open.

Special Brew woman calls out to me. Asks me if I want to fuck her. I move closer, so close her face is a few centimetres away from mine. Her glassy eyes are rolling around in her head and there is spittle trickling down the side of her mouth. She stinks of piss, fags and vomit all rolled into one. My nose wrinkles in disgust. The revolting creature reels off a long list of things she'll let me do to her then clutches at her top and pulls it down, forcing me to stare at her emaciated breasts and hollow ribcage. She asks if I like what I see, runs a tongue across her chapped lips then leers, showing me a mouthful of rotting teeth. She says she offers the best rates of any slag in this patch and asks me again if I like what I see.

I tell her in a very loud voice that I do not like what I see. I do not like it AT ALL.

She grabs hold of my hand and presses it between her legs. I feel the bile rise up my throat. My skin feels tight and itchy. I'm going to throw up. I try to shake myself free of her clammy body, but she is clawing at me with sharp nails, her laughter rings in my ears. You'll not get any cheaper than me, she says again.

In the distance I see two circular lights.

She's trying to force me down onto the cardboard. The figure on the ground groans then rolls over so their spine is facing me.

The lights are moving closer.

Is this my first time, she asks. I'll take care of you.

The sound of an engine gets louder.

Fuck off, I say, and she cackles and says I already owe her for touching her pussy.

The edge of the tunnel is suddenly awash with light which spreads closer, like someone has spilled a pot of white paint across the bricks.

The woman's grotesque face is lit up as though she is on a stage about to perform and, in that exact moment, I have never hated anyone so much in my entire ten-year-old life. My body quivers with rage. Rage for this pathetic, worthless woman who had the precious gift of motherhood and threw it all away. I push her into the road as hard as I can then run.

I hear a screech of brakes then a loud thud followed by several softer ones, but I don't look back. I run into the darkness, heading towards one of the many back entrances to the pastureland on

Walkers' Common. I am skipping over brambles, and twigs snap beneath my feet as sharp foliage digs into my trainers which are growing wetter by the second. As a large thorny stem tears at my cheek, I start to regret my decision to come here but then the kind moon comes out from behind a cloud and bathes the wood in its silvery glow. Now I see the stubby thicket ahead and, as I trot along the path, little tufted tails dive out of sight. I smell earth and damp ferns and, though the gorse scratches my legs, I don't care. I feel safe.

No one is following me, but I don't slow down. Something else is spurring me on: Aslan. I have to see him – he will make things okay – he always does. I turn right out of the meadow and the ground is uneven and I am stumbling, but I carry on. I slip and slide over the cattle grid, and soon I am tearing through the blackthorn arches which run alongside the fence at the back of Millionaires' Row. I hear the fabric on my coat rip and, as I move, specks of fluff catch on the thorns, dangling there like tiny lambs' tails.

I stand in front of Aslan's fence and peer through the hole in the wood. It takes a few seconds for me to spot him. He is in his inner sanctum; a kennel made of corrugated iron, set in the far corner of the cage. He is lying on a blanket and his feet are twitching. He is having a dream and I wonder what he is chasing and if he will catch it. I pat my pockets and find a stray dog biscuit wedged into the corner of one of them; the knuckle of the bone stuck in the beginnings of a hole. I tug out the biscuit, one of his favourites, and poke it through the hole in the fence, wiggling it between my thumb and index finger. I call his name and he lifts his head and stares at me; his eyes shining like two ghostly green pools of light in the gloom. He lets out a huge puff of breath and shakes his head making spittle fly in every direction, then turns his body away from me so I cannot see him. He is ashamed of me. My heart sinks down to my stomach and I begin to cry.

Suddenly there is a burst of golden light piercing my eyes, and

I am lifted to my feet by an angel. No, not an angel, she must be a creature from a mythical realm with her red, pixie hair but she's familiar; she smells of birthday cakes, and she's patting my face and calling out to me, slapping me, telling me I'm going to be fine, saying it over and over again.

COMING SOON

Book 2 In The Welland Valley Murders:

The Serpents Noose

Coming Spring 2025

Epilogue

CALLY KNEW it was going to be a strange day when the mist refused to vanish and lurked on the ground, swirling around her feet like a fallen cloud. The sky had started off the day battleship-grey and stayed the same sombre colour, with the sun keeping itself small and remote, as though pretending to be the moon. The grass in the graveyard was drenched from an early rain shower and the soggy gravelled path leading up to the church had stained the soles of Cally's boots with an orangey-brown paste which, by a strange coincidence, matched the colour of her jumper.

St. Cuthbert's Church with its dainty bell tower and cobbled walls, though the other side of town from where Cally and Dan lived, was where Dan insisted they must get married. Dan had told her the wisteria was the prettiest shade of mauve he'd ever seen, and he wanted to have photos of them, standing in front of it; she in her designer bridal gown and he in his morning coat with *jaunty* cravat. Dan didn't mind when the vicar refused to marry them because he was a divorcee, and when the pompous man said he would allow them to have a church blessing Dan jumped at the chance because he wanted Cally to have a 'proper' wedding – experience the whole *shebang*. In fact, Dan said the words in the service didn't really matter and likened it to having Christmas Dinner without the Brussels Sprouts which people thought they needed to serve up, when actually no one cared whether they were there or not. Dan wasn't a religious man.

Now, sombre organ music reverberating inside her chest, Cally sat in St. Cuthbert's breathing in the smell of stale incense, musty books and Dan's pine-scented aftershave which today had a top note of industrial cleaner about it. She stared at the two white coffins side by side in front of the brass altar: one tiny and one big. There were matching wreaths of forget-me-nots lying on their lids, but they hadn't sized the garlands to match the coffins and the one on top of the child's casket looked like it was about to topple. All around she could hear sobbing, sniffing and people blowing their noses, and it irritated her; she wanted to stand up and ask them why they were crying. No one, apart from Misha had really known either of them – Clive with his pinched face and puffy eyes, dressed head-to-toe in a black robe, had never had a glimpse of the real Jay; he'd worshipped a fake. Dan said not even Jay's best friend Max had known anything about Jay's personal life and all the demons he'd carried about with him since childhood. It all seemed a bit hypocritical and made the toast and marmite in her stomach sit uneasily.

A faint burst of sunshine lit up the stained-glass window which depicted a scene of someone, presumably St. Cuthbert, on his knees, whilst a hooded figure stood behind him with an axe poised then, after a few seconds, the light vanished and made the church seem even darker than before. When the vicar asked everyone to stand for the first hymn, she had to drag herself to her feet as though the gloom had chained itself to her ankles. Dan's bass voice boomed beside her, but her tongue felt heavy in her mouth, and she couldn't muster a single note as the image of Jay, lying half-conscious in the squalid flat sprung into her mind; the look of horror on his face as he realised she was rescuing him. Her stomach roiled and then a stark thought struck her: she knew when she walked down the aisle on her wedding day, despite Dan's enthusiastic smiles and him mouthing that she looked beautiful and that he loved her, it was Jay's distraught face she would see burned into the forefront of her mind.

The singing stopped and there was loud shuffling and creaking as everyone sat down in their pews then the vicar started droning on about how death was all part of a plan which we shouldn't begin to try and understand. It wasn't our place. Cally wanted to put her hand in the air and tell him it seemed a bit of a cop out and she was sure everyone there wanted to understand and could he explore the matter further. Dan's knee jiggled up and down and she stared at the gold embossed writing on the front of the hymn book, the knot of anger growing tighter in her chest. What authority did this sanctimonious middle-aged man standing in the pulpit have which meant he could tell her lovely fiancé that, because his marriage to Belinda had gone wrong, he couldn't have a second go at marital bliss with her?

Row by row the congregation began to file out of the church and Dan gently took her hand and squeezed it. They walked along the path towards the empty grave and stood at the back of the huddle, unable to hear what the vicar was saying as his voice was swept away by the breeze. When they lowered the coffins into the ground, Cally was glad Dan had his arm around her. She felt his body tremble and she rested her head on his shoulder, thinking about the pair's sad, short lives. They laid their wreath next to the wooden cross which said Mikey and Jadis Jones on it then stood back from the immediate family and friends. They had intended to slip away, but Henry spotted them and once Aunty Cleo, who in real life was even smaller than Cally, had been entrusted with propping up Misha, he came running over. Cally was surprised to see Val in the crowd – was it normal to come to the funeral of your daughter's murderer?

Henry who was wearing a tweed overcoat and highly polished brogues smiled at them. His cheeks were pink from the cool September breeze and his face was thinner, but the glint was back in his eyes. 'Thank you for coming.' He shook their hands.

'I'm so sorry,' said Cally. 'What a terrible day for you both. How's Misha coping?'

Henry pressed his lips together. 'They made their peace.' He put his hands in his pockets. 'You know, she might not have said it, but she's really grateful to you, Cally, for finding him.' Cally nodded.

'Hmm,' said Dan. 'I don't think Jay was so happy about it.'

'Am I right in thinking that as soon as Misha was back on her feet in the ward, she went to see him?' asked Cally.

'Yes. But by that time, his liver had packed up and he only had a few hours left, but he was able to forgive her and she him. That's why Misha insisted they be buried together. He loved both those little girls so much and Jadis' death was never his fault. Just a horrible chain of incidents he had no control over.'

Dan clicked his tongue and Cally could feel his body stiffen. 'He didn't have to kill or kidnap though.' He nodded his head towards Val whose face was hidden by a net veil trailing down from a black pillar box hat. 'She didn't get justice for Luella.' He paused. 'Or Bill, for that matter.'

Cally interlaced her fingers with Dan's.

'Val and Misha have spoken at length,' said Henry. 'To say it's complicated is a total understatement. She's here, today, for Jadis; her step-daughter, and to support Misha. They've a lot to understand and process about what happened when Misha was working for Bill. Val's experiencing a lot of guilt about not realising the extent of Bill's abuse of Misha.' He shrugged. 'I guess you could say that it's a work in progress.'

Dan gave another loud tut and shook his head.

Cally gave Dan's fingers a hard squeeze. 'He was just a little boy who thought he'd dealt with the situation. How was he to know Bill never made it to the flat so Jadis was left alone for the entire weekend? When he realised and went back it was too late, so he hid her in the building site and no one apart from him ever knew about it. Just think how much that dreadful secret must have damaged him and eaten away at his conscience over the years. Without someone to confide in, or an adult to help him process what happened, it was always going to affect how he turned out.'

Dan broke free of her grip and folded his arms across his chest. 'But then he decided to worm his way into the family via Di and coldly, and calculatingly, set up a dog cage as a prison for his own sister. And he killed not only Luella, who was a completely innocent victim in all this, but Bill who did deserve to be punished, but not by his own hand.'

Cally could feel the anger building up inside her. She turned to face him. 'I'm not excusing his actions one bit, Dan, but when Misha refused to acknowledge Jay, something within him broke. He always thought they'd be reunited and could go back to playing happy families – it would have made what happened to Jadis less painful for him. When Misha wanted him cut out of her life he couldn't cope, hence why he channelled it into the need for revenge. He couldn't think of an alternative way to deal with what he was feeling. He never grew up emotionally because he didn't know how.'

'Yes,' said Henry, his voice almost a whisper.

Cally stopped and turned – colour flooded her cheeks; she'd forgotten she was at a funeral and there were other people who were still suffering and would forever be suffering because of the events which had recently unfurled. She hung her head. 'I'm so sorry. I shouldn't have said any of that. It was totally inappropriate and unprofessional.'

Henry sighed. 'I agree with you Cally. I think Misha's really struggling with what her brother went through and how her rejection of him played such a huge part in what he went on to do.'

Dan coughed and put his hands in his pockets. 'What about Misha? Will she be okay?'

Henry shrugged. 'She's a strong person.' He tilted his head on one side. 'I think so...eventually. We're together and she's beginning to deal with her past so...'

'Once again, our sincere apologies,' said Cally. She turned to go, and Henry reached out and pulled her back into a hug. The velvet collar of his overcoat smelt of apples. 'Thank you, Cally.'

Despite Henry imploring them to join him, Dan and Cally decided it didn't feel right to attend the wake and, as it wasn't raining, they pulled back the roof of the car and headed for home. It was the time of year Cally adored when the leaves were turning golden and the hedgerows were full of berries and she gulped in the fresh air, trying to get the cloying smell of the church out of her nostrils. She leant forwards to shut the glove compartment, accidentally turning the cd player on and Jay's terrible song started blaring out of the speakers. She hit the off button, pulled out the CD and threw it into the heap of other debris in the back of the car.

She gave out a yell then turned to Dan whose eyes were wide with alarm. 'Tell me something good. Anything.'

Dan pressed his lips together for a few seconds then cocked his head to one side and winked. 'Well, funnily enough, I do have something very amusing to tell you. You see, our friend, Bulag, has been having a bit of a purge of conscience and is singing like the proverbial canary.'

Cally clapped her hands together. 'Oh, that's exciting! And why's he suddenly decided to spill all?'

Dan grinned. 'Well, it just so happens that in amongst Bulag's blackmail dvds we found lots of them which film him having it off.'

'Ewwwwww,' Cally covered her face with her hands. 'What, you mean, sex tapes?'

'Yes, but there's more to it than that. The very lucky woman who features in most of them is the wife of one of The Cobra's most senior players and I just happened to mention to Bulag that I was thinking about passing it onto his boss.'

Cally snorted. 'You didn't?'

'Yes, I did, and now Bulag's telling us everything, everything we need to know to make a few more arrests.'

'Every cloud...and all that.'

Dan threw back his head and laughed. 'There's more.'

Cally's eyes widened.

'The thing is – Bulag's into role play and dressing up.'

Cally put her fingers in her ears. 'La. La. La. No. No. Don't tell me.'

'Think Tarzan,' shouted Dan. 'Think jungle and very, very small leopard-skin pants.'

Cally made a gagging sound and looked at Dan whose face had turned serious. 'What is it?' she asked.

Dan reached out and grabbed her hand, keeping his gaze fixed on the road ahead. 'You're still going to marry me, aren't you? I mean, I feel recently you might have been having second thoughts.'

She squeezed his arm. 'It's true. I have been having second thoughts but not about you, you daft thing.'

'What then?'

'Working in the wedding industry has kind of done it for me – it's lost its magic and what with Luella's death, it just doesn't feel right. And, as for that vicar...' She crossed her eyes. 'He belongs in the Middle Ages, and I thought he was super depressing and sanctimonious. I don't want him lecturing us on morals and how to live our lives and I especially don't want to be grateful to him for allowing us to set foot in his church – it's not the right way to start our married life. We do this our way, or no way.'

Dan blinked. 'So, what are you saying? That you don't want to get married.'

'No. I do want to get married, but I don't want a wedding.' She turned to him, staring into his silver eyes. 'So, Dan Mackey, would you mind awfully if we eloped instead?'

He gave a huge grin. 'Of course, I was only pushing for it because I wanted you to have the whole big white meringue thing. I thought that's what every woman wanted.'

Cally sighed. 'You're such a chauvinistic pig, but I do love you.'

'And I bloody love you, Cally Simmonds.' He let go of the steering wheel for a few seconds and pounded his fists against his chest then made a Tarzan cry; so loud a pedestrian tripped over their feet.

Cally threw back her head and joined in, knowing full well they weren't driving off into the African sunset but to pick up two doner kebabs from *The Olive* instead.

Acknowledgments

Thank you to the wonderful Sumaira Wilson and Nikki East at SpellBound Books for your wisdom, talent and energy in bringing *The Tangled Mane* to life.

Thanks to Robbie Glen for the countless emails and FaceTime chats. To Tina Orr Munro for your kind words, and to Kath Grimshaw for your creative input.

Debbie James from Kibworth Books (the best book shop in the world) – you are a star!

Thanks to Amanda Taylor and Amanda Phillipson from my book group – thank goodness you're kinder about my writing than we are about everyone else's.

Thanks to Rhian Goodman (my partner in everything true crime) for always being there for me, with or without coffee. To Nicola and Matthew Hopkinson for everything you do for me and my family. To James and Emily Murray for your friendship and for Chantal – I know you'll never read this, but thanks anyway. To Rachael Mack for being a best buddy and to Gillie Tyler for your support over the years.

Walking with Otto is my lifeline to staying sane so thank you to Sarah Koeberle, Sarah Mettrick, Becky Bennett and Viv Alston for keeping me company across the Leicestershire countryside throughout every possible weather condition.

To dearest Mum and Dad for being my truest champions closely followed by James, Natalie and V.

Hattie, Gigi and Ollie. You're all so fabulous. I love how enthusiastic you are about my stories and I'm sorry I've 'borrowed' so many things from the Tyler household!

Finally, thanks a million to my husband Will. I'm very, very lucky to have you in my life.

Printed in Great Britain
by Amazon

61294962R00160